An
Accident
in Paris

An Accident in Paris

GAVIN COLLINSON

WELBECK

Published in 2022 by Welbeck Fiction Limited, part of Welbeck
Publishing Group
Based in London and Sydney
www.welbeckpublishing.com

A CIP catalogue record for this book is available from the
British Library

Paperback ISBN: 978-1-80279-360-4
E-book ISBN: 978-1-80279-361-1

Printed and bound by CPI Group (UK) Ltd., Croydon, CR0 4YY

10 9 8 7 6 5 4 3 2 1

OPENING STATEMENTS

'This particular phase of my life is the most dangerous . . .'

– Diana, Princess of Wales, less than a year before the 'accident' in Paris.

I suspect many of the things you've been told about the death of Diana, Princess of Wales, are untrue. Certainly, it can be argued that the stories spun by those in authority about that warm, terrible night in August 1997 are fictions. And not particularly good ones, falling apart under the slightest scrutiny. But that's often the case with propaganda, isn't it? Big on bombast and fancy terminology, but shaky on little things like truth and credibility.

An Accident in Paris is a work of fiction inspired by, and incorporating, real-life events. It draws heavily on official reviews into the Princess's death, including her inquest in 2007/08, Operation Paget (the Met's investigation, initially published in part in 2006) and various French inquiries. The story, through its central character and his ragtag bunch of allies, delves into the contradictions, inaccuracies, cover-ups, mysterious deaths and unanswered questions that were triggered by that tragedy in Paris.

Whilst researching the horrific crash in the Pont de l'Alma tunnel, I avoided conspiracy sites and theorists peddling lurid and outlandish notions. Believe me, there are more than enough obvious inconsistencies in the official records to fuel any engine of suspicion. In fact, this book emphasises that so many authorised statements surrounding the deaths of Diana, Dodi Fayed and Henri Paul are contradictory – not just in that slightly 'off' manner that differing recollections will often engender, but on a dizzying, staggering scale – that it seems bizarre *anyone* could entirely believe the 'accepted' version of events.

And so, if you're interested, here's a sense of what really might have happened.

Gavin Collinson
2022

DISCLAIMER

The following photostat is understood to be a two-page 'briefing note', which is essentially what intelligence personnel call memos, or memoranda. It is published here in the spirit of public interest and all rights remain with its legal owners. No copyright infringement is intended.

The document was redacted at source.

Brief   **TOP SECRET / ARTEMIS**
                                                World Wide Distribution

Page 1 of 2 pages

All Hands Brief – Global Distribution   From: [REDACTED] HoR

File reference: [REDACTED] AD/C5

4 July [REDACTED]

Handling and distribution of ARTEMIS Information

Issue

1.   In light of recent events, namely [REDACTED] [REDACTED] this brief serves as both a reminder and final warning in regard to the handling of ARTEMIS material.

2.   <u>You are prohibited from passing on information, opinion or speculation relating to the death of Diana, Princess of Wales, formerly Lady Diana Frances Spencer.</u>

3.   This directive is binding worldwide, in perpetuity and relates to any form of communication or expression including but not limited to spoken word, written text and online content.

4.   Failure to observe the proper security rules for protection of the ARTEMIS materials in your care could allow access to the very persons to whom it is necessary to deny this information. Should such a situation occur you could be charged with offences under the Official Secrets Acts of 1911 and 1989, and a custodial sentence of up to fifteen years imposed.

5.   If you discover that you have unintentionally caused a compromise, or you become aware of a compromise, it is essential (and mandatory) that you immediately inform your departmental PSyA. He/she will be responsible for raising a LOST HIND event with the ARTEMIS Directorate.

AN ACCIDENT IN PARIS

TOP SECRET / ARTEMIS

██████████████ - World Wide Distribution

Disclosure of ARTEMIS information

Should you believe it is legally or operationally necessary to release ARTEMIS material, authorisation must be gained in advance from:

a. ████████████ HoR;
b. Personnel of Grade RDHB7 or higher.

Case officers and Line Managers are not eligible to grant release of ARTEMIS material.

Should dispensation be permitted you must adhere to the sanctioned narrative, namely:

a. Diana, Princess of Wales, was tragically killed on 31 August, 1997, following injuries sustained in a crash in the Pont de l'Alma tunnel, Paris, France.

b. The crash was a direct result of the driver, Henri Paul, being severely intoxicated. Mr Paul was a known alcoholic. He was not in any way connected to the intelligence community.

c. No other agencies or individuals were responsible for, or involved in the fatal collision.

d. The unexpected and premature deaths of individuals connected to Diana, including but not limited to ████████████████ ████████████████, her ███████████████, ████████████████ and ████████ ████████████, are entirely coincidental and in no way relate to the Princess' untimely passing.

e. In the words of Michael Burgess, Royal Coroner in August, 1997, the events which ended the life of Diana, Princess of Wales amount to a 'relatively straightforward road traffic accident in Paris'.

These facts have been authorised as truth. Any deviation from this official narrative will be considered a breach of the Official Secrets Acts of 1911 and 1989 and will incur all the attendant penalties.

Signed

████████████████

████████████████

Cc: ████████, ████████████, ████████

'Wouldn't it be funny if I jumped out of the cake in a bathing suit?'

– Diana, Princess of Wales, on hearing her former husband, Prince Charles, was throwing a birthday party for his partner, Camilla.

CHAPTER 1

My name is Marc Novak and I've got the best job in the world. The hours are horrendous and the death threats a bit of a bore, but I never know what the day will bring and I often meet the most interesting people. Like the man in front of me now, jabbing a Glock 17 into my ribcage. He's anxious and twitchy and regrets kidnapping his employer's wife because he thinks she might die, and suddenly his old life doesn't look half bad.

He believes I'm a doctor and says, 'What's wrong with her?'

'It's her heart.'

'What's wrong with her heart?'

'Well, I'm going to take a wild stab in the dark and say the fact that she's gagged and tied to a chair, and your girl-friend's pointing a gun at her head won't be doing it the world of good. Why don't you untie her and let her go, Max?'

When Fay Cromwell was abducted two days ago, her wealthy husband, Douglas, received an email telling him no police and half a million in cash would secure her release. He phoned me and, following my instructions, told the kidnappers that his wife had a heart condition and by now would need a doctor. Long story short, I'm here to either save the day or get us all killed. Like I said, I just never know what the day's going to bring.

I've identified Max's girlfriend, Gina, as the more dangerous of the couple. She's been inside and didn't mind it one bit. But worse, she hates seeing the man she trusted go to pieces, and so feels compelled to overcompensate. 'I don't like this,' she tells her boyfriend. 'There's something wrong. We should do them both and get out of here.'

Their captive's eyes widen in terror. I give her a reassuring wink and mouth the words, 'We'll be fine.' And to the Bonnie and Clyde tribute act, 'Not your best plan. My tie clip is fitted with a camera and my associates outside are watching and listening to every word. If you leave now, Mr Cromwell promises he'll take no further action. He just wants this to be over. I think you do, too, Max.'

He's wavering and Gina yells, 'He's bluffing!'

'Yeah,' says Max. 'Prove it!'

We're in an abandoned warehouse and my associate, Mishka, should be in a van just a few yards from the entrance. 'OK,' I reply. 'Mishka. Sound the horn of the van three times.'

There's a tense silence.

'Mishka! Sound the horn! *Now*!'

Gina looks triumphant. 'Told you he was lying.' She swings her gun towards me and I know with absolute certainty that she would love to pull its trigger.

'*Now, Mishka!*'

Max pleads, 'Don't shoot him!'

'You're pathetic! I should have done this by myself!'

'One second!' I shout and show Gina my palms in a *calm down* motion. I lower my voice. 'Mishka. *Please.*' I shrug and mutter to Max, 'Forgot to say please.'

The van's horn blares three times.

'Thank you, Mishka.'

It's now a toss-up who looks most terrified. Mrs Cromwell or Max. He murmurs, 'They've seen our faces . . .'

I grab his Glock and wrench it from his hand. In the movies, I'd have the two kidnappers covered and would be laughing about the whole thing over a G&T in less than an hour. But here, in this icy-cold warehouse that smells of damp and Mrs Cromwell's lavender perfume, the gun goes off. Its discharge is unbelievably loud and Max goes into shock, back-pedalling away from me.

Gina opens fire.

But it's not a problem – her snazzy little Taurus G2c is aimed at me, so Mrs Cromwell remains safe.

I feel a pain explode in my shoulder and return fire. Gina goes down. She'll be fine but, right now, she's in agony. Before she can react, I tear the gun from her grasp and slip it into the pocket of my suit jacket. Its left sleeve is becoming crimson as my blood seeps through the fabric. Pity. Only just bought it in the Boxing Day sales. I walk across to Mrs Cromwell and lower the gag that's been lashed around her mouth. 'You're safe now.' I hand her a handkerchief. 'Press that against the cut on your temple. Are you all right?'

She nods. 'Thank you, Mr Novak.'

What did I tell you? Best job in the world.

It's been ten minutes since the police took Max and Gina away. Douglas Cromwell's Bentley skids to a halt outside the warehouse and he strides over to me. A paramedic is dealing with my bullet wound so we can't shake hands, but he shows his gratitude in the way very affluent people always show their gratitude. 'Mr Novak. I'm going to make you a rich man. I want you to join my security team.'

'That's a kind offer. But no thanks.'

Mrs Cromwell is being escorted from the warehouse, and she spots her husband. Her face turns to thunder and she screams, 'Why didn't you just pay the ransom? I want a divorce!'

Douglas looks at me and I shake my head. 'I can't help you this time.'

He turns and begins to head towards his wife. He pauses. 'Why are you turning down the job?'

'I'm not really a team player.'

He smiles and chases after Mrs Cromwell.

Now, admittedly, the 'team player' line was pretty feeble, but the truth would have sounded too hokey. Even for me.

The paramedic says, 'You're all done!'

'Thank you.'

I haul my suit jacket back on and look over to the Cromwells, who are embracing. Over his wife's shoulder, Douglas gives me a thumbs up. Yeah, they'll be fine.

The sound of cars speeding towards the warehouse interrupts my thoughts. Probably journalists. I button my jacket, straighten my tie, walk to my car, get in and pull away just as the first reporters arrive.

I declined his offer for one very simple reason.

As far back as I can remember, I always wanted to be a detective.

CHAPTER 2

Three years later

The stranger says, 'Mr Novak? Mr Marc Novak – private detective?'

I reply, 'Guilty on both counts,' and immediately wish I hadn't. It's the kind of thing that sounds good in a film noir but not so much on a cold summer's day in Guildford. So I smile to show I wasn't trying to be laconic. 'How can I help?'

'We have a proposition for you.'

'That sounds interesting.'

And by 'interesting' I mean 'dodgy as hell'. Most clients come to me with a *job* or the occasional *project*. But *proposition* implies an offer that's risky enough to be rejected out of hand.

The stranger picks up on my inference and frowns slightly. 'It's a very . . . delicate matter.'

I nod. *Delicate*. Back on familiar territory.

'It usually is,' I tell him. 'Why don't we step inside and talk about it?'

I get edgy whenever someone I don't know rings my doorbell. I'm not a nervous soul, but it's like police cars in your rear-view mirror or conversations that open with, 'Nothing's wrong, honestly . . .' It's never a promising sign, is it?

So when I arrived home to find these two strangers waiting at my front door, I feigned nonchalance but remained wary.

Not that there's anything threatening-looking about the man who did all the talking. I peg him as late forties. He wears a dull, grey suit and he's all nods and pleasant smiles, as if affability is key to any exchange he enters into. I instinctively distrust the guy, but I'm not worried by him.

The woman's a different matter.

She stood back slightly, not saying a word, simply observing the opening niceties. Somewhere in her fifties, I guess. Expensive clothes, Bond Street manicure and jewellery that she didn't get out of a cracker. But more than that – she carries a certain bearing. Rich and ruthless, confident and dangerous. It's all there in her every glance, but – *dammit!* – there's something impressive about her. I realise I want her to like me.

Maybe to counter this, as I usher her into my hallway, I say, 'You can keep your shoes on. Saves any embarrassment if you've got holes in your socks.'

She smiles glacially.

We walk through to the front room. 'I'm Thom Peters,' the man says and we shake hands. He adds, 'And this is my assistant, Miss Winters.'

I'm not buying the 'assistant' bit and throw her a look that says as much. She pretends not to catch it and peers about the room. She's probably thinking what everybody thinks when they first visit. That it doesn't feel like the home of a guy in his late thirties, but more like the house of a much older person. My front room is large. Tidy. Maybe even a touch sparse. I collect antiquarian books and first editions, and my favourites are housed in a glass-fronted display cabinet. Not many framed photographs, but on a corner shelf, right next to an old wooden clock, there's one of me with a friend of mine. Precious Weeks. We're both wearing broad, authentic smiles but, yes, it's an odd photo of a couple because we're obviously *not* a couple. Not like that. No hand-holding or shoulder-draping. Just a slight leaning-in that suggests a staged closeness.

I say, 'Make yourselves at home,' and offer them both coffee. Peters accepts and Miss Winters shakes her head.

I walk through to the kitchen, pick up what looks to be a TV remote control, press a couple of buttons, then turn my attention to the coffee. I grab a fistful of beans, sling them into a small glass jar, attach it the grinder, crank the handle and let the nitro blades do their worst. The whole process of making the coffee – I go for the pour-over method today – takes less than five minutes. For me, it's a soothing and familiar ritual.

I re-enter my front room armed with two mugs of Aruba blend. The aroma is strong and seductive. I hand one mug to Peters, who murmurs his thanks. 'Sure I can't get you one, Miss Winters?'

She politely, but wordlessly, declines.

I say to Peters, 'Who did you say you worked for?'

'You're a two-man band, Mr Novak? I noticed your agency is listed as Novak & Stewart.'

'Yes. Well, Stewart's been out of the picture for some time. And I have a colleague ... Well, *had* a colleague.

But she's just left the company. Who do you work for, Mr Peters?'

'A collective that prefers to remain anonymous. At least until the appropriate NDAs have been signed in triplicate. I'm sure you understand.'

'Not really.'

I'm starting to get the feeling I'm being pushed around and I don't much like it.

Peters asks, 'Are you busy at the moment?'

'Well, last night's dishes aren't going to wash themselves and I've a couple of series I've been meaning to binge-watch. Look – tell me your proposition or get out of my house. I won't charge you for the drink.' And to Miss Winters, 'No offence.'

But it's Peters who replies. 'None taken.'

I see him dart a look at his colleague, who gives a tiny, affirmative shrug. 'We're prepared to pay you a retainer of £10,000 per month, plus expenses, on the condition you work for us exclusively on one case.'

'Which is?'

Peters takes a long, unnecessary inhalation of air before slowly breathing out. It's his version of a drum roll, but to be fair, his next words warrant it.

'We want you to find out who murdered Diana, Princess of Wales.'

I pause. 'Of course you do.'

'And uncover *why* she was killed.'

'Well, yeah.'

'My assistant and I are quite serious.'

That assistant gag again. OK. I've had enough of this. My voice remains calm, level and low but it's obvious

I'm done with their charade. 'Assistants tend not to wear Manolo mules and rocks that cost more than my parents' house. And collectives trying to find out who killed the most famous woman in the world? Well, they rarely rely on a two-man band working out of a home office in Guildford. Miss Winters, do you want to tell me what this is all about? Or shall we pussyfoot around for another twenty minutes?'

A pause. She won't let me outstare her, which is fine by me. It means she has to react or risk looking weak.

'We want you to seek the truth, Mr Novak.'

At last! Miss Winters has a soft, southern English accent. She probably sounded posher when she left public school but she's been smart enough to tone it down a bit. She talks quickly, as if she has all her words lined up ahead of time. 'If you're no longer interested in the truth, fine. Go back to honey traps and taking photographs of middle-aged men fucking in fancy hotels.'

'I think I preferred it when you let him do the talking.'

'Disappointingly typical of you.'

'Yeah. Self-preservation often comes across that way.'

'So,' she says, as if she's slapping me across the face with a kid leather glove, 'are you interested?'

She's trouble – and I can't shake the feeling their whole proposition is an unexploded bomb that's about to start ticking.

I smile. Look over at Peters. 'Can I get you a refill?'

CHAPTER 3

I've opened up the table behind the sofa and now the three of us are sitting around it. Peters is still working his jovial uncle routine and Miss Winters continues to audition for the role of Snow Queen.

Peters says, 'I imagine you're wondering why we've come to you.'

I'm wondering a lot of things but choose not to reply.

'Truth is,' he continues, 'over the years, we've worked with many different investigators. Crack military teams. Former Scotland Yard men. Even Mossad. And they've all approached the matter in the same way. With the same results. Therefore, we decided to try an entirely new tactic.'

I've never been called an entirely new tactic before. Maybe I should use it as a byline on my company website.

'You're not establishment. You have no agenda. You'll have your own methodology and, we hope, the where-withal to succeed where so many others have failed.'

'Look, I'm not a royalist,' I tell him. 'But there was no mystery about Diana's death, was there? She was in a crash. The driver was drunk. And there was an inquest into her death, so—'

Peters interrupts me. 'An inquest that came ten years after she died. Think about that for a moment! Mr Novak, an

16

inquest is a legal obligation when someone dies unexpectedly, or from violent or unknown causes. Legal. Obligation.'

'I get it.'

Peters doesn't think so and continues with, 'They're
normally held, what, a week or two after the time of passing? With Diana, it took an entire *decade* to get round to
it. And even then . . .'

'What?'

'It was a farce! Out of dozens of key witnesses, why
were only three called? Three. Out of over twenty official
documents relating to Diana's post-mortem, do you know
how many the jury got to see? Two. Literally two. Why?'

He's getting angry and I see this is real for him. In my
peripheral vision, I spot Miss Winters stirring slightly. She's
considering intervening, but Peters ploughs on.

'The driver you mentioned was called Henri Paul. He
was behind the wheel of the Mercedes that crashed, killing Diana. He was the fall guy. They branded him an
alcoholic. Everything was blamed on him, but it simply
does not add up.'

'How so?'

'Well, why did the coroner in charge of the inquest,
Lord Justice Scott Baker, tell Paul's parents that he was *not*
drunk when he was driving the Mercedes? Records confirm
he said this. He told them Henri Paul was blameless and his
name would be cleared. Then, just days later, at the close
of the inquest, he does a total about-face and officially pro-
claims Henri Paul was blind drunk – and makes *him* the
scapegoat. Makes him culpable for the whole thing.'

It's beyond obvious Peters is growing more livid with
every recollection, and I know I should make him calm

down. But there's something magnetic about a genial man's fury and I simply ask a question I already know the answer to. 'You think Henri Paul was sober that night? When he drove Diana through Paris?'

Peters leans forward. 'Look, he drove her from the Ritz, right? Well, on his way to there, he stopped and chatted to an old friend – Josiane Le Tellier. She said, and I quote, *"I've known Henri for years, and I've been tending bars for twenty-five years. I can tell when somebody's drunk. He wasn't."'*

Peters moves back in his chair. 'He. Wasn't.'

CHAPTER 4

Peters pulls his phone from his jacket pocket. 'Once he gets to the Ritz . . . Well, look at the video.'

'Sure.'

He hands me his phone after lining up an MP4 file. I press play and see grainy security-camera footage of a suited, bespectacled guy walking purposefully through high-ceilinged corridors and an opulent foyer. Peters tells me, 'That's Henri Paul at the Ritz, shortly before he drove Diana and her party away. Does he look even remotely tipsy to you?'

He doesn't, but it's hardly conclusive. 'I could fake it if I'd had a few.'

But now I see footage of Paul bending down and tying his shoelace. He deftly transfers his weight, shifting his body – whilst he's still low – to tie his other set of laces.

I hand the phone back to Peters and say, 'Look, he could have been sober earlier in the evening, then had a few drinks when he reached the hotel.'

'What? He doesn't have a drink until he knows he's going to be driving the Princess of Wales across Paris?' Peters' sarcasm is more exasperation than withering rejoinder. 'Actually, that was the official line. That he could have downed up to six measures of Ricard at the Ritz shortly

19

before driving away.' Peters shakes his head. 'Rubbish! Not one single camera caught him buying drinks and the bodyguards with him said they don't recall him drinking at all, and that he certainly wasn't drunk.'

'But he was an alcoholic, right? You said something about—'

'Again, that was the official line, but it's a total fabrication. His friends all denied it and his autopsy showed he had a perfectly healthy liver. So – what? He had a magic body? He could be an alcoholic for years and somehow the booze diverted past his liver? No, Henri Paul was not an alcoholic and he was not drunk on the evening of 30 August, 1997.'

I try to break this down one last time. 'The police must have searched his flat. Did that give any indication as to whether or not he was a heavy drinker?'

Peters' eyes light up like we're playing gin rummy and I've thrown down the card he needs for a winning hand. 'Oh, his flat was searched, all right. On 3 September – that's just three days after the crash – it was searched by the French Brigade Criminelle. Paul's parents were present.'

'And did they find booze?'

'They did. But hardly an alcoholic's stash. Just one bottle of Champagne and enough Martini to make a couple of cocktails.'

'That mitigates in his favour, I suppose.'

'But,' Peters wags a finger at me, 'his flat was searched again a few days later. This time there were no neutral witnesses. And this time the police came out with more booze than an off-licence! Said they found liquor all over the place. Bottles of red wine, crème de cassis, Ricard, port, vodka, beer, bourbon and God knows what else. You can't tell me the police simply missed that massive hoard of alcohol the first time around?'

'It seems unlikely.'

'The guy leading the first search called it "surprising".'

'Very diplomatic.'

'So, people are already trying to establish a narrative: that Henri Paul was a drunk, that he was unfit for the role of driver. That he caused the crash and we should all just move on . . .'

'It poses a very obvious question,' I concede. 'Who planted the bottles of alcohol that were found at Henri Paul's flat during the second search?'

CHAPTER 5

Earlier that Day: Novak's Story

Marc Novak didn't consider himself a sentimentalist, but when he looked back on the events of the day he first met Miss Winters and Thom Peters, his subconscious added a touch of romance. He'd visited Hyde Park in the morning and strolled past the Diana, Princess of Wales Memorial Fountain, that huge, oval water feature constructed from over 500 pieces of glimmering Cornish granite. One side of the stream bed descends smoothly to allow a gentle, uninterrupted flow. The opposite side comprises rills, curves and steps, forcing the water to tumble and cascade. Its designer, the American architect Kathryn Gustafson, revealed this was intended to reflect the two sides of Diana's life. The tranquillity and the turmoil.

Novak remembered passing the memorial and pausing by a signage conveying facts about its creation and thematic aims. The information posts carry a photograph of the Princess and he recalled looking long and hard at the face of Diana. It hadn't happened that way, of course. He'd simply glanced at a picture of her and carried on walking, oblivious to the fact that, very soon, her death would become central to his life.

Novak was, like many men in their late thirties, aware he was on the point of not being young, but uncertain what to retain of his youth. Life had happened quickly. It seemed so recent that people were always asking him what he was going to do. What did he want to be? Now people only asked what he had done. What he was. He wanted to reply, 'A work in progress.'

The old-fashioned suit-and-tie look he always favoured had once contrasted his youthful good looks, as if his clothes were an irony. Now they suggested a man who had settled down. They were the uniform of any middle-aged male seeking to fit in. An outmoded disguise. He had broad shoulders, tidy dark hair and wore nondescript glasses. Friends had urged him to try contact lenses, but he'd grown used to treating his spectacles as a prop – besides, they were easy to remove when he didn't want to see the world in focus.

'Marco!'

Mishka Ramakrishnan invariably called him Marco. He looked up and saw her bounding towards him. She wore trainers, skinny jeans and a Blondie T-shirt under a light-grey hoodie.

Novak nodded. 'Morning!'

'How's it going?'

'Not so bad. You all packed?'

'Nah. I only ever take hand luggage. Anything else slows me down. Got the shots?'

Novak handed her an A4 manila envelope and asked, 'Where are we meeting her?'

'Serpentine.' Mishka slid a sheaf of photographs from the envelope and began to leaf through them. 'Well, he definitely has a thing for blondes, doesn't he?' She continued her perusal. 'Oh. And brunettes . . . And whatever *that* is . . .' She turned the final photo ninety degrees, as if trying to decipher the image. 'You made copies for us, yeah?'

She'd asked the question to tease him, but he seemed unamused. 'Serpentine. You mean the gallery?'

Mishka returned the photographs to the envelope. 'Look, I can handle this, man. You can go get the first round in.'

'It's part of the job.' He hesitated and tried to lighten the mood. 'Copies for us?'

'Don't pretend you haven't.'

'You're an animal.'

'Er, racist.'

'Sexist.'

'Cyclist.'

'Oh, that *hurts!*'

A light glinted in the distance, but Novak was distracted by something else. Looking ahead, he saw their client had already reached the meeting point. He felt a familiar nausea in his stomach and throat.

Perhaps it was that sense of dread, or maybe he was tired from a late night. Either way, on another day he might have been sharper and more curious about the source of the glint. It had, in fact, been sunlight reflecting off a Zeiss telephoto lens, attached to a Nikon DSLR. The person behind the camera was part of a two-man team. One photographer. One spot man. Novak had noticed neither, despite the fact they'd been monitoring and recording his movements all morning.

CHAPTER 6

Novak's Story (cont.)

Novak, Mishka and their client were sitting at one of the metal tables clustered outside the Serpentine Gallery. Anna Brandon looked like a woman with a very rich husband. Casually elegant. Poised but fragile. Mid-thirties, fair hair and Jackie-O sunglasses that she wasn't wearing for the bright weather. There was the normal, perfunctory small talk, someone fetched coffees and then the business began. Anna was handed the envelope but was clearly reluctant to open it, handling it cautiously, as if suspecting it was booby-trapped. Novak gave her an encouraging but solemn nod and she finally removed the photographs.

He studied her as she slowly went through the pictures. Even with her eyes masked by sunglasses, he could easily discern her disbelief and distress. It was inescapable. Each new photograph brought fresh revelations and all she whispered was, 'Oh, no . . .' over and over.

It was like watching a car crash at about two frames per second. Novak's feeling of nausea grew worse. He looked down at his coffee, then glanced across to Mishka who was using a wooden stirrer to doodle in her latte's froth.

Eventually, very carefully, Anna returned the photos to the envelope. The shock in her voice was raw. 'I thought he was having an affair, but . . .'

Mishka looked up from her artwork. 'Yeah, well, I think we've mopped away any doubt.'

Novak said, 'Mrs Brandon, you're going to need time to process all this. I'd recommend not confronting your husband about it straight away. At least, not until you've devised a strategy you're happy with.'

Anna was staring at the envelope. 'I'm sorry.' She looked up. 'What?'

'Don't let on you know, until you've figured out what you want to do next.' Anna nodded and Novak added, 'I'm sorry for what you're having to go through. If I can help in any way . . .'

'You've got our number,' Mishka said.

Anna removed her sunglasses. Her eyes were red and Novak guessed she'd been crying before she'd even reached the park. She spoke to him directly. 'Thank you.' She gripped his forearm and then, with that sincerity and gratitude unique to the vulnerable, added, 'You've been very kind.'

A couple of minutes later, Anna Brandon replaced her sunglasses, lightly held the envelope by one of its corners and dropped it into her Hermès Picotin handbag. As she walked away Novak muttered, 'Well, that felt shit.'

Mishka shrugged. 'Least she knows where she stands.'

'Yeah. On a landmine.' Novak gazed across the park. 'I don't know if I can keep doing this job. I mean, what's the point?'

'You used to love it.'

'Where's the . . . meaning?'

'You thinking of jacking it in?'

A long pause. 'I don't know.'

'What would you do?'

'Join a circus.'

Mishka grinned. 'Could I come with you?'

'No.'

'Why not?'

'You'd distract the daring young man on the flying trapeze.'

Another pause. Shorter this time. 'You're not serious about leaving.' It was unclear whether her words were a question, statement or plea.

'I try not to be serious about anything. Besides, you can hardly talk. You're taking six months off!'

'Serves you right for not hiring me full-time.'

'You said you enjoyed the freedom of being a free-lancer.' Novak finished his coffee. 'Remember the first job we worked together?'

'The Cromwell case! You almost got killed. Good times.'

Novak smiled. 'Come on. Let's get a couple of farewell drinks in. I'm buying.'

As they walked through Hyde Park, the two-man sur-veillance team took several more photographs before con-tacting their superiors for instructions on how to proceed. They were told to drop off – for now. The next phase of the operation was about to begin.

CHAPTER 7

'Mr Novak, the situation poses *many* obvious questions.'

I say to Peters, 'Look, after the crash, they must have tested Paul's blood. Checked for traces of alcohol.'

He tugs his tie down a little and undoes the top button of his shirt as he replies with fervour, 'The testing was another joke. Another raft of mistakes. Even the scientist giving evidence at the inquest admitted that if the analysis had been done in an English laboratory . . . well, the errors were so serious, it would have been denied a licence to operate! Mixed-up samples, items mislabelled – shambolic.'

'In which case, I suppose there were requests for independent testing, to verify the official findings?'

'Of course there were – from multiple parties – but all requests for independent tests were refused. Henri Paul's personal effects that he was carrying at the time of the crash – wallet, keys and so on – were all returned to his parents. Everything except his security pass. It held a photo of him. Henri's dad said he liked that picture and made an official request to have the pass handed over. It was denied.'

Peters is looking at me and I recognise the test. 'I'm guessing the pass had blood on it?'

He's delighted by my shot in the dark. 'Exactly. The authorities officially revealed it was spattered with Henri's blood. So, you see, they're caught between a rock and a hard place. They either wipe down the pass and return it – in which case, it looks like they're tampering with evidence. Or they take the safer option, hang on to the pass and never release it. Now why would they do that?'

My tone is a little more waspish this time. 'Because Henri's parents were highly critical of the investigations that followed the crash?'

'Correct!'

'And so the authorities were worried they might have the blood analysed and thus prove he was sober.'

'Well, it's fairly obvious that's what happened. Why else wouldn't they release the pass?'

I rise from my chair. 'It's not obvious. It's just a possibility.'

Peters is wide-eyed. 'You don't get it! Once you accept the driver wasn't drunk, the entire thing starts to unravel. And the things I've told you, they're all in the public domain. All are from sources like the official inquest and Operation Paget – the Met's inquiry into Diana's death.' I hover over him, but he can see I'm impatient. 'From the friends who say Henri Paul wasn't a drunk or an alcoholic and all the witnesses who testified he'd not been drinking that night. The autopsy that proved he wasn't even a habitual drinker. All those bottles of booze that mysteriously appeared in his flat, that hadn't been there during the first search? Hell's teeth, man! What other evidence do you need?'

Miss Winters says one word. 'Peters.'

But he's in full flow. 'And just think of it from a common-sense point of view. This guy is Deputy Head of Security at the Paris Ritz. A trusted, well-thought-of security professional without a stain on his record. Are we seriously suggesting that he's asked to drive Diana and her party across Paris and at that point – *at that point!* – he quickly downs enough alcohol to be about three times over the limit? That no one sees him doing this, no one smells it on his breath and none of the hotel cameras catch him at the bar or looking even slightly the worse for wear?'

'I get it. You think they made Henri Paul the patsy.'

Peters can only repeat his earlier assertion. 'Once you accept the driver wasn't drunk, the entire thing starts to unravel.'

I tilt my palms. 'So what else have you got?'

His eyes have that winning-hand glint in them again. 'Oh, so much more . . .'

'Let's hear it.'

'The actual crash itself. My God, it's so—'

'Enough.' Miss Winters speaks the word quietly and without force, but it's enough to keep Peters in check. He looks at her, silently urging her to let him continue. She gives no such indication.

Deflated, Peters mumbles, 'Sorry.'

'The whole point of hiring Mr Novak is that he approaches the case with a fresh mind, not one guided by unanswered questions from the past.' She addresses me. 'Three people were killed in suspicious circumstances. We simply want you to find out what happened.'

I'm still hovering over the table. 'I'm just getting a top-up,' I tell them.

I don't offer my guests one, but Peters feels the need to say, 'I'm fine,' which wouldn't have been my diagnosis.

I wander through to the kitchen. At least they've ditched the sham about her being his assistant, but that begs another question. If she's happy for Peters to take the lead, and she wants to remain in the background, why did she come at all?

I pour coffee into my mug and switch the kettle on. It's obvious I'm buying time, because I know damn well what Miss Winters' next question will be, and I don't have an answer. Sure, the two strangers in my house are evasive and manipulative, but there's something intriguing about the mystery they're asking me to examine. And there's a more personal factor that draws me to Diana's death. Always has done. Yet a few minutes ago Peters spoke about common sense. And using that arbiter, there was one element which suggested any investigation would be a waste of time.

I pour a little hot water into my coffee, walk back, take my seat and say, 'It was twenty-five years ago.'

'You think justice has a sell-by date?' Miss Winters' question isn't rhetorical.

'No. But I think most people can't remember what they had for breakfast. I'll be asking about an event from another century.'

Peters replies, 'The death of the most famous woman in the world? People remember, Mr Novak. Even people who never met her. Everyone remembers how they heard the news. Where they were. How they felt. How people around them reacted.'

This hangs. I think back, too, to where I was on that sunny summer morning when the whole world reeled. That day was the first time I saw my father weep and, a quarter of a century later, I can't bear to think of my mother as—

31

'Where were you?' Miss Winters interrupts my recollections with her question. She's seen the look on my face and now there's one of curiosity on hers.

'Well, I wasn't in Paris,' I tell her. 'So I guess that rules me out.'

Peters says, 'But your point's well-made. It's been twenty-five years. For us, that's two-and-a-half decades of searching for a solution that makes sense.' He looks at Miss Winters. Again, the question is implicit and, again, she wordlessly indicates it's acceptable for him to continue. 'The collective has decided that if you fail to uncover the truth, well, we'll move on. It's been a long journey, leading us nowhere. I mean, God knows we've sought justice by every way possible, but you'll be the last one.'

'No pressure, then.'

Miss Winters asks, 'Do you accept the case?'

I should say no. I really should say no.

'OK,' I reply. 'Give me a couple of weeks to see what I can find. If I'm just getting a load of conspiracy theories and sob stories, I'll let you know and you can keep your money. If I think I'm getting somewhere, I'll take the case. Deal?'

Yes, I know it's a stall. All three of us do, but Miss Winters and Peters are evidently satisfied, which I find oddly unnerving.

They pause in my hallway. We confirm the protocol for keeping in touch and Peters swings open the front door. We shake hands and for some reason he says, 'I have faith in you.'

I catch one of Miss Winters' precise eyebrows rising for a moment. We share a look that confirms we both know how much Peters' faith means to me. He releases my hand, hesitates, and seems to pick up on the fact his colleague wants a private word with me. He nods and sets off down my driveway.

Miss Winters steps closer to me. Did I mention she wears expensive perfume, that's strong without being cloying? If I said it was Chanel No.5 I'd be taking a random punt but, whatever it is, as she leans in, it's almost aphrodisiacal.

'I said I didn't want you encumbered with questions that weren't your own,' she says and I nod. 'There's one exception. Just before she was killed, Diana told the press she was on the verge of surprising them. With something new. With something that would shock them. It would be interesting to find out what it was, don't you think?'

'What's your best guess, Miss Winters?'

'Good luck.' As she moves past me, on to the driveway, she adds, 'And remember what's at stake.'

'I get it. I'm your last chance.'

She stops, looking mildly surprised.

'No, Mr Novak. You're Diana's last chance.'

CHAPTER 8

Now that my guests have left the house, I return to the living room, cross to the windows and check they've really gone. A lot of my clients linger. There's normally something they've not told me and, as they walk away, they begin to have creeping doubts about keeping secrets from someone who's committed to helping them. But Miss Winters and Peters aren't hanging around.

Good.

I close the curtains and go to the old wooden clock on the corner shelf, stealing a look at the photograph of Precious and me. But it's no more than a glance, I promise. I'm over that whole thing. Got over it ages ago, in fact. By the way, the clock is a genuine eighteenth-century antique. Or at least, its casing is.

I carry it to the table. There's a small aperture to the right of the clock face that people always assume is the keyhole for when it needs winding up. It's actually a 2.5mm lens that can be operated manually or by using a device that looks like a TV remote control. I'd used the latter method when Miss Winters and Peters arrived, but now I remove the clock's back panel and slide the power to 'off'. I pluck the USB from its tiny hard drive, fire up my laptop and stick it into a side port.

I watch the recording I'd initiated just before making the coffee. The first couple of minutes show my guests having a nosey round the front room, and I freeze the footage as they approach the shelf, doubtless to check out the photo by the clock. The frame effectively captures them both head-on. It's a good, usable shot. I do a screen capture and open up my facial recognition software. The programme I use isn't *strictly* illegal, in the same way diverting company profits to an offshore account in the Caribbean isn't *strictly* breaking any tax laws.

But the software doesn't resemble the magic face-finders you've seen in cop shows. When facial rec started coming of age, the systems were largely outsourced by government departments that tended to award the contract to the tech firm submitting the lowest bid. To make up the shortfall, these companies offer access to a version of the programme, which is what I'm using now. They're slow but thorough and I set it running with the faces of Thom Peters and Miss Winters.

I grab my phone and call Precious. She picks up and I say, 'Hi,' which feels like enough small talk. 'I need your help.'

'When do you not?'

'Are you free tonight?'

'No.'

'It's important.'

I hear her sigh and know she'll help. 'What is it?'

'What time do you finish work?'

Turns out she's on an early and we arrange to meet when she's left her office. After the call, I check out how the facial rec search is coming along. It's finished.

No matches.

Now, that's strange. Pretty much everyone has an online presence these days, whether they know it or not. And somewhere in the vastness of the internet, there's almost certainly at least one photo that includes your face. But the search has given me no names or possible matches to the shots of Thom Peters and Miss Winters. According to the available data, they don't exist.

I've just been hired by a couple of ghosts.

CHAPTER 9

Dealing with an ex of your current partner is invariably tricky, isn't it? Their latent intimacy always feels intrusive, no matter how much bonhomie and bullshit we deploy to make the social interaction a little easier. I understand this.

So when I meet Precious in the foyer of Guildford Cathedral's refectory, I'm not put out by the fact that her current boyfriend is less than thrilled to see me. Cy Hillier is a big guy. Good-looking. When he spots me, he reacts like he's just found a parking ticket stuck to his car windscreen. As I approach, he says, 'Don't get her involved in anything dangerous. Not again.'

Before I can answer, Precious replies, 'I can look after myself, Cy.'

He doesn't look convinced. 'I'll wait for you in the car, yeah?'

She nods and he leaves.

'Good to see you, Presh. Thank God that wasn't awkward.'

She gives me a pantomime scowl. 'You're buying.'

We go to the counter, where I order for her and she orders for me. That sounds cutesy, I know, but it's just something we've done for years. I carry our tray over to the far end of the room and we sit at a large circular table. To our right, through large windows, the cathedral looms.

'Cy's looking well.'

'How's Jill?' I've no idea what she's talking about, and noticing this, she adds, with a touch of incredulity, 'The girl you were seeing.'

'Oh! Gillian. Yeah. We didn't . . .' I shrug. 'How's your mum's leg?'

'You said you needed my help with something. Sorry – I've only got a minute. I did say we had plans.'

'It's a case I'm working. A murder.'

'It's always the husband.'

'She was divorced.'

'Do I know her?'

'The whole world knows her. I'm looking into the death of Diana.'

I'm curious what her reaction will be, but there is none. 'Diana who?'

'*The* Diana. The Princess of Wales.'

The reaction arrives and it's textbook scepticism. 'Someone's hired you to find out what happened to Lady Diana?' She could have added '*Yeah, right!*' and it wouldn't have sounded out of place. She sees I'm serious and after a moment ventures, 'Oh, is it like research for a documentary or something?'

'I expect so. Do you think I should take it?'

'The case? Yeah. Why wouldn't you?'

I shrug. 'It's dangerous, isn't it? Asking questions about powerful people.'

She laughs. And when Precious laughs, she really commits. Always a big smile followed by head-back hoots. 'Dangerous? Listen to yourself!' She regains her composure. 'Why do white guys always think the world's out to get them?'

Oh God. I don't want one of those conversations. 'Well, it's not that! It's—'

'I'm yanking ya chain!' That broad smile again and she rests her hand on my forearm, just for a moment. 'So, how can I help?'

'You're a journalist.' Actually, that's not technically true. Precious *had* been a journalist, and a good one, in London, for several years. She'd been forced to move back to Guildford when her mum's health started to decline and she needed to be on hand. She now works as an editorial assistant at a local radio station. It's fine, but I know she's desperate to get back to her 'real' job.

I continue, 'I'm trying to cut through the bullshit documentaries and everything about the crash. I wondered if you knew any old journos who actually worked the case?'

She ponders for a second. 'Well, a friend of mine did some digging into it a couple of years back. She turned up some pretty interesting stuff that implicated the Royal Family.'

This sounds like a terrific lead. 'You're joking!'

'Yeah, but they caught on and had her taken out with a poison-tipped umbrella.'

She starts laughing again, and this time I join her. For a moment, it's like old times, and I hate the fact I can't allow myself the luxury of feeling like this. I've no idea whether she picks up on my mindset, but she switches to serious mode.

'Joking aside, there was a guy when I was at uni. Frank Harvey. A real old-school hack. He used to come in and teach us about the practical side of the business. I think he was working on the red tops in the 90s. *Think* he wrote a book about Diana. Might be able to help if it's the inside goss you're looking for.'

'He'd be perfect.'

'Good!' She smiles, as though she's been happy to help with a recipe I'm having trouble with. And here, by the cathedral, having a laugh and a chat with Precious, it strikes me that she might be right. That I might be being over-dramatic and that this is just another case. A little strange, but essentially a research job with no sinister or dangerous elements embedded within it.

'I'll give you his details.' She starts to write something on a scrap of paper.

'There was one other thing,' I tell her.

'There always is with you.'

'I wondered if you could take a look at it yourself? The death of Diana, that is. Just have a poke around at what's out there in the public domain. I'd value your . . . over-view.'

'Frank's details.' She hands me the paper. 'Why do you want me looking into it?'

'You're a strong investigative journalist. Look, I'll pay you if—'

'It's not that. You know it's not that. But I promised Cy I wouldn't get involved. Not after what happened last time.'

'It's hardly getting involved.'

She pauses. Gives me that sigh again.

I smile. 'Thank you. And relax! What's the worst that can happen?'

CHAPTER 10

In my line of work, people pay a lot of money for facts. Clients usually want to know about someone: is a prospective partner everything they claim to be? The answer's normally no, of course, because no one is ever truly the person they choose to project. But clients want exactitudes, so they can decide whether it's worth their while to maintain a façade in order to attract the individual they no longer trust.

But with this case, facts are in abundance. The internet is awash with details about Diana and, given time, anyone can get to know her better than they could a close friend or family member. The problem is, the 'facts' about her are often contradictory. Even a question as simple as 'What were her final words?' throws up differing answers, and good luck trying to establish what condition she was in during the immediate aftermath of the crash. Doctors and witnesses disagree and the only man to survive the collision, bodyguard Trevor Rees-Jones, has no recollection of the event, let alone the specifics of those fateful few minutes.

It's clear, incidentally, that Rees-Jones was lucky to leave Paris alive. His face was obliterated in the crash, leaving him unrecognisable. Surgeons needed family photographs to establish what they were trying to recreate, and used about 150 pieces of titanium for the restoration job. *Ouch* doesn't begin to cover it.

I know this, because after Precious left me at the refectory, I got another coffee and, as it cooled, idly googled facts about the Princess's death. Then I loaded YouTube, slipped in a pair of earphones, and searched for news bulletins. The first video I watch is a British news item delivered by a male presenter. He's slightly shaken, but we're not talking Walter Cronkite levels.

'W-we have reports from Paris,' he stammers, 'that Diana, Princess of Wales, has been killed in a car accident . . . And that her partner, Dodi Fayed, has also been killed. They were apparently being pursued by paparazzi on two motorcycles.'

Quite a lot to unpack there. So, Dodi was Diana's *partner*. That's unequivocal. Not friend or companion. But I know that in early August he'd been engaged to American model Kelly Fisher, dumping her days before they were due to be married. She'd been in France at the same time as Diana, staying on one of the Fayeds' yachts. According to Ms Fisher, Dodi had been two-timing her with the Princess, and he broke off their engagement over the phone on the 7th the day before his royal relationship hit the headlines. So, Dodi and Diana had officially been a thing for less than a month before their deaths, but their relationship seems to have been established and unquestioned.

And there's something else: 'pursued by paparazzi on two motorcycles'. Even I remember there'd been more than a couple of motorbikes trailing the Mercedes. It seems an odd detail to get wrong.

The newsreader continues, 'Reports are that Diana has been killed. Dodi Fayed also died, as did the driver of the car . . .'

The driver of the car. I hit pause and say to no one, 'Henri Paul. His name was Henri Paul.'

The next bulletin I watch is from another British channel. This newsreader remains serious but not emotional – she's professional and unmoved, and at first glance she could be announcing a minor economic downturn. She says, 'Confirmation that Diana, Princess of Wales, has, in fact, been killed in that car accident in Paris, France, just a few hours ago. There had been extreme concern that Diana was very seriously injured when she was taken from the wreckage. There was a news blackout, to all intents and purposes, for a significant amount of time. Now there is confirmation that Diana, Princess of Wales, has died . . .'

Again, I hit pause.

Sip my coffee. It's gone cold.

Rewind. '*There was a news blackout . . .*'

I don't recall that detail, but it strikes me as curious. *A news blackout.* As I get up to leave, I wonder who imposed it, and why.

CHAPTER 11

I first visited Soho when I was in my early teens. I was a callow youth, as they say, but tall for my age. That's important. I remember heading to a shop on Brewer Street that I was told sold movie ephemera and old books about classic films. I guess that, even as a kid, I had the bug for collecting rare editions. Anyway, after leaving the seemingly huge HMV store on Oxford Street, I cut down Poland Street and walked through Berwick Street market. It was like entering a different world.

It was before all those chi-chi street food vendors dominated the market. Back then it was all yelling greengrocers, butchers, stalls flogging tatty underwear and cheap jeans, knock-off jewellery merchants, fishmongers and blokes shifting electronic goods made by companies you'd never heard of. It was lined with rough pubs, second-hand record shops and dimly lit cafés. We got on immediately. The smell of fruit and veg and cigarette smoke. The stallholders' constant shouting, chattering and laughter. The vague sense of threat. It felt authentic and thrilling.

At the bottom of Berwick Street, I reached Walker's Court. Another new world. Neon signs advertising sex shops, tattoo parlours and theatres that certainly didn't look anything like the theatres I'd visited on school trips. There was the Soho

Cinema ('Adults Only') and lots of doors that were anonymous, except for pieces of card pinned to them, revealing the name of the 'model' who was available on the other side.

Sensory overload. I remember a woman staring at me. At the time I thought she was impossibly glamorous, but looking back, I'm guessing she just had big hair and wore a lot of make-up. She seemed to be weighing something up, then came to a decision. She approached me.

'Do you want a girl?'

I replied, 'What for?'

And I swear she actually said, 'A good time.'

Oh. The penny dropped. I can't recall what I told her, but I hurried away. It was the first time I'd ever been propositioned and it added to my understanding of Soho being a place of forbidden delights.

It's different today, of course. Westminster City Council kicked out all the dodgier market traders and gradually my old haunts like The King of Corsica were rebranded, renamed and finally deconsecrated. My favourite second-hand record shop became a craft store and the dark, quirky cafés morphed into delis and coffee shops. The world moved on. In case you're wondering, the movie shop on Brewer Street is long gone. The building had a 'To Let' sign on it last time I passed, along with hopeful imagery suggesting what could be done with the premises.

It's all been gentrified, which is another way of saying homogenised. After a couple of pints, I've even been known to get nostalgic for the fabulously confident working girls who clustered around the (now defunct) bookshop on Walker's Court and, opposite, on the corner of Rupert Street.

But parts of Soho retain an edgy charm and it can still be dangerous, if you know the right places. Or, I suppose, the wrong places.

The pub I'm heading to is the John Snow, named after the doctor who made the connection between contaminated water and cholera, as opposed to the guy off *Game of Thrones*. It's an unpretentious watering hole full of nooks and crannies and corner tables. It's all mahogany fittings and etched glass, and has never felt the need to modernise. They don't play music and there's pie and mash on the menu. Perfect. The 'Snowy' was one of my regular pubs when I had an office in Soho, and as I step inside via the Lexington Street entrance, I'm relieved to see it's unchanged.

The downstairs bar is divided by a wood and glass partition with a bizarrely low doorway. This side of the room is empty, aside from some young women drinking at the bar. So I duck under the doorway and immediately see Frank Harvey at a corner table.

He's in his early seventies. Tough, tall and wiry and dressed in an old-fashioned grey suit that looks too heavy for the good weather. White shirt. Black tie. Sartorially, it's a similar look to mine, and I know he's not wearing it to appear smart. It's his uniform.

Frank is sitting with his back to the wall so he can see everyone in the room. There's a trio of pint glasses on his table, but only one with any beer in it. Next to this, a broadsheet newspaper, open on a completed crossword. I can't help thinking I'm looking at a vision of my own future.

'Frank Harvey?'

He makes no secret of looking at me, with his sharp blue eyes running some kind of assessment. He drains the remaining beer from his glass and puts it back on the table. 'Get 'em in, lad.'

'Sure. What are you drinking?'

He gives me the order and a couple of minutes later I'm back from the bar with a trayful of booze. Two pints and four shorts. I sit down and Frank takes one of the shot glasses. I instinctively realise the protocol, which in itself is part of his test. As I grab one of the other shots, he says, 'Cheers.'

'Cheers. And thanks for seeing me.'

We clink glasses and down our whiskies in one, simultaneously slamming our glasses down on to the tray. Frank reaches for one of the beers, sips it and nods. 'Pleasure. You stepping out with Precious, then?'

'No. Well. We . . .'

Frank nods. 'She's a smart lass. Bit lippy, but . . . So how can I help you, young man? Diana, wasn't it?'

'Precious said you covered her death.'

'Aye. Well, we all did, back then. I wrote a book on it, mind, so I . . .' He shrugs to indicate he might know more than most. 'What d'you want to know about?'

'Mr Harvey . . .' I take a mouthful of beer and decide to go for it. 'Can you tell me who killed the Princess of Wales?'

CHAPTER 12

The wily old soldier has been in too many campaigns to be caught off guard by a direct question. He replies, 'Call me Frank.'

'Will do.'

He glugs down some more beer. 'What was the question again?'

He's joking of course, and the line makes me smile. He seems to enjoy my reaction.

'You must have read all the books.'

'What really happened, Frank?'

'*What really happened?* You said you're a private detective?'

'Yeah. Been hired by people making a film about the Royal Family.'

Frank nods again. Doesn't believe me for a second. 'So, let me guess. You've watched a load of dodgy docs and you want to know if they're all true.'

'There's a lot of rubbish in them, but . . . I just think there are a lot of questions that were never really answered.'

'Like what?'

I think back to the more puzzling elements that I've read about. 'Why did it take the ambulance team over an hour and a half to get Diana to the hospital, when it was only four miles away? Were Diana and Dodi about to get married?' I lower my voice. 'Was the Royal Family involved in the crash?'

Frank looks disappointed. 'Why would they be?'

'Because they wanted her out of the way.'

'The Royal Family didn't give a shit about Diana. People forget – before Paris she'd become a laughing stock for some folk. They made out she was borderline loony. She even made jokes about it herself.'

I remember seeing an online video of Diana addressing an audience, opening with, 'I'm supposed to be dragged off the minute I leave here by men in white coats!'

Frank shakes his head. 'Poor thing. No. The crash was the best piece of publicity she ever got.'

'I doubt she'd agree.'

'Her martyrdom was a right old shitstorm for the Palace. Christ, Charles would have given her mouth-to-mouth himself if it'd have brought her back to life. Sorry to disappoint you, lad. The Windsors didn't have her taken out.'

'So they were fine with the prospect of the future king having siblings whose dad was an Egyptian Muslim?'

'They couldn't have cared less. Look – just before Dodi, Diana had been seeing a British-Pakistani heart surgeon for two years. Hasnat Khan. Now, that relationship *was* serious. Diana was smitten. She talked about marriage with him. Word on the street was Charles was fine about it.' He takes another sip of beer. 'The Royal Family may be a lot of things, but they tend not to be racist. They condescend to everyone equally. Don't forget, it was Diana's own mum, Frances Shand Kydd, who called her a whore for' – he uses

49

air quotes for his next words – 'messing around with effing Muslim men.'

'Christ.'

'That came out at the inquest.'

'Who ended the affair? Khan or Diana?'

'Khan. Couldn't stand the loss of his privacy. She was gutted.'

I'm getting a taste for the beer, a Sam Smith bitter, and take another sip. 'What about the ambulance thing?'

'Folk make a song and dance about that, but it was no big deal. In this country, ambulance crews' number-one priority is to get the patient to the nearest hospital, right?'

'Right.'

'But in France, it's different. Their crews try to treat the patient in situ. So, after the Princess had been cut from the wreckage, she was treated at the crash site by Dr Jean-Marc Martino. But as he did his stuff, she went into cardiac arrest and he twigged they had to get her into theatre, pronto. So she was moved into an ambulance at 1.18 a.m. The time it then took to get to the hospital was what? Twenty-six minutes? That feels about right.'

'Witnesses report seeing the ambulance driving pretty slowly.'

'Sure. Martino ordered the ambulance to go slowly because Diana's blood pressure had dropped – he was worried about the effects that acceleration and deceleration could have on her. She reached the hospital at 2.06 a.m. Doctors did all they could. At 4 a.m. she was pronounced . . .' And after such a precise, detailed recollection, he falters, before adding, 'She was at rest.'

'Do you believe she was pregnant?'

'Not a chance. Diana's friends gave evidence during Operation Paget. They all dismissed the idea. They had no reason to lie.'

Operation Paget, I recall Thom Peters telling me, had been the Metropolitan Police's investigation into Diana's final days.

'And you don't think she was going to marry Dodi?'

Frank shakes his head again. 'Nah. She'd only been seeing him for a few weeks. He was a rebound thing, if you ask me. She wasn't over Khan.'

'The heart surgeon who broke her heart.'

'You look a bit heartbroken yourself, lad.'

I guess I'd been hoping for insider revelations, and not just a rebuttal of some of the more eye-catching theories that circulated about the Princess's death. 'So, you don't think she was murdered?'

Frank's next words are delivered as if he's confirming the most obvious thing in the world.

'Oh, Diana was murdered,' he tells me. 'No doubt about it.'

CHAPTER 13

Frank shifts in his chair and tells me, 'Film companies don't hire private detectives.' He pauses. Most people give advice to make themselves look important, or because they want that *Yeah – you're right!* moment. But I can tell Frank's advice is a heartfelt warning. 'Let this one go.'

I remind him, 'You wrote a book on it!'

A shrug and a grin. 'I gave it the Hollywood treatment! The big bad Royal Family! Imminent engagement! I studiously avoided the truth.'

'You're a journalist. I wouldn't expect otherwise.'

'Cheeky bugger.'

'Come on, then. What *is* the truth about Diana's death?'

'If I knew that, I wouldn't be here.'

I nod. 'You'd be living it up on the proceeds of your book.'

I see that disappointed look in Frank's eyes again. 'That's not what I meant.'

'You don't honestly mean—'

'Best not ask dangerous questions, son.' He leans back. 'So, you were sweet on Precious, were you?'

His diversionary tactic is a little obvious.

'What are the dangerous questions?'

I sense he's thinking about walking away, just for a moment. But he can't let it go and leans back in. Lowers his voice. 'You want dangerous? Well, ignore the speculation. Focus on the facts and what we know actually happened that night.'

'OK?' I make the word sound like a challenge.

'The Mercedes carrying Diana, Dodi, Henri Paul and the bodyguard, Trevor Rees-Jones . . . It entered the Pont de l'Alma tunnel at about 12.22 a.m.'

It's not a question, but I say, 'Sure. That's one of the indisputable facts.'

'Yeah. But you might want to ask why; because if they were heading to the Fayeds' place just off the Champs-Élysées, as we're supposed to believe, they were going way off route. But we'll let that slide.'

Christ. If we're letting that slide, what's he building up to?

'At approximately 12.23 a.m. the car crashes into the tunnel's thirteenth pillar. The question is: why did it crash?'

'To get away from the paparazzi?'

'How do you conceivably get away from people following you in a tunnel? It's the one stretch of road where you can't shake off pursuers.'

'OK. Don't shoot the messenger, but maybe Paul was drunk, like the authorities claimed.'

'Really? He somehow keeps the fact he was three times over the limit a secret from security staff at the hotel? And from Dodi and Diana? Bollocks! Check out the security footage and read the eyewitness accounts. He's fine when they leave the hotel. And his driving – we know! – is fine on the way to the tunnel. He's fine driving along Rue Cambon. Fine crossing the Place de la Concorde. Fine along the Cours la

Reine and fine along the embankment running alongside the Seine. But then, after all that, he what? Suddenly becomes so drunk he can't even steer straight, and just decides to swerve into a concrete column? Does that sound remotely plausible to you?'

It doesn't, but I know questions are sometimes more use than agreement. 'So, what made him crash?'

'Examination of debris in the tunnel, and samples taken from the Merc's door, side panels and wing mirror all indicated the involvement of a white Fiat Uno in the crash. Now, that's not just far-fetched fodder dreamt up by conspiracy nuts. That was the conclusion of Operation Paget – the Met Police's own investigation back in 2004.'

I recall that briefly, back in the 90s, that Fiat had been the second-most-talked-about car in the world, right behind the Mercedes that had been carrying Diana. It achieved smoking-gun status. Whole books were written about it, as though that vehicle alone held every answer to every question posed by events in the tunnel. These days, it barely merits a footnote. It's suffered the evidential equivalent of falling from A-list celeb status to officially opening a nail salon in Woking.

'The mysterious white Fiat,' I murmur. 'Yeah, I remember hearing something about it . . .'

'Yeah, people remember "something" about it, but it's absolutely crucial. It's just that so many other trivial little things have clouded its significance.'

'Go on.'

'So, we know the Fiat collided with Diana's car in the Pont de l'Alma tunnel. Some people have said a Fiat couldn't impact on the direction of a Merc – rubbish! Diana's car was motoring at speed. A sharp nudge from *any* vehicle would have had an effect.'

'I'm guessing the crash-site investigators would have gone into that, though?'

'The crash-site investigation was a bloody scandal! How long do you think they kept the tunnel closed? For their thorough investigation?'

He's itching to tell me when the tunnel was reopened, but I work through the scenario as I'm aware of it, partly to demonstrate I do have a vague notion about such things. 'Well, members of the press were arrested right after the crash, so it was officially a crime scene involving unexpected deaths. In the UK, I guess the tunnel would have been closed off two or three days, minimum. The FBI tend to be more thorough – so, maybe four days, if it had been a US investigation.'

'Right.'

I was hoping for a bit of surprised respect, but I'll take 'Right' and move on. 'So how long *was* the tunnel closed for, after the fatal crash?'

'It was closed in the early hours of the Sunday. It reopened later that morning. By 10 a.m. it was as though nothing had happened.'

I assume he's exaggerating. He must be. The most famous woman in the world has been killed in unnatural circumstances and the authorities are acting like someone's spilt a tin of paint? It feels beyond belief.

I narrow my eyes. '*At 10 a.m.*? They reopened the crime scene just a few hours later?'

Frank gives a slow nod.

'But what about due process? Every square inch examined . . . Tyre-mark analysis in a tunnel that busy alone should have taken—'

Frank interrupts with, 'Should have taken days. Maybe weeks. Even then, you'd normally have had a senior SC Manager reviewing strategy before reopening was even considered.'

'That's outrageous, to put it mildly.'

I think for the first time he twigs this isn't just a distant historical event to me. It's the death of innocent people followed by a sequence of baffling responses that suggests no one really cared.

'Oh, Novak. It gets worse, much worse . . .'

CHAPTER 14

Frank Harvey presses on. 'Just a few hours after the crash that killed Diana, Princess of Wales, they got a cleaning team in. The whole crime scene was doused in water and disinfectant.'

'Jesus . . .'

Frank's angry. He reaches for the tray, picks up his second whisky and knocks it back in one. As he puts the glass on the table, he says bitterly, quoting Lady Macbeth, 'A little water clears us of this deed.'

'What were they wiping away?'

He's gone quiet.

Maybe he's reluctant to exacerbate his own sense of ire. So I give him a little nudge with, 'If this is the stuff they're not bothering to conceal, it makes you wonder what they're actually hiding . . .'

'Ah, but they *are* concealing it! Burying it in an avalanche of facts and half-truths.'

I take his point. Even in the few minutes I've been talking with him, it strikes me that I've been bombarded with anomalies and overlooked facts that each deserve closer inspection, until they get thrust to one side by another incongruity.

There's another one heading my way as Frank mutters, 'Like the guy driving the Fiat.'

'Go on.'

'Dodi's dad assembled a team. They found the Fiat that collided with the Merc.'

'Owned by?'

'One James Andanson, who swore blind he'd not been in Paris the night of the twenty-ninth.'

'Well, he would, wouldn't he?'

'Yeah, except sometime later, he changed his story. Starts saying he was there. In the tunnel when the crash happened. He shoots his mouth off – claims to have information about what really happened . . . This sounds uncharitable, but it was like he was trying to get in on the act. Get a foothold in the media hoopla surrounding the Princess.'

'How did that work out for him?' I'm asking the question, but I'm pretty sure it doesn't end up with him chatting about the crash and his renewed love for life on *Oprah*.

'He was found in the burning wreck of an old BMW, in a forest in the South of France.'

'Christ, Frank.'

'The investigating officer arrived before the body was completely burnt through. He reported seeing at least one hole in Andanson's head. And one of the firemen on the scene – again, a guy who saw him before the charring was complete – insisted he saw *two* bullet wounds, that Andanson had been shot in the head, twice. The post-mortem also reported carbon monoxide in his blood.'

'Which would suggest at some point he inhaled – or was made to inhale – exhaust fumes.'

'No getting away from it.'

'What was the official verdict?'

'Suicide.'

'So he shot himself in the head a couple of times, poisoned himself with carbon mono and then set fire to his car. That's the official narrative and no one sought to question it?'

He shakes his head and I feel those sharp blue eyes analysing me again. 'So all this is public domain.' I pause. 'Why do I get the feeling you know more?'

'What does it matter? It was a quarter of a century ago, people have moved on.'

'You sound as if you're trying to convince yourself. You know it matters.'

Frank laughs, not unkindly. 'How old are you?'

'Late thirties.'

He nods. 'Still burning with the righteous fire of youth. You remind me of—' He stops himself. But something I've said has broken the spell. He's back in the moment and there's a lightness in his voice as he urges, 'Walk away, Novak. I'm not helping you.'

'Frank, I just—'

'What do you think you can really achieve?'

I recall Miss Winters pausing by my front door and say to Frank, 'Just before she died, Diana mentioned she was on the verge of announcing something. Something big. What do you think it was?'

'I think there's one guy who knows . . .' Almost immediately I see he regrets his candour. 'Every old hack has a theory about that little enigma.'

'And what's yours?'

He lets my words hang for a moment, before declaring, 'I'll have another pint and a couple of chasers. Cheers!' He smiles and downs what should have been my other shot.

The interview is over. I thank Frank for seeing me and for the information he's shared, get to my feet and stand another round. Well, it would be rude not to, wouldn't it?

CHAPTER 15

Frank Harvey's Story

Frank had another couple of beers with the private detective, half expecting he'd loop back to Diana with a skilfully established segue. But she wasn't mentioned again and the old journalist realised that although his drinking companion wanted to discuss the Princess, he was far too polite to crowbar her into their conversation.

Or perhaps it wasn't politeness. Maybe it was patience, part of a shrewder plan intended to win his trust and friendship.

Either way, they chatted about Fleet Street in the 80s. Frank trotted out a few of his top ten anecdotes that he'd polished to perfection over the years. Everything from phone tapping (for the serious student of practical journalism) to wife-swapping backstage at the BAFTAs (for everyone else).

When they rose to leave, they shook hands and Frank braced himself for a final plea. But none came. Novak thanked him. Didn't even say they should do it again. And then he was gone, walking briskly across Broadwick Street towards the market.

Still standing in the pub's doorway, Frank turned towards the barman. 'Cheers!'

'See you next time. Cheers, Frank.'

He glanced across the road, pondering where to go next. And with a slight feeling of disappointment – which he didn't care to acknowledge – that Novak had been too courteous, or astute, to circle back to Diana, he stepped into the dusk of Soho.

Something made him pause.

He rooted around in his pocket for a packet of Camels. He unwrapped it and coaxed out a cigarette. As he slipped it between his lips, he realised what was wrong: a guy on the corner of Poland Street, standing patiently outside a sandwich shop. A moment ago he'd been chatting on his mobile phone. Now he was on the move. Still chit-chatting away, but when he was forced to pause for a van trundling along Broadwick Street, he looked momentarily peeved and darted across the road the moment it passed.

He was heading in Novak's direction.

Frank lit his cigarette. Watched him disappear down Berwick Street. He knew it could be a coincidence, knew it could mean nothing.

He exhaled a nimbus of smoke into the evening air and set off down Lexington. Best out of it.

He hadn't even taken three paces before he stopped dead in his tracks.

He hesitated, but only for a second. Then Frank turned and began following the man pursuing Novak. As he hurried through the market, he reflected that it was just like the old days and he hadn't lost any of his old instincts.

He might not have been quite so self-congratulatory if at any point he'd noticed the woman who had spotted his movements and was now following him.

CHAPTER 16

Novak's Story (cont.)

Marc Novak turned left at the bottom of Berwick Street Market and hung another left when he reached Wardour Street. Five minutes later, he was sauntering down Carnaby Street, then cut across into Kingly Court.

The man tailing him – a cautious operative called Edwards – was able to keep a reasonable distance behind his quarry because he was so easy to pick out. Novak was tall, toned and lean and stood out as he strode through the busy Soho streets. Even so, Edwards almost missed him turn left again when he disappeared into some kind of club. He considered his options and decided to follow Novak into the place. He stepped through the front door and found he was in Cahoots, a 40s-themed bar that recreated the spirit and aesthetics of wartime London. An attendant ushered Edwards down a long flight of steps that took him into the main area, a large dimly lit room that was decked out like a disused underground station during the Blitz. Except, of course, this space was full of small tables and chairs and historical paraphernalia. Everything from ornate standard lamps to large, old-style suitcases and stacks of tinned food ostensibly from eighty years earlier.

Edwards scanned the room. No sign of Novak.

A waitress approached him. She wore a red floral dress and black high heels and her raven hair was fashioned into a victory roll. 'Hey! How are you doing?' She was American with a broad New York accent.

'I'm good, thanks. This may seem an odd question, but is that' – Edwards gestured to the door he'd just come through – 'the only way out?'

'Sure is. Do you have a reservation?'

'I'm afraid not.'

'You're in luck. A big party's just cancelled. Follow me, sugar.'

She guided him through the 'station', where drinkers, many of them in period dress, sipped impressive-looking cocktails out of mugs and old milk bottles. He was led into what looked to be a carriage of a wartime tube train. Its interior was divided into booths. 'You're very fortunate, honey.' The waitress stretched the *very* for a couple of seconds. 'This place is normally chock-a-block.' She indicated where he should sit. 'Here's a menu.'

She handed him what looked to be a newspaper, but it actually contained a list of the drinks and snacks on offer.

'Thank you.'

'No problem.'

The waitress disappeared.

Edwards was alone in the carriage and sat in a central booth, meaning he could see the main area fairly well and was still able to keep his eyes on the exit. If Novak left, he'd know about it. Glancing down at the menu, he briefly wondered if he could put an 'Engine Fuel Espresso' on expenses.

Probably not. Typical. He found himself in a cocktail bar, but he couldn't even—

Edwards suddenly felt a tight, intense pain around his throat and was pulled several inches out of his seat. He tried to clutch his throat but a broad leather belt was strangling him. Novak, who'd been concealed in the next booth along, tightened his grip and Edwards felt his eyes bulge. He tried to beg, 'Let me go!' But the gurgle was incomprehensible and he fell silent as he sensed Novak's breath on his right ear.

'Who told you to follow me?'

The belt loosened and Edwards choked.

'Answer me!'

The belt tightened again and Edwards' vision swam. When Novak relaxed his grip a second time, he blurted out, 'I don't know! I'm freelance! It's just another gig!'

'Who do you report to?'

'No idea! It's a dead-drop job!'

'And what do I call you?'

Edwards felt Novak's hands riffling through his pockets.

'My name's Vass. Oliver Vass.'

'No, it's not. You're not carrying any ID. So you're too much of a pro to give me your real name. All right, we're going to pay a visit to your dead-drop site. I'm guessing there'll be some sort of surveillance there that could help us figure out who hired you.' Novak pulled the belt from Edwards' neck and the two men stood up. 'You lead the way.'

'You almost crushed my windpipe.' Edwards stepped out of his booth, paused and rubbed his throat. 'I really thought you were going to strangle me for a—'

Without warning, he whirled around, unleashing a powerful, right-handed haymaker.

Novak ducked and moved forward with a savage upper-cut that broke Edwards' jaw, sending him sprawling into an unconscious heap on the floor.

The waitress appeared in the carriage doors. 'Hey! What goes on, Mr Novak?'

'I haven't the faintest idea, Reggie. He simply collapsed.'

'Oh, yeah?'

'Maybe he saw the prices.'

'Very funny, I *don't* think.'

Novak knelt over Edwards. 'He's out cold, but he'll be OK. Thanks for your help, earlier.'

'You wanna show some gratitude? How 'bout taking me out for that drink you keep promising?'

'I'd love to. But I'm on a case.'

'You are literally *forever* on a case.'

'And if anyone asks how this happened . . .' He nodded to the supine Edwards. 'Remember, careless talk costs lives.'

Reggie tapped the side of her nose. 'I'll keep mum.'

Novak kissed her on the cheek. 'You're a trooper.'

As she watched him weave his way through the tables towards the exit, she shook her head. 'Ain't I just?'

CHAPTER 17

I check my watch – 5 p.m. It's got chilly, which suits me fine – the cold air on my face feels refreshing as I stride through Soho, walk through Leicester Square and on to Charing Cross Road. Years ago, the stretch from Wyndham's to the Phoenix Theatre was rammed with antiquarian and second-hand bookshops. And if I was after something new, the original Murder One, tucked away on the north side, seldom disappointed. Some of those bookshops went out of business, a few switched to online trading only, but several moved to the side streets that run from Charing Cross Road towards St Martin's.

One of them is called Harker & Hay's Bookshop and remains a favourite of mine. I walk in, close the door and say hello to the woman on the till. She looks up and glares at me like I've just tried to set fire to one of the shelves. She's about my age. Long hair tied back. Tortoiseshell glasses. She emanates an air of hostility, as if anyone who sets foot in her shop is somehow trespassing.

I say to her, 'Are you Ms Harker?'

'I am *Miss* Harker.'

'You sent me an email.'

'I doubt that.'

'OK. Your *father* sent me an email, telling me you had some first-edition Doyles in. Three, I think. I'm an old friend of your dad's. How is he?'

'He's on the mend. Wait here, please.'

'Happy to.'

She disappears and I pretend to browse through a shelf of nineteenth-century classics. But I'm thinking about Frank Harvey. He knows a lot more than he's telling me about the crash in Paris, and more importantly, he knows someone who might have information about the announcement the Princess was intending to make shortly before she was killed. Frank told me to drop the case, but I'd be a poor investigator if I didn't follow the lead. And besides, there was something in the guy's manner. Something that suggests the case is still important to him. Out of nowhere, I wonder if he feels he let Diana down.

'These are the books my father thought you might be interested in.'

'Thank you.'

She hands me three old hardbacks. All by Conan Doyle. Two Brigadier Gerards and a Sherlock. I look them over as she surreptitiously looks me over. Her old man and me go way back and I'm guessing she's wondering if all the stories he's told her are true.

'I'll take this one, please.' It's a UK first edition of *The Casebook of Sherlock Holmes*, the final collection of short stories featuring the Great Detective. 'Could you wrap it for me, please?'

Miss Harker gets to work and I glance out the front window, looking up towards the clouds.

I tell her, 'The rain's holding off.' But I don't tell her that the woman who followed me from the John Snow is loitering at the end of the road. She's either plucking up the courage to ask me out, or she's working for the same people who hired the guy currently asleep at Cahoots. Either way, she's not my type.

But she represents a problem. I can hardly deal with her in the same way I handled the man.

'Miss Harker, would you mind if I left by the rear exit?'

She looks surprised, then masks it. 'You're the detective . . .' Her father will have mentioned it. 'Are you in trouble?'

'I'm always in trouble.'

She raises an eyebrow.

'Do you mind if I slip out the back way?'

'All right,' she replies after a moment's hesitation. 'If someone comes in and asks after you, I'll say you're checking out stock on the fourth floor.'

'This is a three-storey building.'

'Who's counting?'

'Thank you, Miss Harker.'

I stay in the area and visit a couple more bookshops before finding the paperback I'm after. The cover has a photo of the Princess of Wales looking forlorn and the words: *DIANA: THE TRUTH by FRANK HARVEY*. And on the back cover . . .

There he is. A young Frank Harvey. His author photograph is ridiculous. He's in a suit and tie, but he's in the field, moving away from a helicopter that I presume he's just leapt from. He's half crouching, half running. The picture couldn't convey 'FRANK HARVEY – MAN OF ACTION!' any more forcefully if the words were popping out on a spring.

Yes, his author photograph is absurd, and I love it. I'd bet good money he does too.

I buy the book, take a photo of the back cover and WhatsApp it to Frank, along with the message: *You handsome devil!*

And now I know, looking at that picture, that Frank Harvey will be on board. Sure, he's knocking on a bit, but he's a man with more helicopters to jump out of.

CHAPTER 18

It's 10 p.m. and I'm sprawled across my sofa, finishing Frank's book. He's one of the few authors who writes about Diana as if she was a real person. So many royal observers simply present her as the figure we've come to know, come to anticipate and, I suppose, welcome. Bashful but brave. Loving mother, wronged wife, woman of substance and fashion icon. Qualities used as props to ensure we recognise the figure being invoked. Like sticking a deerstalker on a serious-looking bloke and handing him a magnifying glass, just to make absolutely certain we're all aware that the character in question is now Sherlock Holmes. The need for and authenticity of the props may be dubious, but it doesn't matter. There is a version of Diana we've come to expect and anything deviating from that would be like receiving an Easter egg on Christmas Day.

The more I read about the Princess of Wales, the more I like Frank. Check out any book or article that centres on the writer meeting Diana. How is their first face-to-face conveyed? How is Diana introduced? Through her beauty? Through her down-to-earth nature? Or her ability to put you at ease?

All fine, of course. Possibly even true. But anodyne and unhelpful.

Frank Harvey, on the other hand, describes the room where they met and the security presence that followed her everywhere. Those men who are just out of shot on most photographs and almost all recollections. But with Frank, there they are: vigilant, slightly pompous, a touch complacent. He notices how they move and the cologne they wear. To him, the two seem equally important, and I respect that level of insight.

I pull out my phone and call his number. He answers almost immediately.

'It's Novak. Don't hang up!'

'I told you before, lad. Walk away. I can't help you.'

'I know! Yeah, I'm not calling you about any of that. I'm reading your book.'

He pauses. 'Yeah, well, I don't give refunds.'

'No, I'm enjoying it.'

'Thanks. But don't get too invested in the central character. Spoiler alert – it doesn't end well for her.'

'You say in the book that you met her a couple of times.'

'Yeah. That bit's true.'

'What was she like?'

'How d'you mean?'

'Just . . . what was she like? As a person.'

There's silence on the other end of the phone. I'm hoping I made a good impression, that he's a bit drunk and a lot sentimental. That way, he might open up. But the silence stretches and I think I've called him too soon. I'm about to change the subject and bail when:

'Well, she really and truly cared. She made you feel like you were the centre of the universe. You know when you're a kid, you do something really well and just for a minute or two it feels like the world is yours and everything . . . just kind of glows?'

'Yeah, I do,' I lie.

'Well, Diana, she gave you that feeling. She was beautiful. I mean, a looker, sure, but I mean . . . she was beautiful, you know?'

Frank stops. Expects me to say something, but when I don't, he continues.

'I only met her twice, but even today . . .' He sighs. 'I still miss her.'

There's another silence. I let this one stretch even longer before risking it. My voice is low and urgent. 'Help me find out what happened to her, Frank. Give me the name of the guy who knew what Diana had been planning to announce . . . We can still help her.'

Frank exhales, and even in that release of breath I can hear he's annoyed. Probably not so much with me for pursuing the personal angle, but with himself for being suckered into sharing his feelings. He hangs up.

My doorbell rings and I'm glad of the distraction. I rise, slipping my phone into my pocket as I go to the door.

Even as I open it, I'm thinking about the call, wondering if I could have played it more shrewdly with Frank. I don't see who's on my doorstep, just feel the force of the attack as I'm struck in the face. I stagger back slightly, but my assailant moves forward in a blur, fast with violent intent.

CHAPTER 19

Precious's Story

Precious Weeks' stance on royalty hovered somewhere between apathy and antipathy. As a group of wealthy, whining individuals, their attempts to appear 'of the people' appalled her. Their diamond-encrusted lives bore no relation to the day-to-day reality of anyone she'd ever met. And their high-profile pleas for privacy, running alongside their relentless monetisation of their status felt like the antics of a crass, cosseted elite.

And yet, when she'd worked at a food bank, she'd seen first-hand the fillip an unpublicised visit by one of the Queen's daughters-in-law had given her fellow volunteers. And like many non-royalists she had an almost guilty fondness for the old girl herself, with her stoic endurance and unwavering sense of duty.

Precious knew very little about Diana, so when Novak had asked her to look over her death, she began with the basics. She, too, watched the bulletins that had aired shortly after the crash in Paris and had been struck by the mention of a news blackout.

On a whim, she Googled one of the most famous quotes associated with the Princess, 'Whatever love means', which was – she recalled – how her husband-to-be responded when they'd both been asked if they were in love.

The conversation the quote is from took place in February, 1981 on the day her engagement to Prince Charles had been made public, and Precious found it on YouTube without any problems. Lady Diana, as she then was, wore her iconic blue suit and white blouse, and early on in the recording she showed off her engagement ring – fourteen diamonds surrounding a 12-carat oval Ceylon sapphire set in 18-carat white gold. The future princess looked startlingly young.

But what struck Precious hardest was the fact that Diana and Charles were completely, *glaringly* different and so obviously mismatched. She was an anxious teenager, caught in the headlights of global attention. He was an assured man in his thirties. A prince and public figure, careless of the world's inquisitive gaze.

Precious fast-forwarded the video, hitting play as Charles replies to some banal question with a smiling, 'I'm amazed she's been brave enough to take me on!'

The male interviewer asked, 'And I suppose, in love?'

Here it comes.

Diana dipped her head, as if embarrassed by the question. 'Of course!'

The man she's soon to marry replied, 'Whatever *in love* means.'

Precious frowned. Rewound the video to a section where Charles talked about Diana's recent holiday to Australia, which she visited without him. They'd both been quite open about the sojourn, so it was obvious that, for a couple of supposed soulmates, they'd kept in touch surprisingly little during Diana's absence. Charles talked about having difficulty phoning his then girlfriend and recalled, 'But I rang up on one occasion and I said, can I speak . . . and they said no. We're not taking any calls. So I said, it's the Prince of Wales speaking! How do I know it's the Prince of Wales, came back the reply. But I am!'

Diana laughed dutifully at the anecdote. Genuine, infectious laughter.

Her fiancé continued, 'Eventually I got the number because they were staying somewhere else. But they said the phones are tapped, or something, which I found highly unlikely . . .'

The Prince and the interviewer both chuckled at the suggestion of phone tapping, as if the notion was absurd. Charles looked amused. Precious rewound the moment and focused on Diana's face. She's far from amused. *'They said the phones are tapped, or something . . .'*

She hit pause. Studied Diana's reaction. There's no mirth on her face. She's serious.

She knows.

Precious reflected that although royal historians may choose to wrap Diana up in cotton wool, she really didn't need it. The so-called People's Princess was a lot sharper than most people imagine.

The truly interesting takeaway from the interview remains universally ignored, whilst the Prince's ill-judged words became infamous. And as she considered this fact, a realisation hit Precious.

When it comes to Diana, we often look in the wrong places.

She briefly wondered why that should be the case, unaware, of course, that the conclusion she arrived at would prove pivotal to Novak eventually unravelling the truth about Diana's death.

CHAPTER 20

The blow to my face has sent me reeling back. The strike wasn't particularly hard, but it caught me off guard. I see another slap heading in my direction, but I'm prepared for this one and catch my assailant's wrist.

'Good evening, Mrs Brandon.'

I unfurl my fingers, wondering if she'll have another go, but she just stands in my doorway, breathing heavily through rage and exhaustion.

'You lied to me!'

I instinctively touch the side of my face that she struck and glance down at my fingertips. They're coated in blood, but it's nothing serious. Her wedding ring caught the corner of my lip, opening a small cut. I pull a tissue from my pocket and dab away the blood whilst asking, 'Are you all right, Mrs Brandon?'

'*No!* I trusted you! I needed you! And you let me down!'

She steps forward into my hallway and for a second I think she's about to hit me again. But she kind of slumps. 'Damn you!' It's the last crackle of a sparkler before it burns itself out. She's deflated. Shakes her head. 'I . . .'

I know that look. She's about to weep and my first instinct is to wrap my arms around her, squeeze her into me, and tell her I'll take care of everything.

Yes. I know. That would be unprofessional. Relax! I did say *instinct*, didn't I?

Instead I tell her, 'Whatever's wrong, I can fix it.'

But she's already turning away. 'No one can.'

Anna Brandon is hurrying down my driveway and I jog for a couple of seconds to catch her up.

'Well, that's useful,' I assure her.

She stops. 'How is that useful?'

'Because the problems that no one else can help with – they're my speciality.'

'Do you mean that?' They're the words of a woman who is desperate to believe.

'It's the first line on my CV,' I reply, and this wins a little laugh. 'Why don't we go back inside? I can get a drink and you can hit me again if it'd make you feel any better.'

Another small laugh, but she shakes her head.

'Mrs Brandon, I never lied to you. And I meant what I said at the Serpentine. I will never let you down.'

She's looking up at me and, in the moonlight, I can see her eyes have welled up.

'Mr Novak,' she says, 'the worst thing in the world has happened to me.'

I slowly nod. She looks as though she means it. And I thought I was having a bad day.

CHAPTER 21

She's removed her coat, but remains standing, gazing around my front room like it's the first time she's encountered wallpaper. My place is not what she's used to, but I'm not about to apologise.

'What can I get you to drink, Mrs Brandon?'

'What have you got, Mr Novak?'

'Whisky or wine.'

'I'll have a whisky. With water.'

I guess she'd prefer wine but thinks asking for a cheeky Sav Blanc would make her sound feeble. 'You sure?'

'I know what I want.'

'I'll just be a tick.' When I'm in the kitchen, I call through, 'So what do you think I lied to you about?'

She shouts, but not in a shouty way, 'You gave me your word your services were confidential!'

'They are!' I pause. 'Glenlivet's all right for you?'

'Perfect! Then how come my husband knows you found him out?'

'Ice or no ice?'

'No ice.' She wanders through to the kitchen. Leans against the door frame. Brushes a stray strand of blonde hair from her face. 'He told me he wants a divorce. It's a pre-emptive strike. He *knows*. And I didn't tell anyone. So either you or your partner . . .'

I hand her a large whisky and water. 'How's that? It's a decent enough drop, but probably not the calibre you're used to.'

She takes the tumbler. 'Don't worry about me and liquor, Mr Novak.'

There's that spirit again. It's one of the reasons I like her. 'Would you like more water in there?'

She sniffs her drink and, in a show of bravado, takes a hefty gulp. For a moment she's OK, and even manages to reproach me with, 'You've already drowned it!' But then the burn hits and she starts coughing.

With what I believe is known as *faux concern*, I ask, 'Are you OK?'

She looks at me, annoyed for the briefest of moments before replying with a good-natured shrug.

Ten minutes later, I'm in my armchair nursing a straight Glenlivet while Anna sits on my settee with a glass of Pinot in her hand.

I say, 'I've seen this happen a million times. I know you didn't *mean* to give anything away after we informed you about—'

'I just wanted time to plan!'

'But your husband's an intelligent guy. And women aren't the only ones with intuition. He's acted first so his counsel can claim your demands are motivated . . . A woman scorn'd and all that.'

She shakes her head. 'I should have listened to you.' I suspect this is the first time in a long time that the socially sorted Mrs Brandon feels quite so lost and confused. 'I don't know what to do . . .' As her immediate plight occurs to her, she adds, 'I can't go home tonight.'

'Yes, you can. It's your home as much as his. You've got to make that clear from the start.'

'I will. I'm just not sure how.'

She looks into her wine as if a glass of Sainsbury's own Pinot might hold all the answers.

It's almost midnight; as we stand in my hallway, she says, 'My driver's waiting outside.'

'Of course he is.'

I swing the front door open. My guest steps outside, takes a pace forward, pauses, turns.

'I'm sorry about—' I never find out what she's sorry about because she moves swiftly back to me. Plants a kiss on my cheek. She lingers a microsecond longer than necessary then whispers, 'You're my absolute saviour.'

And with that, she hurries away.

I remain in the doorway, watching her go. As she turns at the end of my driveway, she looks back at me. A moment later, she's gone. She arrived slapping my face, and left kissing it. I'm grateful, not for the first time, that it's a woman's prerogative to change her mind.

As I close the door, my phone beeps with a WhatsApp from FRANK HARVEY. I open the message. It contains just three words: *Colonel Gerry Whittaker.*

I murmur, 'Thanks, Frank.'

I'm a step closer to finding out the truth behind Diana's death.

CHAPTER 22

I wake up early, but know calling Frank before 10 a.m. would be bad form, so I make a coffee and take it back to bed where I finish *Diana: The Truth*. The final few chapters are a disappointment and it's clear Frank was more interested in writing about the Princess than the conspiracies tied to her. He's disparaging about the way French authorities handled the aftermath of the crash, but his overwhelming emotion is sadness. Not about how she died, but simply the fact that she *had* died. Or, as he wrote, a profound loss that '. . . her young life should be cut short in an incident that seems so meaningless'.

I read that line again. Interesting that he opts for the word 'incident' as opposed to 'accident'.

It's 9.30 a.m. I shower, shave and get dressed. Open up my laptop and log on. I've played so many Diana videos that YouTube is now suggesting I watch a whole load more. Who am I to argue? The algorithms don't lie, right? I click on the one at the top of its recommendations. It's dated 1997, the year she died. I'm not sure whether it's from a news report or an extended look at her life, but it shows the Princess in formal mode, giving a short speech about landmines.

I remember they were one of her things, but don't recall ever seeing her speak at length about them. In the video, she reaches a lectern and, using written notes as a prompt, gives a calm, lucid address and within two minutes I understand why she wanted the bloody things banned. She outlines that the damage they do is often inflicted on 'some of the poorest people on Earth' and right from the off, she admits that prior to her recent visit to Angola, she'd been unaware of the issue, because in her words:

'. . . the mine is a stealthy killer. Long after conflict has ended, its innocent victims die, or are wounded singly, in countries of which we hear little. Their lonely fate is never reported. The world, with its many other preoccupations, remains largely unmoved by a death roll of something like 800 people every month, many of them women and children . . . I went to Angola earlier this year in January with the British Red Cross – a country where there are fifteen million landmines in a population, ladies and gentlemen, of ten million – with a desire of drawing world attention to this vital, but hitherto largely neglected issue. Some people chose to interpret my visit as a political statement . . .'

I pause the video, rewind it and hit play, because I'm fascinated by her facial expression as she says those few last words. It's the one time her demeanour changes, and it does so for literally a second. An interpretation of that expression, in modern parlance, would run along the lines of: *'Really?!'* It's an insight into what she thought of people who didn't understand her motives. She continues:

'But it was not. I am not a political figure. And as I said at the time, and I'd like to reiterate now, my interests are humanitarian. That is why I felt drawn to this human tragedy. That is why I wanted to play my part in working towards a worldwide ban of these weapons.'

It's hard to view her desire as anything approaching contentious. In fact, it seems so obvious, it's difficult to see how anyone could object to her stance.

But when the next video plays, I'm reminded of how *anything* Diana said or did was perceived in some quarters as controversial. This second video is an amalgamation of soundbites reacting to her campaign. Labour MP Des Skinner looks furious, which is bizarre because his first comment indicates he agrees with her. 'I want to ban landmines!' he rages. 'But I don't need a member of the Royal Family telling me what to do!' It's a mystifying response, as if he's livid that she's correct, and more than that, she has no right to be correct! There's a suggestion that being guided by 'humanitarian' impulses signals a very low state of affairs.

The next guy up sounds very pleased with himself. He breezily opines, 'I would compare her action this week with that of Brigitte Bardot in support of cats. It's very emotional and very media-worthy, but it doesn't add anything to the sum of human knowledge.'

Whilst I don't recall any of these clips specifically, the next one stirs memories. It shows Diana, presumably in Angola, wearing torso protection and a flimsy transparent face mask, walking through a stretch of crops that war has transformed into a field of death. She stoops to examine an exposed landmine and the whir of a dozen cameras, snapping the sight, is clearly audible. Yes, I remember these moments on the news and on the front pages of tabloids and broadsheets alike. I recollect the next exchange, as well.

It's part of the same news item, and Diana is walking through a broad, beige town street, after seeing for herself the nearby minefield. A journalist puts it to her that she's been called 'a loose cannon' because of the trip, and that 'back home' her actions have been labelled political. The journo doesn't have the nerve to make the accusations herself. She just fires them in the young woman's face, because anything positive would have been unthinkable, of course.

Diana is the epitome of grace, however. In a low, gentle voice, she replies, 'I'm only trying to highlight a problem that's going on all around the world.' Now she smiles, as if to say, *It's really very simple!* And she adds, 'That's all.'

My emotional response to the videos is, I'm mortified to confess, very different to my reaction back in 1997. All these years later, it feels insane that she could be castigated for suggesting that unnecessary weapons that destroy thousands of lives should be banned.

Something crucial occurs to me. If her views on something so obvious caused such an outcry, what would the response have been if Diana had done something truly controversial? And what could—

My phone rings. It's Frank and he's blunt and to the point. 'What time were you going to wait until to call me?'

'Eleven o'clock.'

'You're a rubbish liar.'

'Thanks for the name, Frank.'

'What's in a name? That which we call a lead by any other name would smell as sweet. Have you got a pen and paper?'

'Yep.'

'Then throw them away. Anything I tell you has got to go into your noggin and stay there. I don't want any paper trails. Deal?'

'Deal.'

'You give me your word?'

'Yes. I give you my word. But you know that I'm not doing this out of personal curiosity. When I get to the bottom of how the Princess of Wales was killed, I'm going to shout it to the world.'

'No matter what the cost of taking that action may be?'

'Absolutely.'

'All the way, lad?'

'All the way.'

'Novak – this won't end with all your questions being answered, neat and tidy, like. It won't be a game of Cluedo with you left holding cards at the end saying who did it, where and how. Real life doesn't work like that.'

'I know that, Frank.'

'It will end in death. I don't know how or whose, but it will, you know. Are you prepared for that?'

'Just get on with it.'

'OK,' he says, 'let me tell you about Colonel Gerry Whittaker and how he might help you find out who murdered Diana.'

CHAPTER 23

'So, Gerry Whittaker,' I ask. 'How did he know Diana?'

'The Princess was surrounded by military intelligence. Some she knew about, some she didn't. A handful were bona fide undercover operatives, but most were just assets.'

'Assets? What d'you mean?'

'Well, a bodyguard or someone in a civilian role close to Diana would be expected to report to someone in the service. They'd pass on bits and bobs – if something seemed odd or inappropriate. Trivia, mostly. Thoughts. Opinions. The occasional good piece of intel. Now, don't get me wrong, Novak, that's standard for Royal Protection. But the situation meant a load of normal people became assets to the service.'

'When you say service . . . ?'

'The intelligence service. Yeah. And all those assets were assigned the same case officer. That's to say, they all reported to the same guy, who acted as a buffer between the asset and the rest of the service.'

I grasp the sense of the arrangement. 'A nice, friendly face who remembers how you take your tea.'

'Exactly. If you're a butler or a bodyguard or something like that, you have to be handled with sensitivity. You don't want to be dragged to some big scary building for a debrief.

That'd just freak you out. You want a friendly face, as you say, to chat with about the Princess. And the information you provide? Well, it's not done because the British Intelligence service is monitoring her . . .'

'Heaven forbid!'

'It's done because some nice people want to keep her safe, and so they need all the gossip you can share.'

'And that case officer was Whittaker?'

'I think I was the only one in the press pack who knew he even existed. The Official Secrets Act wasn't just a piece of paper to him.'

'So what happened to the amiable Gerry Whittaker?'

'Christ, Novak! You're gonna have to do some legwork yourself!'

I smile. 'I knew there'd be a catch. Do you have contact details for him?'

'Yep. And you're the first person I'll be sharing them with in over twenty-five years.'

'Well, it's appreciated.'

'OK. First of all – his phone number. Do you have a pen and paper?'

I pause before replying, 'Is that a trick question?'

The moment my conversation with Frank is finished, I call Gerry Whittaker. He doesn't answer and I leave a non-committal message, asking him to get back to me.

As I'm heating up the coffee I brewed earlier, my phone rings.

It's the Colonel. I crowbar Frank Harvey's name into our conversation as quickly as possible, shamefully calling him 'my old chum'.

Gerry asks, 'What's the blessed rogue working on at the moment?'

I haven't the faintest idea what 'my old chum' is up to professionally, and reply with a breezy, 'Oh, this and that! You know Frank!'

There's a beat and I'm sure he's aware that I'm lying. 'All right. Let's meet.' I'm taken aback by the offer and he adds, not unkindly, but he has a tone of *let's crack on, chaps!* 'I'm assuming that was where this was heading, old man?'

I like being called that by this velvet-voiced colonel. It makes me feel as if I'm in the mess and he's just offered to stand the next round.

'That would be fabulous, sir. Thank you.'

'Jolly good!'

He gives me his address. 'Is 2.30 all right for you?'

'Today?'

'May as well. Quick sticks and all that.'

'No, that's perfect. Thanks again.'

'Good-oh. And Novak.'

'Yes, Colonel?'

His tone changes very slightly. 'Come alone.' That's not an instruction. It's a warning.

I start to say, 'Of course,' but he's already hung up.

CHAPTER 24

I drive a mustard-coloured Morris Marina that rolled off the British Leyland assembly line back in the 70s at a time when they were outselling pretty much everything else on UK roads. I call it a classic. Others call it one of the worst vehicles ever manufactured and wonder why I drive a car that's older than I am – although, to be honest, it's a question I ask myself every time I have to fork out for its MOT.

The Marina may be iconic, but I ended up with it quite by chance. I once spent months working a case, and when my client 'couldn't' pay, I ended up with my current mustard motor in lieu of hard cash. It's not all bad news, though. Its former owner was crazy about cars from the pre-BL era but hated how they drove. She therefore gave it what she called an 'invisible upgrade'. A kind of pimp for introverts. As a result, my 70s four-door has a powerful BMW engine under the bonnet, electric power steering and an autonomous emergency braking system that's been tweaked for off-road performance. The bodywork looks great, thanks to a thin gel that's been applied, which bats away the elements and keeps it in tip-top condition. I don't know what the gel is called, but I could sure as hell do with a coat of it myself.

Gerry Whittaker's based in Foxglove, a small village I've never heard of. Finding the village is one thing, but locating the Colonel's house – 'The Lines' – is another. There are no street names in Foxglove and its houses, cottages and terraced homes aren't numbered, as if a numerical signposting convention would be too much of an indignity.

After ten minutes of peering at nameplates, I find a big, old thatched cottage that adheres to the chocolate-box school of aesthetics. White stone and rose bushes. A small wooden front door and chintz curtains. If you weren't trained in such matters and you weren't looking for it, you wouldn't spot the state-of-the-art alarm and surveillance system that keeps it protected. I park a little way away, lock my car and walk back to The Lines.

The Colonel had asked me to use the back door – 'Not that it's the tradesman's entrance, Mr Novak!' – and so I push open the side gate and circle the building. It's an impressive pad.

I ring the doorbell. There's a metal grille, half-hidden by trailing ivy, and Gerry's voice crackles out of it. 'Hello?'

I lean in. 'Colonel Whittaker? It's Marc Novak. We spoke on the phone, earlier today.'

Although I've not pinpointed any cameras, I know damn well there's at least one trained on me right now, and I imagine Gerry is giving me the once-over.

'Mr Novak. Won't be a mo.'

Several seconds later, I hear the rattle of locks and the door is swung open. Gerry Whittaker is younger than I'd anticipated. Late sixties, but spry and in obvious rude health. He's diminutive. 5'8"tops. Wears a blue blazer and tie, and beige slacks like he's about to leave for a 70s-themed dinner party. He says, 'You found me all right, then?' and offers a welcoming smile.

He's understated. Amiable. But he's also shrewd, always watching. Nevertheless, there's something soothing about him. I can see why he got the case-officer gig and I instinctively like the guy.

You found me all right, then?

Maybe I'm being paranoid, but I wonder if he's referring to more than my ability to reach Foxglove. I play it safe with, 'Yes, thanks. It was a pleasant drive.'

'Yes, it's rather a pretty part of the world. Come in, come in!'

He steps back and opens the door wider. Even from the entrance, I can see his cottage is larger than it looks from the outside. The hallway is tastefully furnished and three framed posters hang on the wall to my right. One is a rather gorgeous, blue-toned piece of artwork advertising a production of *Iolanthe* at the Mendelssohn Theatre. The second is a poster for the ENO's recent revival of *HMS Pinafore*. I can't make out the third.

I step inside. 'You have a beautiful home. Should I remove my shoes?'

I can hear music coming from further inside the cottage. It's familiar but I can't place it. And the smell of bread baking wafts through from the kitchen.

'No, you can keep your clogs on!'

My host is never anything less than courteous, but he wordlessly shepherds me into a corner of the hallway. I find myself standing next to a mahogany tallboy. Gerry slides open one of its drawers and produces what appears to be a small paddle.

'And thank you! It's not a bad little billet.'

He begins to run the paddle over me and I tell him, 'I'm not armed.'

'Oh, sidearms don't vex me in the slightest. But I have an aversion to bugs.'

The noise emitted by the electronic 'paddle' becomes higher-pitched as it passes over the region of my groin. Gerry pauses. We exchange glances.

He says, 'Would you mind getting it out?'

'I'd prefer not to.'

'I'll take good care of it.'

Reluctantly, I remove my phone from my trouser pocket and hand it over. Gerry places it in the tallboy's lowest drawer. This one is metal-lined and when he closes it, I hear an efficient hiss that suggests it's hermetically sealed.

Gerry straightens up. 'Excellent. Well, let's go.'

'Yes, let's go.' I nod to appear amenable. 'Where, exactly, are we going, Colonel?'

And as though it's the most obvious thing in the world, he replies, 'Church, of course!'

CHAPTER 25

Gerry drives a big old Land Rover Defender. Of course he does. I strap myself into the passenger seat as he says, 'Left something in the house! I'll be right back.'

He disappears inside and I wonder what he's really up to. There's an efficiency about him that's hard to explain – from the way he puts on his jacket to the way his cottage is presented. He's an exercise in time-and-motion optimisation.

For the first time, I wonder how I'm going to broach the subject of Diana. There's a very real possibility that Colonel Gerry Whittaker is the last living soul who knows what she was planning, and it feels highly likely that whatever it was played a huge role in her final days. I also believe it might be what got her killed, but I don't want to marry that theory just yet. What was it Sherlock Holmes always said? '*It is a capital mistake to theorise before one has data. Insensibly one begins to twist facts to suit theories, instead of theories to suit facts.*'

But still . . . I mull over my conversation with Frank Harvey and all the elements of the crash he outlined. Elements that suggest it was something more sinister, more orchestrated than the official reports would have us believe. It's not just the big stuff, like the fact it seems improbable that Henri Paul was crazy-drunk when he got behind the wheel of the Mercedes, or the French authorities' suspicious haste to

94

wipe down the entire crime scene and reopen the tunnel as if nothing had occurred. No. The small things bother me, too. If Henri Paul wasn't driving the Princess and her party to the Fayeds' apartment, as officially claimed, and their route implies very strongly that he wasn't – then where were they heading?

I see Gerry emerge from his cottage. How much does he know? And, more pertinently, how much is he willing to share?

'Got it!' he calls across to me and waves a CD case in the air.

A minute later, we're heading out of Foxglove, zipping through the winding country lanes of rural Surrey.

'So, Frank tells me you're operating as a journalist.'

'Yes.'

'What does operating as a journalist entail?'

'I'm researching Diana, Princess of Wales,' I reply truthfully.

'Hell of a woman! Ever meet her?'

'No. No, I never had that honour. But I believe you knew her?'

'You never met the lady, but I'll wager you can remember where you were, and what you were doing, when you found out she'd been killed.'

'I remember it very well.'

'How old will you have been in 1997, Mr Novak?'

'Call me Marc. Were you still in touch with her during her final days? When she was in France?'

'Oh, she never took me to France!'

I know he's being evasive but press on, asking casually, 'Did you know Dodi?'

'Dodi Fayed?'

Before I can stop myself, I snap, 'No, Dodie Smith.'

Gerry roars with laughter. 'Oh, very good! As a matter of fact, I'm very fond of her stuff. Ever read any of her books?'

'No.'

'Operating as a journalist.' We take a left and we're back on a road I vaguely recognise. 'How long have you known Frank?'

Telling the truth might be the best tactic now, so I admit, 'Not that long. But I like him. What about you?'

'Oh, donkey's years. He's a good chap. Came from an era when journalists saw their role as reporting the news and not somehow being a part of it. Or simply cutting and pasting a few tweets as if they sum up the mood of the nation.'

'You were with Diana for a fair few years. You never felt compelled to write a book about her?'

'What would be the point?' I can feel he's bracing himself for more questions, so decide to give it a rest.

'How long have you lived in Foxglove?'

He seems to appreciate the change of subject. 'Don't worry, Marc. I'm sure we can do business.'

He's the kind of man that imbues you with confidence. Not just in him, but in the situation, as if he can lead you out of any maze, no matter how labyrinthine it feels, or how heavy the fire that you're under may become. Not for the first time today, I truly feel as if I'm inching closer to the truth about the crash in the Pont de l'Alma.

CHAPTER 26

We drive along in comfortable silence, heading to higher ground and more arresting bucolic views. Gerry ferrets in his pocket and retrieves the CD he brought from the cottage. Without looking away from the road, he hands it to me.

'Stick this on, will you, old man?'

'Sure.'

I take a peek at the cover. It's *The Mikado*, as performed by the D'Oyly Carte Opera Company in 1973.

Gerry asks, 'Are you a fan of Gilbert and Sullivan?'

'My parents were.'

I won't burden him with any more details, but my mum and dad owned the vinyl version of the album that's now in my hand. I remember it being played on Sunday afternoons, my parents shrieking with laughter at jokes they'd heard a thousand times. I liked that about them. Their willingness to let go and guffaw, even at a punchline they knew was coming before the needle was lowered on to the record. My friends' parents were always perfectly pleasant, but mine had a vibrancy about them. A joy of life that other grown-ups seemed to have jettisoned as they entered adulthood.

I slide in the disc of *The Mikado* and the overture begins, followed by a couple of numbers that work their lemon madeleine magic on me. The Colonel sings along to a few lines. I accompany him and, as the song finishes, he roars with laughter. I want him to like me but, more than that, I need him to trust me, and demonstrating a fondness for something he's passionate about will help me get both. Sure enough, he exclaims, 'Good show, Novak! Good show!'

As 'Our Great Mikado, Virtuous Man' begins, the Defender reaches the top of a plain and the Surrey Hills stretch ahead of us. Glorious.

We chat about Gilbert and Sullivan, then satire in general, the press and modern warfare. It's one of those free-flowing conversations where we disagree about very little, although just enough to make it interesting.

We finally take a left and drive up a steep little lane that brings us to an ancient church, perched on top of a hill. It's small. Medieval. Seemingly deserted. Gerry pulls up, sticks the handbrake on and listens to the end of 'Behold the Lord High Executioner!'. In the lull that immediately follows it, he turns the engine off, which also kills the CD player.

He takes a deep breath and, whilst looking dead ahead, says, 'Well. This is the end.'

It's a mild day, but up here the wind is chilly and noisy as it ruffles my clothes. I turn up the lapels of my suit jacket, which feels like it should help but never does. We're walking through the graveyard. I know some people find these places spooky or downright depressing, but something about the stones and the tranquillity has always drawn me to them.

Gerry glances across at me. He can discern I find the place pretty and serene and he nods. I get the feeling I'm passing a lot of tests, but I'm not trying to, and I've still no idea what he meant by 'This is the end'. But I do know it would be clumsy to ask.

I'm starting to think Gerry brought me here because I might like old churches, but he pulls me back to reality as we reach the far end of the graveyard.

'Here's how it works. You write your article. Write whatever you want. Doesn't bother me, as long as you're respectful to the Royal Family and Her Majesty's armed forces. Take whatever tack you like.'

He hasn't been looking at me, choosing instead to study a gravestone as he speaks. 'You cite an anonymous source – that's me – for any bits you make up.'

Does he *really* believe I'm a journalist? Or, at least, that all this is simply about an article I intend to write?

'If you get any flak, I'll speak to your editor and swear blind it's all true. You'll find my credentials are pretty good.' Gerry nods. Finally looks at me. 'Served all over the globe. Belfast to Baghdad. And I was in the Falklands show. In the first wave when we said *hands off*! to the Argies and mounted the final push into Port Stanley.' And now his gaze reverts to the gravestone. 'Sound pukka to you, Mr Novak?'

'Yes, Colonel. Very pukka. But I'm after the truth.'

'The truth?' He scrutinises my face. 'But I thought you were a journalist?'

'I never lied to you, Colonel. But I'm afraid I misled you, slightly. I'm a private detective.'

He's aghast. 'A gumshoe?'

From nowhere, an appropriate quotation comes to me and I tell him, 'I don't think much of my profession, but contrasted with respectability, it is comparatively honest.'

After a split second of worrying silence, Gerry laughs, delighted. 'My favourite line from *Pirates!* Ha! You really are an aficionado of the Savoy Operas, then?'

'My mum and dad used to play them constantly. They were . . . Oh, it doesn't matter. I think you'd have liked my parents, Colonel.' I say this because it's true and I hope Gerry can tell I'm not just soft-soaping him.

'Are they still with us?'

'My dad is. Mum, no. Sadly.'

'You still miss her.'

It's not a question, but I give him an answer. 'Yes. Very much.'

'You'd have made a good soldier, Novak.'

Now I guess why we're here and the inference takes me aback. It seems appropriate to simply reply, 'I'm not very good with orders, Colonel.'

'So, what do you want to know?'

'Diana.'

He nods. 'Did Frank Harvey—'

I interrupt him. 'Before she died, Diana told the press that she'd be making an announcement – something big that would astound them. Do you know what it was?'

Gerry considers the question but says, 'I'm here to pick out a spot.'

'I guessed. Cancer?'

He nods.

'And if you think the game's up, you must have beaten it already.' His expression tells me I'm right. 'Twice, I'd imagine. But it's returned and realistically . . . I'm sorry, Colonel.'

'Don't be.'

'And I hope my guesswork doesn't offend you.'

'Not a bit of it. I'm impressed. Come on.' We begin walking through the churchyard again. 'I think I'm the only one left who knows Diana's final secret. I swore I'd take it to my grave.'

I take a look around at our surroundings. 'Well . . .'

'I'm a man of my word.'

'I'm not doing this for some book or cash or a tawdry exposé. I'm doing it because it's been twenty-five years, and I think the truth deserves sunlight. She was a remarkable woman, Colonel. Help me give her justice.'

'I could go to the papers and get a king's ransom for what I know. What she was planning to announce . . . What she intended to do . . .' His voice trails off.

'Is it tied up with her death?'

And what he tells me changes everything.

'Of course,' he replies. 'It was the *reason* she was murdered . . .'

CHAPTER 27

Gerry's statement of fact hangs for a moment. I think he wants to tell me more, but at the same time he regrets telling me anything.

'Then share it with me, Colonel . . . Doesn't she deserve justice? Doesn't Dodi Fayed deserve it? And Henri Paul? I need to find out who killed Diana, and why.'

He moves forward, as if trying to literally walk away from the topic of conversation. I remain at his side. 'I have a young daughter, Mr Novak, the result of an old man's foolish fling. But I love her very much. I'd like to help her, after I'm gone.'

'Which won't be for quite some time yet, I hope.'

'I have a few months. Maybe a year or two. I hope to get to know her in that time.' His tone has been growing gentler, but he shakes away any sentimentality as he states, 'I'll give you the information for £100,000. That should see her through university and get her started.'

'A hundred grand?! Colonel, that kind of money . . .' I've no idea where the sentence is going so I'm pleased he interrupts it.

'It's worth ten times that and you know it. The only reason I'd divulge it to you is that I rather think you're chasing this rabbit for the right reasons.'

I nod. 'Thank you, Colonel.'

He stops walking. Pauses. Looks about himself. 'How about here?'

We're at the edge of the graveyard, on the side nearest the church's chancel. There's barely a spot in the grounds that doesn't boast a superb view of the Surrey countryside, but the aspect from this location is particularly striking, offering the full gamut of woods, hillsides, broad meadows and a couple of distant villages.

I say to Gerry, 'Give me your bank details and the money will be in your account by midnight.'

He nods. 'That should give me enough time.'

'To do what?'

'There's one other chap who knows a great deal – but not all – of what happened that night in Paris. Matter of fact, he's probably the only other living soul who knows what Diana was going to announce. I'll need to give him the heads-up about you going after the truth. If he promised anyone he'd maintain his silence, he'll doubtless welcome my reassurance that you'll be open and unambiguous that you received your information from me, and nobody else.'

'Understood.'

'And I'll check my bank account first thing in the a.m. – just to confirm there's been no cock-ups with the transfer. I'll then let you know we're good to proceed and I'll share Diana's secret with you. And more besides, my friend. Make sure you use the intel wisely.'

'I promise you I'll do the very best I can with it. For you, as well as her.'

Colonel Gerry Whittaker looks like a traveller who's unexpectedly had a huge weight lifted from his backpack.

'Good man. We can meet here tomorrow at eleven hundred hours. And I'll tell you everything you need to know.'

'Thank you.'

He starts strolling back to his car but I linger for a moment.

'And Gerry . . .' I call across to him.

He turns. 'Yes, Novak?'

'It's very pretty.'

He takes this in. Nods his gratitude. He turns, resuming his walk back to the Defender, and shouts over his shoulder, 'Do not leave flowers!'

CHAPTER 28

As I'm driving home, I call the number Thom Peters gave me. Out of habit I use 'caller withheld'. After a couple of rings a woman with an RP accent answers. 'Hello. How can I help?'

'Could I speak to Thom Peters or Miss Winters, please?'

'Who's calling?'

I give her a fake name, again out of habit, but when Peters eventually comes on the line, he already knows it's me. I tell him I need a hundred grand and he tells me he'll need to check with his superiors. I give him very vague details about what the money is for, but stress its importance.

Next I call Frank.

He picks up and doesn't waste time with pleasantries. 'How did it go with the Colonel?'

'It went well. Look, I'm calling you about other stuff, as well.'

'Sounds intriguing. Go on.'

'What I told you about being hired by documentary makers to get background info on Diana? Not strictly the case.'

'And in other news, I wasn't born yesterday, lad. Let's have it.'

I tell him the whole thing. Arriving home to find Miss Winters and Thom Peters on my doorstep. Their job offer.

The unanswered question of who they work for. My suspicions. Miss Winters raising the question of the announcement Diana had promised to make. I don't neglect any detail. And it's not through any sense of moral obligation. I trust Frank and feel he's the kind of person I want onside.

'I guessed it was something along those lines.'

'I'm sorry I wasn't open with you.'

'Don't worry about it. These two characters – Winters and Peters. Do you think they're dangerous?'

Without thinking, I reply, 'Yes.' I suppose it's the first time I've considered them in such straightforward terms.

'And who do you think they work for?'

'No idea. Like I said, they're ghosts.'

'I don't believe in ghosts. I'll have a word around. See if I can turn up anything.'

'Thanks, Frank.' I say I'll send him the photograph I have of them, taken from the recording made in my front room, then add, 'But be careful. I'm still not entirely sure what I'm getting into.'

'Don't worry about me, lad. So, come on. What did the Colonel say?'

'He said—'

I break off as I hear a series of beeps that indicates I've got another call coming through.

'Frank – can I put you on hold for a sec?'

'No!'

'Thanks!'

I take the incoming call. It's Miss Winters. 'Peters tells me you're asking for a considerable amount of money.'

'I need it for the case.'

'Elaborate.'

106

'I think I'm on to something. But it's beyond a door at the moment. And I'm going to need some capital to unlock it.'

Miss Winters asks, 'How much?'

'A hundred grand.'

She doesn't hesitate. 'That's quite a key.'

'It's quite a lock.'

'Before I authorise that kind of sum I'll need more information. How are your investigations progressing? Have you found anything that points to murder?'

'Pretty much everything about this case points to it. But you knew that already. All the blatant lies and question marks concerning the crash in Paris? They're out in the open.' I pause. 'So why do you even need me? Why isn't there a full-scale governmental investigation into the three deaths? Why are the authorities not doing anything about it?'

Miss Winters sounds perplexed. 'I don't understand your question.'

'Well, it's obvious that the truth about Diana's death has been – if not covered up – let's say . . . *obfuscated*. Why doesn't that bother anyone in authority? In fact, why doesn't it bother *anyone*?'

'It's 2022. No one's interested in the truth any more. Broadly speaking, the truth is irrelevant. At best, *truth* has become a niche commodity.'

She's not saying this to appear fashionably cynical or insightful. The world view she outlines lies at the heart of her belief system.

'In years to come,' she continues, 'I think it will be accepted that Diana was murdered. But her killing will be treated with the same lack of solemnity that we afford . . . the murder of the Princes in the Tower. Or the assassination of John F. Kennedy.' I imagine she's shrugging. 'Just another story. Another diverting puzzle. The killer's identity sought in the same way that some people hypothesise about the identity of Jack the Ripper. Not because they want justice for the victims. But because, well, it's a fun game. Now, let's get back to the matter of £100,000.'

'I need that money, Miss Winters. Transfer it or I walk away.'

'If I authorise the outlay, will it take you closer to finding out who killed the Princess?'

'Yes.'

'Then the money will be in your account within the hour. Call me when that door is unlocked.'

She hangs up and I'm back with Frank. 'That was Winters,' I tell him. 'They're transferring the money to my account.'

For a moment I assume he didn't bother staying on the line, then he says, 'Oh my God. Novak! This could be it. If the Colonel tells you what he knows . . .'

'I'm pretty sure he will. We got on well, but it's more than that. He's a dying man who wants the best for his daughter *and* his conscience.'

'If he tells us what Diana was going to announce, we could actually work out why she was killed. And who by.'

'Agreed,' I reply. 'After all these years, this could be it.'

I park my car on the road and traipse up my driveway, looking forward to an indecently large whisky and soda. But my plans are derailed when I spot a familiar figure stood in the shadows by the side of my front door.

My visitor steps forward and even before either of us has spoken a word, I've got a whole new set of priorities.

CHAPTER 29

As Anna Brandon walks towards me, my home's security light comes on, and it's as though a torch has been shone on to her face. She has dark, ugly bruising over her left eye.

'Mr Novak, I hope you don't mind me coming over but—'

I'm striding towards her. 'Who did this to you?'

'It was an accident!'

I reach her. 'May I?'

She nods, and I gently tilt her head towards the light. Her skin is unbroken but the bruise looks bloody awful.

'Did your husband do this?'

'It was my fault as much as his. We got into an argument. I pushed him and he defended himself.'

'He'll be defending himself again very shortly,' I tell her and turn away. I march down the driveway towards my car.

'Mr Novak, no! Wait!' She reaches me as I'm opening the driver's door. 'No! No, for God's sake! Please!' There's a sob in her voice. She brings it under control – just about – and continues, 'The last thing I need tonight is another man trying to solve a problem with his fists!'

She puts herself between me and the Marina, then stumbles and I catch her. I can feel how unsteady she is and guess she's exhausted, mentally as well as physically. I move her slightly, so she can lean back on the car's bodywork.

'God, I just need a . . . a haven.' She puts her palm on my chest. 'I'm so tired.'

'Is your driver around?'

'I came alone. I didn't know where else to go. My family think I'm crazy for wanting to walk away from a rich husband, and my friends . . .' She shrugs. 'I'm so sorry for—'

'You did the right thing, Mrs Brandon.'

'I can't face a hotel tonight.' She shakes her head. 'I don't know what to do. My life is totally . . .'

Anna Brandon sways and I lightly rest my hands on her upper arms. 'Can you walk?'

'Thanks. And yes, I think so. I'm so sorry.'

'You don't have to keep saying that.' Then, fearing I sound brusque, I add, 'Sorry.'

She offers a smile. 'Must be contagious. The saying *sorry* thing.' She runs a hand through her hair. 'I shouldn't have come. God, my life is ruined.'

'I'll take care of you. Come on.'

'May I lean on you?'

'Always.'

I help her into my house and guide her to the sofa.

'Can I get you a drink, Mrs Brandon?'

'A cup of tea would be heavenly.'

'Give me five minutes.'

I'm back from my kitchen in four, armed with a mug of Earl Grey. 'Do you take . . .'

But Anna Brandon is half reclining across the sofa, her eyes closed. Her soft, regular breathing indicates she's asleep.

'. . . Sugar?' I whisper, finishing the question, but she doesn't reply.

I fetch a blanket from upstairs and drape it across her, pour the tea away and open my drinks cupboard. Looks like that whisky and soda is back on. I fix myself a large one, take a seat at the kitchen table, and call the Colonel.

CHAPTER 30

After a couple of rings, I'm clicked through to the Colonel's voice message service. 'I'm phoning about the matter we discussed earlier today. To confirm it currently embodies the law.'

In other words, the plan is progressing just fine and he'll get the money as requested. If his phone is being bugged, it won't take long for any snoop to work out what I'm trying to convey, but hopefully the message will make Gerry smile. The lines I'm referencing are:

> 'The Law is the true embodiment
> Of everything that's excellent.
> It has no kind of fault or flaw
> And I, my Lords, embody the Law.'

. . . And are from *Iolanthe*. If nothing else, I'm sure he'll appreciate the irony of the allusion. I hang up. Gently massage my eyelids. Think about Gerry Whittaker. What takes a man like him from the frontline of the Falklands War, to a role protecting royalty and finally to a village in the English countryside that practically screams, *'Leave me alone!'*

And his daughter. I hope it's not too late for her to get to know her father. Not just the military man with a penchant for Gilbert and Sullivan. But the man with wit, warmth and compassion that I met and respect.

'You look tired.'

I open my eyes. Anna Brandon is leaning against the door frame of my kitchen, just as she did the previous night when she brushed aside a stray lock of hair. She's not wearing make-up this time and, of course, there's bruising over her eye. Same person. Different face.

'I feel tired,' I concede.

'Is it a case?'

'It's always a case. I thought you were out for the count.' I hold up my tumbler. 'Want one?'

'Why not?'

Why not, indeed. I mean, what could possibly go wrong?

'And do you have a pair of pyjamas I could borrow?'

'I don't wear pyjamas.'

'What do you wear?'

'Daring cologne and a cheeky grin.'

She laughs. 'No, I meant—'

'I know what you meant. I'll dig you something out.'

'Thanks. I know it's an imposition, but *do* you mind if I spend the night with you?' She almost falls over herself to clarify, 'I mean here. With you. As in, in your house. Not *with you*, with you.' She shakes her head. 'That *would* be wrong. Obviously.'

There's a silence I'm in no hurry to break.

She nods to the tumbler I'm nursing. 'How is it?'

'Stiff.'

'I meant your drink!'

'So did I. Whisky, no mixer.'

'Are you teasing me, Mr Novak?'

113

'Uh-huh.'

She looks serious for a moment, then begins to laugh.

After she's changed, we find ourselves in the spots we occupied last night. Nothing was said, but she's relaxed on the sofa and I'm sitting in the armchair.

She looks up, in my direction. 'Aren't you going to ask me?'

'Ask what?'

'Why I married him?' She sips her whisky and water. 'Men always ask. Women never need to.'

'Let me guess. He was lovely. You were in love. There were warning signs but . . .' I shrug. 'He changed. You don't know why, but it's probably work. And, of course, you can fix him.'

'Well, not really. He was never that lovely. I mean, he was generous and liked to make sure I was happy, but that was him showing off, I think. It was nothing to do with kindness. No. Not *showing off* as such. He wanted to prove that he could make me happy.'

'Why? Was that a first?'

'Not really. But it's unfair that you say there were warning signs. I mean, what does that actually mean? That he wasn't a saint? Well, true, but the fact that someone isn't perfect . . .'

'I take your point.'

'Those imperfections can't retrospectively be labelled as *warning signs*, can they? As if I should have seen what was coming?'

'That's not what I meant.' It probably was. 'Has he hit you before?'

'I've hit him.'

'And did he enjoy that?'

'I think he did, yeah.'

'You striking him doesn't excuse that' – I tip my tumbler towards her bruising – 'in any way. Period.'

'Men always talk a good game. Have you ever hit a woman?'

'Yes.'

This shocks her. 'Badly?'

'She went down and stayed down.'

'Did you enjoy it?'

'She had a Webley & Scott trained on a bunch of innocent people. She was about to pull the trigger.'

'And did you stop her?'

'Not exactly.' I open a couple of shirt buttons to expose the scar made by the 8mm bullet that had torn through my upper torso.

'OK. So you took a psycho down. But you know what I mean. Have you ever hit a girlfriend?'

I button my shirt up, slightly miffed that my Webley & Scott bullet wound didn't impress her. Maybe I should have shown her the one Gina gave me at the end of the Cromwell case, as well. 'No.'

'Have you ever hurt one?'

I think about Precious. 'Yes.'

'Was it your fault?'

'Probably. Can we change the subject, please?'

'Did you mean to?'

'No. Can we change the subject?'

She makes sure I'm holding her gaze. 'You feel more comfortable sympathising about the hardships I've endured than admitting to the hardships you've caused. Typical man.'

I try not to register my surprise at where she's taking the conversation. 'I'm sorry if I've offended you.' I get to my feet. 'I'll prepare your bed and make sure—'

'Oh, sit down!'

That smile again. I realise she's probably a little woozy.

'I'm just getting a top-up,' I tell her, wander through to the kitchen, refill my glass and return to my armchair.

She says, 'I'm sorry if I offended *you*.'

'Hey, you're the client.'

She sits bolt upright. 'That's a cheap shot.'

But this time I don't apologise. 'I think we should both turn in, Mrs Brandon.'

'I like you.'

'You're only human.'

She finishes her drink. 'Top-up, please.'

'You know where the bottle is.'

She gets to her feet. 'Thank you.'

'Pleasure.'

She walks through to the kitchen and I pop upstairs, straighten my bedroom and by the time I'm downstairs again, she's finished her nightcap.

We both understand the evening is over and say 'Good night' simultaneously.

She walks from the room. Pauses halfway up the stairs and, without looking back at me, murmurs, 'I still want to fix it with my husband. Stupid, isn't it? That I still love him?'

I shrug. 'Whatever love means.'

CHAPTER 31

I grab my three-season sleeping bag from the boot of the Marina, lay it out across my sofa and fix myself one for the road, get changed and finally hit the hay. But I'm so tired, I fall straight to sleep, my whisky untouched on the coffee table.

The sunlight through the curtains wakes me at 7.10 a.m., but that's fine. There's a lot to do. I shower and change into a suit, then knock lightly on my bedroom door. I hear movement.

'Come in!'

I push the door open. 'Morning! How are you feeling?'

Anna Brandon tilts her palm to imply 'so-so'.

'Can I get you anything?'

'Got any orange juice?'

'No, sorry. Coffee?'

'Actually, do you mind if I get a little more shut-eye? I hardly slept a wink last night, thinking about . . . you know.'

'Take as long as you like. I've got to nip to the bank. I'll see you when I get back.'

'Sounds good.'

Yeah. It does.

I close the door so she can get back to sleep.

*

It's a glorious day and I walk to the bank, enjoying the sunny stroll. I'm the first customer through the doors and even the bind of having to fill out half a dozen documents in order to transfer the £100,000 doesn't dent my good mood.

'Right, Mr Novak. The £100,000 is now in the account of Colonel G Whittaker.'

'Let's hope he doesn't spend it all at once.'

In the bank's foyer, I phone Gerry. As usual, he doesn't pick up and I leave a message, obliquely letting him know that the money has been transferred. I step into the sunlight and walk home. My phone rings just as I put the front door key in the lock.

'Morning, Colonel!'

'Novak!' Gerry sounds a little out of breath. 'I'm afraid there's been a change of plan . . .'

CHAPTER 32

'What?'

There's suddenly a ball of dread where my stomach used to live.

'Nothing for you to worry about.'

'Yeah. That line always worries me.'

'Just a last-minute thing that's cropped up with my gardener. We can still meet at the church. But let's make it noon. That suit?'

'That suits fine. You're sure everything's all right, though?'

'Everything is more than all right.' He pauses. 'You're waging a war I should have fought years ago.'

'You're worrying me again.'

'Sweep away the lies and the shams and the injustice. You'll be restoring natural law. I thank you for that, Novak.'

'Just doing my job.'

'I said yesterday that you would have made a good soldier.'

'I took it as a massive compliment.'

'Well, perhaps I should have said you *are* a good soldier. I'm proud to serve by your side.'

'Thank you, Colonel.' I can see why men would follow him into battle.

'Happy landings, Novak.'

'Goodbye, Colonel.'

At 10.15 a.m., I'm in my kitchen making coffee, more out of habit and to kill time than anything else. I brew about half a litre and pour most into my battered Hammertone Green thermos flask and a little into a mug. Take a sip. Perfect. I prepare a little something for my guest. She's still sleeping, snoring ever so slightly. So I scribble her a quick note and leave it on the bedside cabinet.

Sitting at my kitchen table, I enjoy that mug of freshly brewed coffee and allow myself the luxury of speculation, wondering what the Colonel will impart when we meet.

What was Diana, Princess of Wales, planning to tell the world before she'd been killed in Paris? What was the new, next chapter she'd intended for her life? I blow on my coffee. How had she presaged the announcement?

Something that will amaze you all.

I know Frank pooh-poohed the idea, but I still wonder if she was about to reveal she was pregnant. If she had been expecting when she'd stepped into that Mercedes, and the car had emerged from the Pont de l'Alma Tunnel and taken her to wherever Henri Paul had been driving them – let's see, that kid would be in his or her mid-twenties today. I picture a good-looking, confident young person. Friend to the Royals? Thorn in their side? Not so sure. Media darling? Truculent recluse? Probably a combination of the two.

But Frank Harvey's rebuttal of that theory feels sound.

Something that would have amazed us all . . .

I try to make sense of the picture by holding it a different way. Could it have been something she knew, as opposed to something she planned to do? A secret about her former husband, Prince Charles, perhaps? It's possible, but feels too much of a soap-opera twist. I finish my coffee. Whatever her last secret was, I'm about to find out.

I leave my mug in the sink and don't need to walk up the stairs again. My guest's soft purr is audible from the downstairs hallway. I grab my thermos and head to my front door, where I pause. Should I wake her? No. I step outside and head to my Morris Marina.

I'm sure Anna Brandon will be fine.

At 10.43 a.m. I drive out of Guildford, head towards Shalford, veer right at the green and I'm soon hurtling through the meandering lanes of Surrey's verdant countryside. It's a beautiful day and I wind my window down. The sun is warm on my skin, but the onrushing air provides a welcome, bracing chill. I've got plenty of time and a flask full of good coffee. Plus £100,000 worth of secrets waiting for me in a pretty graveyard.

I put my foot down.

Life is good.

At the end of the road, I bear left, speeding towards Shamley Green.

Maybe I'm driving too fast, but it's a day made for driving too fast. The road narrows, making it difficult for two cars to pass and pretty much impossible for two vans to negotiate the same stretch. But at this time in the morning the traffic is usually light and it's possible I won't even pass another vehicle.

I consider the prize that awaits me and press the accelerator a little more. The thick hedgerows become a threshing, green blur.

My phone rings.

It's on the passenger seat next to me and I glance across at it.

CHAPTER 33

My phone continues to ring, insistently. The screen reveals the caller is Frank Harvey, so I'm tempted to pick up, but the roads are too tricky. Any lapse of focus could be disastrous.

'Sorry, Frank.'

I ignore the call for the moment, but reach Shamley at about 11 a.m., which means time remains on my side. I pull into the car park of The Red Lion, a top-drawer pub just off the village green. It's your classic 'wooden beams and flagstone flooring' type of place, and I've enjoyed a fair few meals and pints in its beer garden over the years.

Stepping from the car, I call Frank. As it rings out, I look over at the green. There's a cricket match in progress. Amateurs, although not half bad. The bowler's pretty fast but the old guy at the stumps has the measure of his yorker and wallops it hard. There's the evocative sound of leather on willow and a smattering of cheering from both sides.

Frank doesn't pick up. Strange, given that he was calling me less than five minutes earlier. I don't leave a message. I'm soon back in the Marina and the village is behind me, sealed shut, with shop-keepers and doctors dreaming of hitting that perfect six.

*

I have this tendency: when things are going well, I always expect something to go terribly wrong. Maybe that's why Frank's failure to answer my call bothers me. I leave the roads I'm pretty used to and begin covering the final stretch that leads to the church. It's about fifteen minutes away and I'm still making good time, so when I'm forced to stop as a farmer shepherds a flock of sheep across the narrow road to an adjacent meadow, I'm not unduly concerned.

My phone rings. It's Frank. I pick up and give him a cheery, 'Good morning!'

'Well? What did he say, son?'

'Nothing.'

'What?'

'I've not seen him yet. The meeting's been put back till noon.'

'Dammit!'

'I know, right? But I wanted to have a quick word with you before I got there, anyway.'

'What about?'

'Just wanted to thank you.'

'What for? Not writing another book?'

The last few sheep are meandering across the lane.

'Well, there is that.'

'You're welcome.'

'Seriously though, Frank. I did want to say thank you. For seeing me in the first place. And your help. And the lead you gave me. I think together, we may have just—'

I stop speaking. I've seen something. That ball of dread returns to my stomach.

'Novak! What is it?'

'I'll call you back, Frank.'

I hang up. The farmer tips his trilby in my direction and follows his flock into the field. I put my foot down.

I reach the end of the lane and hang a right, following the two police cars I spotted tearing along this wider road. They're out of sight now, but this stretch, although broader, only has a couple of turn-offs and its aspect changes. To my left, an incline; the edges of a forest border the bottom of the slope. It's a 50mph zone. I'm shifting at around 80.

And then, that horrible deceleration. Horrible, because you know the traffic ahead is slowing down to have a good gawp at an accident. I make out a cluster of police cars at the side of the road. Blue lights spinning. I'm down to about 20. A bunch of police officers – all pointing and nodding and looking professionally grave – stand by the side of the incline, just a few yards ahead of me.

I see the slope is about to get steeper, but where I am now, I can safely pull off the road. I make a snap decision to do it, crunching over bracken until the Marina clears the path of traffic. I'm immediately out and jogging towards the police presence, but I still can't tell why they're here. Apart from their cars, there are no other vehicles – aside, that is, from the slow stream of traffic dribbling past them from both sides of the road.

A couple of coppers are setting up a cordon. They're unspooling that familiar yellow and black 'POLICE: DO NOT CROSS' tape and I hear its sticky shriek as the constable furthest from me stretches a length across a trio of trees.

One of the officers, who appears to be in charge, is co-ordinating something with a woman I'm guessing is his second in command. The guy half turns. Three chevron stripes on his sleeve. A sergeant. He spots me, so I get in first.

'What's happened, sarge?'

'A crash. I'm afraid you can't park there, sir.'

A crash.

I hear myself say, 'It's all right. I'm a doctor.'

And now I spot a break in the roadside foliage where bracken and bushes have been torn away, tyre marks on the soft earth.

I feel sick.

The woman says, 'Got any ID?'

I don't stop walking, but I do stop thinking, just for a moment.

'Sir! I'm going to have to see your ID!'

It might not be Gerry. And he might be alive.

I say, 'Sure . . .'

Behind the sergeant, I see a group of teens. All of them are holding their phones aloft, filming and photographing the entire scene.

I stop and make a big deal of searching my pockets for ID. 'I don't think that's helping, officers . . .'

I nod to the youths.

The sergeant mutters, 'Jesus!' and to the woman, 'Clear them out, would you?'

They both turn away and I start scrambling down the incline. A couple of paces in and the forest begins, its trees partially shielding me.

'Hey! You can't go down there!' It's the sergeant's voice. I ignore it because of what I see.

I half jog, half slide down the embankment. It's become steeper and there's a small lake ahead. Not a gleaming,

126

glistening pool of silver, but a shallow, muddy patch of water that's dark and heavy with dead leaves. On the edge of it, there's a car on its side.

A Land Rover Defender.

I'm moving too quickly, slipping every other step. I think my hands have landed on loose rocks or something, because I vaguely notice my palms are bleeding.

From back on the road I can hear someone shout, 'Where the hell is that ambulance?'

But I keep sliding, running, falling.

Two policemen are heading away from the Defender, back up the slope, back towards their colleagues, so for now at least, there's no one else near the overturned vehicle. It's on its side and thick grey smoke billows from its underside. There's something grotesque and forlorn about the sight.

From the angle I'm approaching the Defender, I can only see the underneath section of it.

One final fall. I pick myself up and move quickly on to level ground.

'Gerry!'

My pace slows as I approach the Colonel's car.

I can see it's definitely his, now. The vehicle I was being driven in yesterday, whilst reminiscing about my parents and singing songs from Gilbert and Sullivan. A couple more paces and the driver's side of the car comes into view.

I can see Colonel Gerry Whittaker. His car is bent to hell. The front windscreen is mainly an opaque honeycomb of cracks. But his driver's side window is largely intact. It's cracked, but holding firm. Which is why I can see him.

The glass is smeared with blood and Gerry's face is pressed hard against it. His forehead is a mangled, horrific wound. His face slashed and smeared red. His neck is twisted, wrenched unnaturally across his right shoulder. His mouth gapes open.

'Christ . . .'

Despite my aversion to corpses, I move swiftly towards the car. The Colonel is dead, but there's still something I need from him.

CHAPTER 34

I try the driver's door and it opens. His body slumps towards me and I catch it by the shoulder.

'Jesus . . .'

Very gently, I slide my hand into Gerry's inside pocket. Nothing. I try the pocket on the other side of his jacket and find his phone. As I stash it and close the door, I hear a voice.

'Step away from that vehicle!'

It's the sergeant. No 'sir' this time, as he makes his way down the incline.

The investigator in me realises I should be snapping away or filming the wreckage, but the sergeant is nearing the scene and I don't particularly want to explain what I'm doing here or how I'm acquainted with the deceased. Besides, I know with stone-cold certainty that I won't need to take a photo of the Colonel's face to remember every detail of it.

I turn to go. Pause. Turn back. I take it in one final time. The scene I caused. And the guilt I feel threatens to—

No. This isn't on me. *His death is not on me.*

Not for a single second do I think the Colonel simply slid from the road and, facing him this last time, I silently make a vow. I will see that natural law is served.

The sergeant has almost reached the level ground. This time when I turn, I don't stop, half circling the Defender and plunging swiftly into the woods. I doubt the policeman will follow me. He'll dismiss me as another rubbernecker trying to take ghoulish pics to bolster a Twitter account or footage to flog to the press. The forest becomes denser and I begin jogging up the incline, quickly putting distance between myself and the overturned Defender. I don't stop until I've almost reached the top of the slope. I survey the land below me but there's no sign of the sergeant.

I'm forced to give the police presence a wide berth, so reaching my car takes longer than expected. I half sit, half lean on its bonnet, watching as an ambulance finally draws up to the cordon. A couple of paramedics leap out and race down the incline. They could stop, chat and pass around a cigar with the coppers for all the difference it would make. Hurrying at this point isn't helping anybody.

My guilt and shock have been subsumed by rage and melancholy.

It's 12.02 and I should have been meeting the Colonel around now. We should be shaking hands. Conducting our business. Then promising one another we'll keep in touch.

I take out my phone and call the number Peters gave me. RP woman picks up. 'Hello. How may I help you?'

'I need to speak to Miss Winters. Now.'

'Who may I say is calling?'

'Marc Novak.'

A pause. 'Oh. It's you.'

'Is she there? It's urgent.'

'Hold the line, please.'

Some godawful recording of Rachmaninov's *Rhapsody on a Theme of Paganini* clicks on. I'm only subjected to it briefly before Miss Winters cuts in. 'Mr Novak. What's happened?'

'You asked me if I'd take the case. Take it fully, that is. All the way.'

'Yes?'

'Well, I've an answer for you. I'll take the case. On one condition. I can take it all the way – whatever happens. And whoever happens.'

'Agreed.'

'Do I have your word on that?'

'You have my word.'

'Good.'

'What's happened?'

'I swear to God I will find out who murdered Diana . . . and Dodi and Henri. And Gerry Whittaker.'

'Novak! What's going on?'

'I'll find them. And there will be justice. Not the justice of courtroom judges and governments.'

'Novak!'

'Natural law.'

I end the call and close my eyes.

CHAPTER 35

Miss Winters' Story

Miss Winters had a corner office – some of her staff whispered she *lived* in that corner office – with windows that could offer a spectacular view across London. She kept the blinds permanently closed, however, so the room, although large and expensively furnished, possessed a forbidding air. She sat behind a wide, curious table that more closely resembled a piece of modern art than a standard office desk. A good two metres by a metre and a half, its surface appeared to be ebony shot through with tiny capillaries of red. It hinted luxury, whilst her chair – an antique, but plain wooden seat – suggested the reverse.

The room's whole aesthetic, from the Ligne Roset sofa to the monochrome print that hung on the wall – one of Doré's illustrations for Dante's *Inferno*, sometimes referred to as *I found myself within a forest dark* – suggested Miss Winters had been behind the design. But there were no cheap tricks. The two chairs in which her guests were seated, for example, were comfortable and slightly higher than her own. Yet it always seemed – as it did to the pair in front of her desk on that morning – that Miss Winters was forever above them. A presence that could never be transcended.

Her phone rang and she lifted the receiver. 'It's the call you were anticipating, Miss Winters.'

'Thank you. Put Mr Novak through immediately.' The line went quiet. The next moment, her voice's timbre changed from icy imperiousness to flummoxed concern. 'Mr Novak,' she said, 'what's happened?'

'You asked me if I'd take the case. Take it fully, that is. All the way.'

She actually widened her eyes as if Novak was in the room with her. Peters smiled, enjoying the performance. 'Yes?'

'Well, I've an answer for you. I'll take the case. On one condition. I can really take it all the way – whatever happens. And whoever happens.'

She nodded hastily. 'Agreed.'

'Do I have your word on that?'

She paused. Squinted, as if confused, then fell back into character, replying with an ecclesiastical solemnity. 'You have my word.'

'Good.'

'What's happened?'

'I swear to God I will find out who murdered Diana . . . and Dodi and Henri. And Gerry Whittaker.'

She rolled her eyes, clearly growing bored with the exchange. 'Novak! What's going on?'

'I'll find them. And there will be justice. Not the justice of courtroom judges and governments.'

'Novak!'

'Natural law.'

She rolled her eyes again. Heard the line go dead. 'Natural law! God help us. What era is the man from?' Miss Winters replaced the receiver and said to Peters, 'Well, he's already found Whittaker.' She sighed. 'That crash – it was a great shame we had to . . .'

Her voice trailed off, and a startled Peters replied, 'Yes indeed, but . . .'

'That Defender of his,' Miss Winters continued, 'was a beautiful vehicle. The new ones have got no class. But it can't be helped.'

Peters felt a modicum of relief that his view of his boss remained intact. 'No. Couldn't be helped.'

Miss Winters looked at the two women sitting opposite her. 'You know, Novak . . . Is he genuine?'

They both nodded.

'He actually asked me for my word. I mean . . .' She seemed unable to even grasp the concept. 'He does know this is the twenty-first century, doesn't he?' She shook her head, as if to displace the mysteries this man Novak presented. She addressed the woman to her right. 'Do you foresee any problems with him?'

There was a slight pause. 'None whatsoever,' Anna Brandon replied. 'He'd ride into hell for a woman he thinks he can save.' There was a look of disdain on her face. 'Dinosaur!'

'And you?' Miss Winters addressed the woman sat to her left. 'You can control him for your side of the operation?'

'Yeah. Of course.' Mishka nodded. 'No problem.'

CHAPTER 36

I drive to the church. The car park's empty and I can't see anyone in the graveyard, so I don't even bother getting out. I speed back the way I came. The ambulance has gone but the police presence remains. The annoying sergeant is chatting to a colleague, and he looks up. Catches my eye. I slow down immediately, so the car behind me is closer to my boot, effectively concealing my licence plate.

I give him a final glance in my rear-view mirror, so I almost don't see the kid on a bike. He's travelling towards the cordon, but the car in front of him swerves into the middle of the road. This flusters him, and he pulls out to avoid whatever the erratic driver is trying to dodge. Upshot. The boy on the bike is right in front of me. He's in his late teens. There's a satchel slung around his neck with the words 'Rudy the Foodie' printed across the side. He's wearing a fancy modern helmet but his bike is older than me. That's lucky, because it means it's slow. This gives me time to neatly swerve around him.

An already bad day had almost got a whole lot worse.

No one touches Gerry Whittaker for twenty-five years. Then I turn up and he's dead within twenty-four hours. There is no doubt that his murder is linked to what he knew.

Whoever wants that information to remain a secret clearly prioritised his death as a means of achieving it. But it won't take them long to accept that even with the Colonel out of the way, it's possible that he left a record, or some kind of clue, as to his insight into Diana's intentions.

So I drive like I'm in training for the Monaco Grand Prix, careering along the straighter stretches at full pelt and powering through the windier roads at a lick that makes every corner an invitation to join Gerry in the morgue. More through luck than expert driving, I roar into Foxglove relatively unscathed. I park opposite The Lines, race across the road and circle around the back of his cottage.

There's an open window on the first floor. Could be useful.

I reach the back door and, just to be on the safe side, ring the bell. A couple of seconds pass. Glance to my left, then right. Coast clear. I pull a set of lock picks from my inside pocket. I'm guessing Gerry was big on security, but a lock remains a lock, no matter how high the hi-tech that supports it. I've just started work on the problem when I hear movement from inside.

Are they here already?

Someone's walking towards the door. I slide my picks back into my pocket. Take a step back.

'All right! I'm coming, I'm coming!' The shouting is from the cottage's hallway.

An uncertain rattle of locks and the door opens a couple of inches – as far as the safety chain will allow. Through the gap I see a woman who looks to be in her seventies. Diminutive, but no pushover. She's looking at me like I've got a nerve ringing anybody's doorbell without her prior permission. By way of introduction, she snaps, 'He's not in!'

She's wearing an apron. The kind I thought nobody went near any more, except in sitcoms and sketches. The Colonel's cleaning lady, then? Probably, although I doubt she'd call herself that. I give her an apologetic smile and say, 'No, I was supposed to be meeting the Colonel at the church. But he phoned and asked me to meet him here, instead. He said it was important.' She looks unconvinced and I add, 'But I can come back another day. I'm sure he wouldn't blame you for being overcautious.'

I quite like that last touch, but Gerry's faithful guardian isn't budging. She sighs and thinks aloud, 'I could phone him . . .'

'If he voices any objection to me waiting here, well, I'd be very surprised.'

That much *is* true. I try another smile, but she simply closes the door. A moment passes. I hear the metallic jingle of the safety chain being unlatched. She swings the door wide open.

'Make sure you wipe your feet. Been like Piccadilly Circus here, this morning.'

I step inside and do as instructed. 'Really?'

'Yeah. Two other gentlemen came calling. Didn't like the look of them.'

I wipe my feet like I'm trying to wear out the hessian mat. 'Why not?'

She wrinkles her nose as if smelling yoghurt that's gone off. 'Didn't let 'em in.'

'Very wise, er . . . ?'

'Edna.'

'Very wise, Edna.'

She walks through to the front room and I follow her. The fact that two men have already tried to gain entry means I need to work quickly and take chances.

'Don't know who you can trust and who you can't these days, can you, Mr . . . ?'

'Ferguson. James Ferguson. Call me Jim. And you're right. Things are seldom what they seem. Skim milk masquerades as cream.'

She pauses. Smiles, recognising the quotation. 'Aw. *HMS Pinafore*. I can see why the Colonel likes you. That's one of his favourites. Can I get you a brew, Jim?'

'A cup of tea would be lovely – thanks, Edna. And do you mind if I use the . . .' Observing the time-honoured rule of avoiding the word *toilet,* I point to the ceiling. 'I know the way.'

'Go ahead. I'll stick the kettle on.'

She turns away and begins humming 'I'm Called Little Buttercup' from *HMS Pinafore*. I watch her walk to the kitchen, blithely unaware that her employer is dead in the back of an ambulance. I shake my head. I need to focus.

The two guys Edna sent away will have reported back to their boss and I doubt they'll let an old woman in an apron stop them from coming in next time. I don't have long.

CHAPTER 37

I nudge open the door to the Colonel's study, peeking over my shoulder to check I'm alone. Edna is in the kitchen, cheerfully and noisily attending to tea-making duties. I slip into the room, taking in the lack of clutter, the clarity. I push the door behind me, leaving it an inch ajar so I can hear anyone climbing the stairs.

The air feels cooler in here. It's a spare room-cum-study, with a single bed against one wall, a small mahogany sideboard adjacent to it and a desk to the left of the door. As with the hallway, framed posters from Gilbert and Sullivan productions line the walls.

There's a computer on the desk. A small, slender laptop connected to a screen, mouse and keyboard. I pull out the seat in front of it. Sit down. Open the laptop. Fire it up. I'm hoping that the Colonel didn't use a password, but realise that's unlikely. And so it proves. The home screen is asking for a password before I can actually access anything. Great start.

I try the usual combinations. PASSWORD. password. PASSWORD1. Variations of 'Monkey' are popular, too, and although that doesn't sit well with Gerry's personality, I run through several variants of the possibility. None of which unlock the screen. Kind of inevitable. The Colonel may have come across as a bluff aficionado of operettas and the occasional bon mot, but he was once a high-ranking intelligence officer who dealt in secrets for a living. Let's face it, GERRY1 is never going to cut it.

I lean back.

'How do you like your tea, Jim?' Edna's voice carries like a town crier's.

'Nice and strong, please! Could you leave it to stew?'

'Aye aye!'

I stare at the winking cursor under the words 'PLEASE ENTER YOUR PASSWORD'.

I try entering YOUR PASSWORD.

Nothing.

There's a Montblanc fountain pen on the desk. I pick it up and check it for an inscription that might give me a clue, but it has none. I run my fingers through my hair. We often choose passwords that have some kind of significance for us. Dates, for example – often birthdays – that resonate. Or names of people that figure in our lives, although they may not be family or even particularly close to us. So, when the late Gerry Whittaker sat where I'm now sitting, what word or phrase occurred to him when he was asked to come up with a password? He probably thought for a moment, smiled and let his fingers tap out – on the keyboard in front of me – the phrase that felt appropriate to him. So, put simply, what resonated with Colonel Gerry Whittaker?

I hear a car engine and freeze. Its roar grows louder. My mind races, flickering through a thousand options, but . . .

The sound recedes as the vehicle carries on through Foxglove. Back to the screen. My eyes drift upwards to the framed artwork hung above the desk. It's an original poster for the movie version of *The Pirates of Penzance*, with Kevin Kline wearing a pair of dangerously tight leather trousers and brandishing a sword like he'll puncture anyone who mentions it.

I type in GILBERT&SULLIVAN. Nothing. But their oeuvre feels like a plausible fit and I begin typing rapid-fire guesses relating to their work. It's hopeless, of course. One operetta alone offers at least a hundred phrases that could have been chosen. I hear another car on the road that runs alongside the cottage. I'm more relaxed about this one, and carry on typing in G and S-related word combinations.

All rejected. I know I'm running out of time. Quite aside from a visit from whoever had the Colonel killed, the amiable Edna isn't going to stay amiable if I remain upstairs much longer. And as if to confirm this latter consideration—

'You all right, up there?'

She's hassling me already.

I type in EDNA.

No dice.

'I'm fine! Just had to take a quick phone call.' No answer. 'Maybe I'm old-fashioned, but I wish whoever invented portable phones hadn't got out of bed that morning!'

I hear her laugh. 'I'm with you on that one!'

'Won't be a sec!'

'Well, don't let your tea go cold!'

'Thanks!'

I stare at the screen, but something's wrong. The sound of the car is gone. But there was no gradual tail-off.

I hurry to the window behind me. It offers a view of Foxglove's main road and I immediately spot what I was hoping wouldn't be there. The car. A squat, dark SUV with mirrored windows. It couldn't appear more conspicuous or dodgier if its licence plate was a row of question marks.

I swear under my breath, stand back slightly from the window, but peer along the edge of the curtain. Two guys climb from the vehicle. Both tall, tanned and well-built. Short hair. Long faces. They're wearing dark suits and I've seen clowns like these a million times. Muscle sent in to get a job done.

I swear under my breath. Again. Move back to the laptop.

'Come on, Gerry!'

Another possibility occurs to me and I type in DIANA.

Nothing.

PRINCESS and variants of the word also get me nowhere and I can hear one of the two suits knocking on the back door.

CHAPTER 38

It's loud, insistent knocking. But I need to focus.

What was Diana's nickname? I remember reading it! What was it? Something regal . . .

DUCH.

I try it. Nothing. Mutter to myself, 'Oh, *come on*!'

Edna shouts to the two guys, 'All right! I'm coming, I'm coming!'

I glare at the screen and the blinking cursor that invites me to try another potential password. Somewhere in this mass of tin circuitry below my fingertips, there may well be information that could dictate how we view a figure who was once the most famous woman in the world. Information that could become a staple of history books across the globe. And I can't access it because a sequence of words eludes me.

I can hear Edna attending to the locks and opening the front door. 'He's not in!'

An East London accent. 'Mrs Edna Baker?'

She replies, 'The Colonel's right-hand woman.'

A Geordie accent this time. 'We're from the police, Mrs Baker.'

From the police. I'm half listening as I continue to type in possibilities. The police would say they *are* the police and operatives from any other legitimate body would specify the organisation they're from. No one is *from* the police.

Edna replies, 'Well, I'll need to see your—'

'Warrant cards?' Geordie interjects. 'No problem, pet.'

A few seconds of silence and I'm willing the old woman to give their ID a forensic examination. I'm typing anything I can think of into the password field, but the impossibility of the task is starting to hit home. Any second now two very big men are going to walk up the stairs and they won't be thrilled to find me trying to access the data I'm guessing they've been sent to retrieve. But the answers that Gerry Whittaker promised to give me feel so close. I try another password. Another fail.

Edna says, 'They appear to be in order. Here you go . . .'

East London already sounds tetchy. 'Can we come in now, Mrs Baker?'

'I told you – he's not about.'

'We're here to speak to you,' Geordie tells her. 'I'm afraid it's . . .'

East London finishes the sentence. 'Not good news.'

And bless Edna! She keeps arguing the toss. 'Yeah, well, if it's about the parking fines, I never pay for parking when I'm going to hospital. On principle. It's not like it goes to the NHS.'

I murmur, 'Good for you, Edna!'

The *Pirates* poster above the desk has a list of actors' names beneath the main artwork. I start trying them as passwords, initially using first names and surnames, and then mixing them up and adding standard numerical additions such as '1' and '123'.

East London snaps, 'It's not about any fines. It's about Colonel Whittaker. We need to come in. Now!'

'All right then.'

I hear the door close, the safety chain swish back and this time the door is opened properly.

'Make sure you wipe your feet!' And as she walks through to the front room, 'Piccadilly bleedin' Circus!'

The two men follow her into the front room. I know I should leave. Leave now. But the answers I'm after about Diana feel almost tangible . . .

Edna asks, 'So, what's it all about?'

Geordie replies, 'Bad news, I'm afraid.'

'Always is! What is it this time?'

'I'm sorry to have to tell you, pet, Colonel Whittaker's been involved in an RTA.'

Edna gives no reaction.

East London says, 'That's a road traffic accident.'

'Oh my gawd – is he all right?'

Geordie says softly, 'I'm afraid—'

He's stopped speaking. I look up, straining to hear what's going on.

What's he spotted?

'Two cups, pet?'

I stand up, move to the door.

Edna says, 'One for me. One for the Colonel's guest. Look, is Gerry all right?'

East London demands, 'What guest?'

'The gentleman,' Edna replies. 'He just popped upstairs. What's going on?'

But the men don't reply and I hear them racing up the stairs.

This is it. Me or them. My eyes linger for a moment on the fountain pen. I remove my glasses and put them in their metal case. The men have reached the landing and I hear them move a couple of steps towards this room.

I take a deep breath.

One of them whispers, 'You see him? Shoot the bastard.'

The other replies, 'Don't worry about that.'

I'm waiting. And one of them pushes open the door.

CHAPTER 39

Molly's Story

Molly Stone had helped found The Next Time Club and, like all its members, was a former journalist, although it was a term she disputed. 'There's no such thing as a former journalist,' she once argued. 'It's just a way of saying a hack who's run out of stories – for the time being.'

Towards the end of her career, she'd grown disillusioned with the state of her profession. Molly noticed that editors were increasingly looking for lighter, easier reads than she was used to putting out. The in-depth articles that had been her bread and butter since she'd started on her local rag as a teen were falling out of favour. One morning, Molly's boss had called into her office. 'I'm going to have to let you go.'

'You make it sound like you're releasing a helium balloon.'

'It's not that I want to, Moll. Times are tight. And I'll always find room for your stuff, if you want to go freelance.'

The arrangement had suited her well. Initially. Her old boss would take a meaty piece of writing from her once a month. Which became once in a while. Which became once in a blue moon. Which gradually became, 'It's a great idea, but not for right now. But keep in touch because, you know, next time.'

That became a phrase many fellow members of the press pack who shared her predilection for substantial features were beginning to hear on a regular basis. 'It's terrific! But no. Next time!' Or 'I would love to, but upstairs have capped my spending. But hey – next time!'

Molly recalled writing a feature on the run-up to the vote for Scottish independence. A good, solid piece of work that looked at the effect a victory for 'Yes' would bring. One editor had blanched when she read it. 'Are you crazy? We can't run this! It would make us look way too biased!'

'But it's the truth!'

'That doesn't matter.'

That doesn't matter.

The writing had been on the wall. Just not in the newspaper.

Molly had officially retired soon after, moving out of London to settle down with her wife in a busy little Home Counties village. She'd helped form the club because she'd missed being around all the other journalists who'd been told 'next time' before eventually running out of time. They met to catch up, drink too much and reminisce about the old days.

They were convening in The Inkwell Tavern, a dusty little pub in Soho, on the day Frank Harvey showed up.

She rose to meet him and they embraced. 'Not seen you for a while. Where've you been, stranger?'

'You're looking well, Moll.'

'You didn't answer my question. We've missed you.'

'Don't talk daft. What can I get you to drink?'

'G&T, please. They do Silent Pool here.'

Frank smiled. 'You and your fancy gins. What's that spicy one you used to like?'

'His name was Frank Harvey and I've still got a soft spot for him.'

'Flatterer.' He paused. 'Elephant Gin. That was it.'

'Ironic name because if you drink too much, you can't remember a thing. You joining us?'

'I was after a quiet word with you, actually. Any chance?'

Frank got them both a drink as Molly excused herself from the other club members. One asked, 'What's he doing back? He must want something.'

Molly replied, 'I wonder what . . .'

She joined her old friend at a corner table. He asked, 'How's the wife?'

'Cut to the chase, Frank.'

They clinked glasses. 'I'm helping out some lad. He's trying to find out who killed Diana.'

'Why not let it lie?'

'Because that's not what we do, is it? You covered it back in the day. You know the official version of events stinks to high heaven.'

'Maybe. But I don't want to see you getting hurt.'

'Only getting old?'

'That's not what I meant. Why haven't you joined us lately?'

'All the old stories . . .' He sipped his whisky. 'Can you help me?'

'Of course I can.' She smiled. 'You're my favourite former husband!'

'Glad to hear it.' Frank handed her a copy of the photograph Novak had sent him. 'Those are the two ghosts I

149

need identifying.' He pointed to the images of Miss Winters and Thom Peters.

'What do we know about them?'

Frank sketched out the details as he knew them.

'Understood. I'll get on it.'

'Thanks. That would be a big help.' He finished his drink. 'Look, I'd best be off. Good to see you, Molly. Always is.'

'So soon? You only just got here . . .' She walked him to the door. 'Just watch yourself, eh?'

'It's been twenty-five years, Moll. Besides, you know what a cautious fellow I am.'

'Twenty-five years, twenty-five days. Makes no difference. Still dangerous.' She kissed him lightly on the cheek and hesitated before asking, 'Why *are* you doing this?'

'Because I've heard all the old stories.' He glanced over at The Next Time Club. 'I want some new ones.'

He winked at her and walked from the pub. Molly watched him disappear into the throng of Soho.

'You may have a point,' she murmured to herself, before rejoining her fellow club members.

CHAPTER 40

For me, the secret of putting up a good fight and succeeding in a relationship is – perhaps inevitably – one and the same thing. In short, it's all about commitment.

I'm not a violent man, but if you're standing toe-to-toe with someone who intends to hurt you, you have to commit mentally to damaging that person. Pushing your opponent away or going for an armlock might sound like the cool and humane option, but when you're lying in hospital with your jaw wired up like a model of the Big Bang, you'll regret not battering the sonofabitch when you had the chance.

The door to the Colonel's study is pushed open. The barrel of a Glock enters the room and pauses. I'm holding my breath because I know the senses of the guy on the other end of the gun will be heightened. No matter how many times he's done this, unless he's a total psycho, he'll be scared. The Glock edges forward by an inch. I see the man holding it has his finger tight on the trigger.

I keep my back to the wall so he doesn't see me.

He steps forward.

And I commit.

I bring my right arm around in a fast, tight arc and plunge the nib and most of the shaft of the Montblanc fountain pen deep into his windpipe. He drops his gun as he raises both hands to his throat, whilst instinct impels him to move back, colliding with the man behind him.

I swing from my position into the doorway.

Christ.

The second guy is huge. A man mountain. But I've committed. He shapes to throw a punch but he's way too late and I headbutt him hard, my forehead slamming down on to the bridge of his nose. I hear it shatter and keep moving forward, shoulder-charging him down the stairs. That should be it. But he tumbles into the hallway below and doesn't even pause.

He's racing up the staircase like a bull that's glimpsed red.

I take a step back, slam the study door shut, scan the floor of the Colonel's study. *Where is it?*

The big man has whirled up the stairs like a tornado and kicks open the door.

I've found what I was looking for, but as I grab it and turn, he punches me hard in the face. I'm sent flying, although the adrenaline means I hardly feel a thing. A dull thud. Nothing more. Which isn't to say I underestimate the danger.

I land on my spine. He's on to me in an instant. His giant right hand grasps my trachea. Adrenaline or not, I feel this. He squeezes my throat and brings his face close to mine.

'You,' he tells me, 'are in a whole world of trouble.'

His right hand still grips my windpipe as he pulls his left back, shaping for another punch.

I can barely breathe, let alone speak, but manage to gasp, 'That's my . . .'

He pauses. Fractionally relaxes his grip. 'That's your what?'

I thrust the barrel of his colleague's Glock into his stomach. 'That's my line.'

I fire twice. His body acts as a silencer, so the discharge is relatively quiet. His screams are much louder. I push him off me and move across to his friend.

'Who sent you?'

I realise two things at once. Interrogating a man who's just been stabbed in the throat and expecting cogent replies is a pretty tall order.

And he's pushing a button on his wristwatch.

I swear to myself.

Because it isn't a simply a wristwatch. It's a Breitling Emergency Watch fitted with a Personal Locator Beacon. Ten grand a pop with titanium casing, cobra yellow facia and military-grade GPS.

Any moment now, this place will be flooded with backup.

Edna appears at the top the stairs. 'Oh my gawd! What happened?'

I grab the Colonel's laptop. 'Call an ambulance. They'll both be fine if they get treatment. I'm sorry, Edna.'

I race down the stairs, dash from the house and jog to my car. My hands are shaking as I open the driver's door.

Well, that was painful and messy but at least it was over quickly and I'm walking away alive. Another four ways that a successful fight is like most of my relationships.

As I tear out of Foxglove, I see two more black SUVs zipping towards The Lines. As the first of them passes me, I glance to my right. The driver's window is down so I can clearly see the man behind the wheel. He's pale and impassive and his appearance has a strange kind of smoothness to it, as if he's somehow been manufactured. There's something eerie, something disquieting about him.

And as if he can intuit my stare, he turns his head. Holds my gaze for a second. I feel a sense of dread.

The next moment, both SUVs have passed me and I floor the Marina, keen to put as much distance between me and them as possible.

CHAPTER 41

Elsewhere: Mishka's Story

Mishka arrived home mid-afternoon and immediately realised something was wrong. It was, she reflected, such a peculiar theft. The plaque that she'd screwed on to her front door when she'd moved in, four years ago, had been taken. It was a house name sign. Wooden. Inexpensive. Missing.

As she approached her front door, she wondered why anyone would go to the trouble of stealing such an ordinary sign. And then something else bothered her. She noticed the truly bizarre element as she reached the wooden door. Mishka touched the space where the sign should have been. She frowned.

'What the hell?'

The two tiny, circular areas where the screws had been lodged in the door had been painted over. Mishka squinted. No doubt about it. The paint had been delicately applied and carefully chosen, almost precisely matching the door's overall colour.

She put her key in the lock. Or tried to. It wouldn't fit, but in a sense, that didn't matter. The lock was on the latch, meaning that as she pushed the door, it opened. Cautiously,

Mishka stepped into her house. She was a naturally untidy person who found comfort in disorder. But the clutter and mess that normally characterised her hallway was missing.

In fact, everything was missing.

She bobbed her head into her front room. Every item of furniture, every book, every lamp, every clock, every keepsake – *everything* – was gone. She stepped into the room, as if her presence would break the spell.

She turned around 360 degrees. It looked unfamiliar. Skirting boards and floor. Exposed walls. Her house, but not her home. And she heard the noise from upstairs.

Mishka moved swiftly through to her kitchen. The built-in units remained, but the cupboards were empty. The pots and pans and plates and cutlery all gone. Her breakfast room stood completely empty and the poster-sized framed photograph that had hung on her wall had been removed, a faint darkening of the patch that it once covered served to emphasise its absence.

And still the sound from upstairs. The low, continuous tapping.

Mishka tried not to panic but could feel her heart pounding. She stood in her hallway, took deep breaths and began to climb the stairs.

The upstairs landing was, of course, clear of its usual clutter. An empty hallway for the first time in years. Mishka could now identify that the tapping was coming from her bedroom. She steadied herself and, very slowly, pushed open the door.

CHAPTER 42

I park my car opposite Rudy the Foodie, a sandwich shop in the next village along from Foxglove. I'm hit by the welcoming aroma of fresh coffee and hot toast as I walk through its door. The place is staffed by two people, both behind the counter. One of them is making sarnies, although as far as I can see, there are no other customers around. The other is a tall, good-looking woman, early sixties, jet-black hair and chunky jewellery.

She puts down a tea towel. 'Hiya! What can I get you?'

'Are you Rudy?'

'I'm Maureen. But Maureen the Foodie doesn't have the same ring to it.'

I smile and hand her a business card that she doesn't bother to look at. 'I'm Bryan Hornleigh, from Bingham Insurance.' I pause, as if expecting her to know the firm. Very often, people will nod and indicate they've heard of a fictitious company, simply because it's the expected response. But not Maureen. 'Your cyclist,' I continue, 'the delivery boy?'

'Freddie? Oh God, what's he done?'

'It's nothing like that. It's actually a long shot.' I describe the stretch of road where Gerry Whittaker's 'accident' occurred and the approximate time it must have happened.

157

I don't mention the incident itself, of course. 'Is there a chance he was there or thereabouts at that time? Heading away from Foxglove, preferably?'

'Why do you want to know?'

'We've a client in the village. And every month we pay him a lot of money because of a whiplash injury he says is so bad he can't even leave the house.'

'Right. So?'

'So, this morning I got a tip-off. Telling me he was out driving, happy as Larry, along that road.'

'Let me guess. You want the footage from our delivery boy's helmet cam to prove it?'

'That would be perfect.'

'He'll charge you for it. £27.50.'

I say, '£27.50?'

Maureen is adamant. 'Not a penny more, nor a penny less.'

As I wait for Freddie, I pull the Colonel's phone from my pocket. It's an ancient model. One of the original Nokia 3310s that were virtually ubiquitous about twenty years ago. The handset has raised buttons, as opposed to touch-screen technology, and peering at the device, I can see the print on the digits '1' and '2' is much more worn than that of the other numbers. So I try entering '1122' for the pass-code. This gets me nowhere. I try '1212' and the phone is unlocked. Pity the Colonel's laptop couldn't have been this obliging.

He told me that only one other living person knew what Diana had been about to announce, and he mentioned having to speak to him after our meeting. His call log shows

Edna phoned him twice yesterday, and he'd made a swift call to a contact listed as 'Leonard Raymond', who'd phoned him back that evening. The log indicates they'd chatted for twenty minutes. I press 'Return Call' and get put through to a voice message.

I hear a man's plummy voice. 'You have reached the Raymond! Do leave a message and I shall endeavour to return your call as and when I am able. Ciao for now!'

'Mr Raymond, my name is Marc Novak. I was a friend of Colonel Whittaker's. Please call me back as soon as possible. Believe me when I tell you, this is, quite literally, a matter of life and death.'

CHAPTER 43

Mishka's Story (cont.)

Mishka stepped into her bedroom. It was devoid of furniture except for a small desk she'd never seen before. Sitting behind it, tapping away on her laptop, Miss Winters didn't bother to look up. She simply murmured, 'One moment . . .'

'What's happening?'

'I said, *one moment*.'

Mishka checked her built-in wardrobes. Her clothes were all missing. She braced herself, daring to demand, 'What the hell have you done with my stuff?'

Miss Winters closed her laptop. 'Hello, Mishka.'

'This wasn't part of the deal.'

'There was no deal. You had instructions. You complied.' Miss Winters leant forward slightly. 'Good doggy.'

'Then why this?'

'We needed you to ensure that Novak took the Anna Brandon case. It's the kind of grubby little investigation he'd normally turn his nose up at. But you convinced him. You made sure he was on hand to record her husband's so-called infidelities, and you made sure he stayed on the case even when he'd done his job.'

'It wasn't difficult. He saw a woman who needed help.'

'The man's a fool.'

'Is he gonna be all right?'

'Ever since we've been friends, we've been very good to you. When your mother had an altercation with the taxman, we made sure there was a nice, amicable outcome.'

'I just want to know he'll be OK.'

'And when those photographs were found on your brother's hard drive—'

Mishka's anger flared. 'Those were not his!'

'But I don't think we need you any more. And believe me, you are a lucky girl.'

'Why?'

'You're still alive.'

'What have you got planned for Novak?'

'However, in order to maintain that happy state, you must move away. I don't want you near Marc Novak or his colleagues.'

'Why?'

'I can't have you thinking foolish thoughts and getting in touch with him. Helping him. Confiding in him. You've played your part – time to exit the stage.' Miss Winters paused and slid her laptop into its case. 'Agreed? And think very carefully before you reply.'

Mishka nodded.

'Excellent!' Miss Winters stood. 'It so happens we have an opportunity in our Birmingham office. I think you'll do very nicely there.'

'Yes . . . I guess so . . .' Mishka tried to take it all in. 'I've got family in the Midlands.'

'Birmingham, *Alabama*.'

'You can't—'

'When I said exit the stage, I didn't mean wait in the wings. Clothes and other items that you'll need have already been forwarded to the States. You will be collected in . . .' She checked her watch. 'Seven minutes. Your escort will give you all the documents you need and you'll be driven to Heathrow.'

'What then?'

'In a couple of days, the life you have led up until this point will be a memory.' She paused, and Mishka sensed a slight softening of her voice. 'Like I said, you're a lucky girl.' But the customary steely tone returned for her last, unambiguous order. 'Do not contact Novak again. Ever.'

Miss Winters brushed past Mishka and began walking down the stairs.

'You promised me he'd be all right!'

Miss Winters paused at the front door. 'I promised you I'd take care of him.' She opened the door, and spared the younger woman a final glance. 'Not quite the same thing, dear.'

CHAPTER 44

Freddie Clarke is seventeen years old and looks it. Some teens appear careworn and hardened. Not this kid. Skinny, fresh-faced and bursting with energy, Freddie arrived about ten minutes after his boss, Maureen, phoned him. We're sitting at one of Rudy the Foodie's tables and he's opened up his laptop. I've just asked him about the footage his camera would have shot earlier, and as he logs on, he says, 'I've already downloaded it.'

Which surprises me. 'Why? Did anything unusual happen this morning?'

'Nah, I always put the morning's recording online at around lunchtime.'

It feels odd to me that a series of mundane cycle rides is the kind of thing that some people like to watch these days. I know expressing that opinion would make me sound like Freddie's great-grandfather, so instead I say knowingly, 'If you don't 'gram it, it didn't happen.'

The kid grins and – not unkindly – replies, 'No one says that any more.'

'Yeah. I get that a lot.'

'I've got a couple of YouTube channels.'

'Just the two?'

'One of them is exclusively footage from my drop-offs, in case you want to check out what happened on other days.'

'I'm only interested in this morning. But thanks.'

'No worries. Here we are. The stuff I recorded today . . .' On the laptop's screen I see the street outside the café. The movement suggests Freddie is mounting his bike, and then his journey begins. He passes the spot where my Marina is currently parked. 'Here it is. I can email it to you.'

'Any chance you could just stick it on this?'

I hand him a USB stick. Freddie puts it in his laptop and begins transferring the video file. 'Yeah, sure. Would it be cheeky if I asked you for a bit of cash for it? Just £27.50.'

'Fair enough.' I'm not entirely sure this is a rabbit hole I want to go down, but all right, I'll bite. 'Do you mind me asking, why £27.50?'

'It's my birthday next month. I worked out if I make £27.50 a day extra, I can afford to take me and my girlfriend to Hay-on-Wye. For the bookshops. I collect old books.'

'So do I!' I like Freddie even more. 'How's your collection going?'

'My parents are getting me a first-edition *Casino Royale* for my eighteenth!'

'Dust cover?'

He shakes his head. 'They're not made of money!'

But that hardly seems to matter to him, and I recognise his joy at such a significant addition to his collection. That's how I started. Picking up first editions that were battered and dog-eared, sans dust jackets and often in such bad shape they were close to worthless on the market. But it's not all about the market, otherwise you might as well never set foot in a bookshop and simply trawl the internet for tomes that you might never even hold in your hand.

'You a Bond fan?'

Freddie nods. 'Do you know the Richard Chopping covers?'

It's like asking an opera buff if he's heard of Mozart. 'I do. I admire his work a great deal.'

'I think his covers are beautiful.' The kid says this as if I should be surprised.

One of my very early acquisitions was a first edition of *On Her Majesty's Secret Service* that I picked up in a (long gone) pokey little bookshop in Balham. No dust cover, but still an absolute steal at whatever I paid for it. Not a lot. I later bought a copy with its dust jacket intact, bearing Chopping's iconic artwork. But it's still that jacketless copy that retains a prominent spot in my cabinet back home.

'I think his *Live and Let Die* is stunning.'

Freddie's face lights up and he scribbles something down for me. 'That's my other YouTube channel. It's about books and stuff.'

After everything that's happened this morning, people like Freddie are a reminder – to me, at least – why we should carry on trying to make a difference. I take back my USB stick and the scrap of paper he's scrawled the information on.

'Here's fifty-five quid.' I hand him some notes. 'Say hey to Hay for me.'

'Top man! Cheers!'

A thought occurs to me. To be on the safe side, I add, 'And do me a favour. Don't post anything for a couple of weeks. Are you good with that? It just means my boss won't be able to ask me to go through the footage.'

'Sure. No problem. Call in if you're in the area again; we can talk books.'

'I'd like that.' We stand and shake hands. 'Good luck, Freddie.'

'And you, Mr Hornleigh.'

I walk to the door. Maureen tracks me as I pass the counter. There's a look in her eye. A look I like. 'You leaving, Bryan?'

'Sadly.'

'You don't fancy a roll?'

'Well . . .' I slip the USB stick into my pocket and glance through the shop's front window. 'I'd be lying if I said I wasn't tempted.'

I see one the two black SUVs driving slowly down the street. 'But I have to fly.'

She gives a little shrug. I shoot her a wink and walk quickly to my car, hoping the men in the dark cars don't spot me.

CHAPTER 45

I get home and pour myself a generous glass of Johnnie Walker Red. Raise it to the Colonel. I try to think of an appropriate line from the Savoy Operas, but nothing springs to mind, so I tip the whisky down my throat, fix another and send it looking for the first.

I'm tired. But there's still work to be done. I try to get hold of Thom Peters and Miss Winters. RP woman tells me they're unavailable. 'That could mean anything!' I argue. 'In a meeting. Dead. Trapped in a toilet cubicle.'

'May I take a message?'

I hang up and phone Frank, who answers after a single ring. 'I'm guessing it's bad news.'

'Yeah. The worst.'

I tell him about the Colonel's overturned Defender and the state I found him in. I tell him about stealing the laptop and dealing with the guys who were presumably at The Lines to acquire it. I even tell him about Freddie's footage and Leonard Raymond.

His reply is simply, 'Join me in London.'

'Why?'

'We can toast the Colonel.'

'It's what he would have wanted.'

'It's probably not,' Frank points out, 'but it's sure as hell what I want.'

Ninety minutes later, we're in the upstairs bar of the Star & Garter, a cosy little pub on Poland Street, about two minutes' walk – or stagger, depending on the time of evening – from the John Snow. It's a strange boozer, with its type of clientele seeming to change whenever I pay its pumps a visit. A few years ago, it was the haunt of young sales execs who worked at Centaur Communications, a media organisation based a few doors down. On most evenings, but especially Friday nights, the pub's first floor became an almost exclusive refuge for its workers. They were a rowdy but good-natured bunch and I often shared a few jars with them in my younger days. Good vibes. Good times.

When Centaur moved on, the nature of the Star & Garter changed. One night it's an old man's pub, filled with guys nursing Guinness and grievances. The next evening it might be overrun by the denizens of Soho's media land, whilst Saturday can see it awash with tourists. It's a weird one, but I'm never averse to popping in for a quick pint or four.

Frank and I raise our glasses. He says:

'Is life a boon?
If so, it must befall
That Death, whene' er he call,
Must call too soon.'

I've no idea what he's quoting, but I'm guessing it's from the pen of William S. Gilbert. Frank continues, 'He called too soon for Gerry Whittaker. But it's not Death we'll hold to account. It's the men that let him in . . . Here's to the Colonel!'

I chime back, 'The Colonel!'

An old boy a couple of tables down overhears, raises his shot glass, shouts, 'The Colonel!' and falls off his chair.

I knock back my drink and Frank shares a couple of stories about Gerry. I listen politely and then say, 'So who do you think killed him?'

'Christ knows.'

'The same people that killed Diana? If it was them, why didn't they take him out earlier?'

Frank looks annoyed. No – exasperated. 'Novak, you're still thinking that this is like, I don't know, a game of chess or something. One side versus another side. One black. One white. Never changing. Every piece controlled and committed. That's not how this works.'

'Fair enough. Tell me how it works.'

'Whichever agency or collective had the Princess of Wales murdered will have been powerful. Probably still is. So, they'll have stakeholders. People who don't want to see them fail.'

'Because its knock-on effect would impact on them?'

'Exactly. Corruption. Killings. Cover-ups. It's like any other business. So these stakeholders will themselves have stakeholders. Ad infinitum.'

'Ad nauseum.'

I lean back and take a drink. Frank's perspective makes sense. It's cynical and hard to stomach, but it's an authentic take on how a secret world operates and thrives. Its rules and regulations to be followed as closely as a high-street café must adhere to food-safety laws.

Frank eyes me to see if I'm understanding it all. He says, 'There's a link between the crash in Paris and the Colonel's car being rammed off the road. No question. But it's not neat and tidy. Life never is, son.'

I try to bring it back to basics and the facts that I think are crucial. 'The Colonel knew what Diana was about to announce to the world. He said it's what got her killed. I think whatever that announcement was going to be might be on his laptop.'

I'm curious to learn how Frank will respond, but the old boy who fell off his seat zigzags over to us. Actually, I now see he's about forty. Athletic build, but he looks three sheets to the wind. The guy stammers, 'Is . . . is this a wake?'

Frank says, 'We'll let you know.'

'I . . . I knew him! Knew . . . Knew him well. Damn well.'

I ask, 'What was his name?'

'He was a good man!'

Frank hands the guy a fiver. 'Here you go, my friend.'

'Is this for a drink?'

'It's for a packet of aspirin. You're going to need it in the morning.'

'You're a gentleman!' He staggers back to the bar.

'You're a soft touch, Frank.'

'Where were we?'

'I was saying that Gerry Whittaker knew what got Diana killed. And I reckon he shared the knowledge with his laptop, so to speak.'

Frank taps his temple. 'Old soldiers keep it up here.'

'He knew he was dying. I think he was the kind of bloke who wanted to set things straight before he snuffed it.'

'You might be right. His laptop – you said it was pass-word protected?'

'Yeah. And my former business partner – Mishka – she's the one who normally dealt with the techy stuff.'

I'm expecting him to know a guy, but he says, 'Don't look at me! Wouldn't have a clue where to start.'

'Come off it! You're a journo, Frank! You must know someone who can hack it!'

'Why's that?'

'Because being able to hack stuff, or knowing someone who *can* hack stuff, is right there on page one of how to be a journalist in ten easy lessons.'

'You have an indecently low regard for the ladies and gentlemen of the press.'

'Can you get it hacked?'

'I'm offended . . .' He shrugs. 'Offended you even have to ask. But . . .'

'What is it?'

'This would mean me joining you on this bloody stupid quest of yours.'

'It's just another helicopter to jump out of, Frank.'

He smiles. Frank Harvey understands I'm trying to rope him into something bigger than individual elements of the case. He takes another mouthful of beer. 'Like I said, the Colonel was taken too soon. And Diana may have been this other-worldly princess, but she was also a good woman. Yeah, I'll help.'

'Thank you.' I feel we should chink glasses to seal the deal but sense he's slipped into business mode, so I crack on. 'The Colonel's laptop is probably the only place he stored the info about what Diana had got planned.'

'Agreed.'

'Drumroll, please . . .' I remove the laptop from my bag and place it on the table between us. 'And if that's what got her killed, this' – I point at the computer – 'could be our last chance to find out who did it and why.'

Frank is gawping at me as though I've started to remove my trousers. 'Have you gone doolally tap?' He shoves the laptop back into my bag. 'You brought that *here*? Knowing how valuable it is?'

'No one has entered this room since I walked in.'

'You've got a lot to learn, lad.'

'I knew I was taking a risk but I had to. Time's against us.'

He shakes his head. 'Still think you're barmy.'

'Still think you're right. Can you get it to your friendly neighbourhood hacker tonight?'

'I can try.' He slips the bag out of sight, under the table, lodging it firmly between his ankles. 'Why does this case mean so much to you?'

'I'm hoping for a knighthood.'

Frank takes another swig of beer. 'So you don't want to say?'

I shake my head.

'Fair enough. Look, I'm going to shoot. Having something this valuable is making me nervous.' He reaches for the bag. 'Hold on . . .' He takes a penknife from his pocket, opens his suit jacket and, after making sure none of the other patrons are looking his way, slashes a horizontal cut across its lining. He removes the laptop from the bag and slides it into the poacher's pocket he's just fashioned.

172

'Nice idea.'

Frank stuffs his discarded broadsheet newspaper into the bag and hands it to me. 'I've finished the cryptic crossword but the easy one's all yours.'

'You're too good to me.'

He stands up. 'Stay for another drink. When you leave, hold the bag like it's the most valuable thing in the world.'

'Yeah, and you look after yourself.'

He nods and takes a step towards the stairs. Hesitates. 'You too, Novak.'

Frank walks away. I knock back the last shot then take my time finishing what's left of my beer. Finally, I grab my bag and saunter to the bar. I should get a soft drink.

'I'll have a large whisky with a splash of water. No ice. Thanks.'

The barman hands me the drink and, just to save time, I ask him to slosh another double in there. As I walk back to the corner table I'd shared with Frank, I notice the guy who'd fallen off his chair has just left. I pause by his table. One of his shot glasses isn't quite empty, still holding half an inch of clear liquid. I don't really care who sees me. I raise it. Sniff it. Taste it. My face flinches.

I never could stand plain water.

CHAPTER 46

Frank's Story (cont.)

Frank Harvey stepped into the chilly night, paused and raised the collar of his suit jacket. He patted its pockets, pulled out a packet of Camels, extracted a cigarette and placed it between his lips. All the while, he'd been surreptitiously scanning Poland Street. There was a blonde across the way who appeared to be chatting on her phone without walking anywhere and Frank stopped a couple of people, asking for a lighter. By the time someone lent him a Zippo, the blonde had strolled about a third of the way to Oxford Street. Frank thanked the passer-by, returned the lighter and set off in the opposite direction, heading towards Broadwick Street.

He didn't notice the man from the Star & Garter following him into the heart of Soho.

Frank hung a right. He made a quick phone call and swore to himself when no one picked up. He turned left and began striding down an unlit alley. To his left, he could see the backs of shops and cafés and he could still hear the pulse of the neighbourhood.

He heard something else. Footsteps. Instinct made him glance over his shoulder and he spotted his pursuer immediately. The man who'd feigned drunkenness back in the pub. Frank swore again and began to run, but the younger man covered the distance between them in a sprint.

'Give me the laptop!' He grabbed Frank's shoulder and spun him around. 'Now!'

But the older man was ready. House keys in his fist, he swung at his attacker and felt his Yale slash into the soft flesh of his opponent's face. The man gasped and took a couple of steps back and Frank turned and began to run again, hoping to reach the main road and the relative safety that other people would afford.

But his pursuer was too fast, reaching him, grasping his jacket and swinging him to the ground. He stood over the journalist and slid something from his sleeve.

Frank saw the cosh. Navy-blue hardened rubber, about 30cm long. He raised his palm. 'All right, all right. Take the bloody thing.'

He pulled the laptop from his improvised pocket and handed it over. The man slipped it into his duffel bag and put his fingertips to his face, as if noticing the deep key cut for the first time. 'You old bastard!'

He kicked Frank savagely in the stomach, raised his bludgeon and swung it on to the back of his skull. More vicious kicks and blows. The assault initially lasted just a few seconds but Frank was able to partly protect himself by placing his arms around his head. For several moments the onslaught was frenzied, then his attacker paused, grabbed Frank's left wrist and yanked it to one side, exposing part of his face. A button was pressed on the cosh's handle and two blades clicked open at its other end.

'You messed with the wrong fella, old man.'

Frank saw his attacker raise the cosh. He spotted the blades but was unable to defend himself as the lethal bludgeon was swung down fast towards his face.

CHAPTER 47

Novak's Story (cont.)

'So did you.'

The voice was close behind, almost upon him. Before he could bring the blades of his cosh down into Frank's face, the attacker felt an extraordinary pain in his side.

Novak was standing immediately behind him. He pulled the steak knife out of the guy's side and, without hesitation, plunged it into his torso again, an inch or two above the first stab wound. The man screamed in pain and Novak snatched his duffel bag a moment before he spun to the ground.

Novak said to Frank, 'Are you badly hurt?'

'What happened?'

'I cottoned on that he was tailing you. Got a friend to ping your phone and grabbed a steak knife on my way out of the pub. Frank, are you OK?'

'I'll be fine.'

He looked up at Novak, who murmured, 'Christ. You look like hell.'

'Talk to that bastard.' Frank nodded to his attacker. 'Find out who he's working for.'

'We've got to get you to a hospital. And if he's got back-up, I don't fancy our chances in this alley. Come on!'

'All right, all right . . . But take it easy. I think he broke a couple of ribs . . .'

Novak hauled Frank to his feet and helped him along the alley. They reached a pub and he eased his friend into one of the outside chairs. 'Stay here.'

He jogged back to the alleyway, but the injured man had managed to crawl away. Novak phoned for an ambulance as he returned to the pub. He found Frank drifting in and out of consciousness, bought a couple of large whiskies and guided one of them into his mouth.

'Drink this . . .'

Frank swallowed. Coughed. Spluttered.

'My head feels like . . . And I've a pain in my shoulder . . .'

'There's an ambulance on its way. It'll be here any moment. You're going to be fine.'

'You stabbed that guy?'

'Twice.'

'You're tougher than I thought.'

Novak paused. 'I don't like to advertise Mr Hyde.'

'But he's always there?'

'Not something I'm proud of.' He thrust the second glass of whisky into Frank's hand. 'Drink your medicine.'

The other man nodded. 'Yes, Dr Jekyll.'

Frank grinned but Novak didn't return the smile.

CHAPTER 48

The ambulance arrives like a shocking headline, drawing everyone's eye. Paramedics leap from the vehicle and begin checking on Frank as most nearby drinkers pretend *not* to have a good gawp over their pint or Pinot. I give a semi-fictitious account of what their patient has just endured, whilst he downplays the damage, insisting he doesn't need to go to hospital.

'I'll be fine. If you want to help, get me another drink.'

I say quietly to one of the paramedics, 'He says he's got a pain in his shoulder. Given the trauma to his torso, I'm thinking it's Kehr's sign.'

She nods. 'You think he's got a ruptured spleen?'

'It's a strong possibility. You need to get him to a hospital as soon as possible.' I turn back to the patient. 'Frank, they're going to have to do a brain scan and make sure there's no blood on your brain. And check for internal injuries and basically keep an eye on you for a bit. Nothing to worry about. You'll be in there for a few days.'

The paramedics reassure Frank and help him into the back of the ambulance.

My phone rings. I check the caller ID: *Leonard Raymond*. The man Colonel Whittaker had spoken to following our meeting yesterday.

'Frank. This is a lead. I've got to take it.'

'Keep going with the investigation, Marc. Give me your word you won't give up.'

'Oh, believe you me, I can promise you that.'

We shake hands and the ambulance doors are slammed shut.

I answer my phone. 'Mr Raymond?'

'Speaking.'

'Thank you for returning my call. I hope I'm able to save your life.'

As the ambulance pulls away, I drift towards Sherwood Street and shift my focus to the phone call with the last living man who might know what Diana had been on the verge of announcing when she was killed.

CHAPTER 49

Leonard Raymond's voice sounds . . . I want to say posh, but I guess it's more theatrical. He says, 'I wasn't aware my life was in any danger.'

'You knew Colonel Whittaker?'

'Gerry was a dear, dear friend.'

'I'm afraid he's dead.'

A pause. 'He can't be! We spoke yesterday. He was in good spirits.'

'He was murdered this morning.'

'How?'

That *How?* is interesting. There's no disbelief or denial at the mention of murder. The Colonel's killing is a shock to him, but at the same time, it's not completely unexpected.

'An RTA.'

'Was it quick? Will he have felt—'

I interrupt. 'Where are you, Mr Raymond? We need to meet and discuss the situation as soon as possible.'

'Who exactly are you, Mr Novak?'

'Your last hope, Mr Raymond. Where are you based?'

'Paris.'

'Well, Mr Raymond. It looks like I'm coming to Paris.'

We arrange to meet tomorrow and he closes with, 'Until then, Mr Novak, au revoir.'

I call Precious and tell her, 'I need another favour.'

'Remember when people used to say hello?'

'Sorry, Precious. Tough day. Someone was killed this morning.'

'A friend of yours?'

'How did you know?'

'Kinda goes with the territory, Novak.'

I reach the steps that lead down to Piccadilly Circus underground station. 'Remember when people used to say I'm sorry for your loss?'

She replies, 'Apols. That was insensitive. What do you need?'

'Where are you?'

'Just left the office.'

'Good. I have to get to Paris tonight. But I haven't got time to schlep home, grab my stuff and get to St Pancras. I know it's a big ask, but could you swing around my place, pick up my passport and laptop and meet me at the station?'

'Why the sudden urge to visit France?'

'I'm following a lead. I wouldn't ask, but I think lives are at stake.'

She doesn't hesitate. 'I'm on it.'

'Do you have a key?'

'Yeah. It's still on the bunch with my house keys.'

'Great – thanks, Precious.'

'I always knew our relationship would be useful for something.'

I know she's joking, but after the day I've had, I really don't need it. I say, 'Phone me when you get to the station,' and take the stairs into the underground.

*

I reach St Pancras and buy a few things for my trip. A fresh shirt and underwear, toiletries and a bottle of Courvoisier. I stuff them all into the duffel bag I took from the guy who attacked Frank. Precious arrives much sooner than I'd anticipated and she's with Cy. I thank them both for helping out and ram my laptop, which she hands me, into the bag. As I sling it over my shoulder I say, 'Thank you both – again.'

And it's only now that Precious gives me the bad news.

CHAPTER 50

'I'm coming with you.'

I look from Precious to Cy, expecting him to shake his head, intimating she's joking. But he looks dead serious.

'What?'

She repeats. 'I'm coming with you.'

In terms of my Paris plans, this couldn't get any worse.

Cy adds, 'And I'm coming, too.'

OK. Just got worse.

'Precious! Why the hell do you want to come?'

'You asked me to take a look at how Diana died. Well, I've read the Operation Paget report and the inquest's findings – and I want in. It wasn't just an accident in Paris.'

'I'm glad you want to help me—'

'I'm not doing it for you. I'm doing it for her and everyone else that suffered because of the cover-up.'

I shake my head. 'But it's too dangerous. Sorry. Absolutely not.' I remember something. 'Could I have my passport, please?'

'Sorry.' She shakes her head. 'Absolutely not.'

'This is blackmail.'

'This is *business*. You get your passport if you agree to let me help.'

184

I check my watch. 'You win. You can tag along. Cy, you *really* don't need to come.'

'I really do,' he replies.

'What for?'

'To look after Presh.'

'I can look after Precious.'

'Didn't do a very good job of it last time.'

We broke up because I'd involved her in a case and made a catastrophic error of judgement that almost cost my then fiancée her life. It's not something I like to think about, let alone talk about. And I sure as hell don't need Cy bringing it up.

Precious interjects, 'I can look after myself, and I don't appreciate any suggestion to the contrary.'

Me and Cy mumble our apologies.

'Now come on,' she urges. 'We've got a train to catch.'

CHAPTER 51

I buy three business premier-class tickets and we just make the last train to Paris. Perhaps because it's so late, we're the only passengers in our carriage. Precious and Cy sit next to each other. I take a two-seater table across the aisle and the train slowly pulls out of St Pancras.

I bring Precious up to date with the investigation and ask, 'So what convinced you to get on board?'

'If you read the official narrative it's impossible *not* to see there's a cover-up in play.'

Cy looks sceptical. 'You think Princess Diana was murdered?'

She nods. 'Yeah. And not just her. The two male victims that were with her in the Mercedes and, well, others.'

I ask, 'What others?'

'Doesn't it strike you as odd that so many of the people Diana trusted and relied on were either moved away or—'

'Killed?' Cy is almost mocking her. 'You can't believe that, Presh.'

She replies, 'Want an obvious example? Barry Mannakee, a member of Diana's security detail. She trusted him, maybe came to rely on him too much – but we know she fell in love with him, because she's on record as admitting it. So, you have this very capable guy that's looking out for Diana on every level. His loyalty is with her, not his employers. So then – surprise, surprise – he's removed from her orbit. Transferred to what was then the Diplomatic Protection Group.'

Cy shrugs. 'So what? He could still advise her. Maybe even get his old job back in some capacity or—'

Precious interrupts. 'Just a few months after he was moved on, he was killed in a motorcycle accident. The driver of the car *officially* involved in the crash – who was perfectly innocent – said she suspected evidence was concocted and *multiple* witnesses reported seeing another car that was involved in the crash. The clue of the second car was never followed up. Never even officially acknowledged. It's as though the authorities wanted to pretend it never existed. The princess herself thought Mannakee had been murdered. And one of Diana's lovers – James Hewitt – claims he was visited by an MI5 officer who warned him he could "meet the same end as Barry Mannakee". So you tell me. Was he murdered?'

Cy remains adamant. 'Official authorities do not kill people! That's something that happens in other countries, sure, but not here.'

I say, 'Cy, we like to think we live in a civilised nation. But murder's a part of how our security services go about their business. It's as much a part of the industry as emails and paperwork.'

'Oh, come on, man!'

'And it's all legal and – well, not quite above board.'

Precious tells him, 'Cy, you don't even need a licence to kill. In January 2021, government lawyers told a court that MI5 officers could authorise informers to carry out murders. Let that sink in.' She pauses. 'A member of the public can commit murder if they get a note from our security services.'

'I don't believe it!'

'This isn't conspiracy-theory stuff,' she says. 'It's acknowledged fact. That same week, by the way, the security service's right to use children as undercover informants was also confirmed. Frightening, isn't it?'

'No. It's terrifying,' I add. 'But it's the accepted, legally recognised truth of the more brutal side of national security.'

'Honestly, Cy.' Precious puts her palm across the back of his hand. 'People of interest being killed in the UK? It's not that unusual.'

He shakes his head again.

I press on. 'You must have heard of the famous cases. The ones that managed to avoid having D-notices slapped all over them?'

'Like what?'

'Like Gareth Williams – seconded to MI6 after a ten-year stint at GCHQ. Found dead in a duffel bag. Scotland Yard reckoned he died after getting into the bag, and that he was alone when it happened.'

Cy shrugs. 'So what?'

Precious replies, 'The bag was locked on the outside.' She gives a second example. 'The MP, Stephen Milligan. Rising star of the Conservative Party. He was another one. Ties to the intelligence world. Rumoured to be looking into arms sales. He was found strangled in his house in Hammersmith – put down to death by misadventure. Sexual misadventure. Former girlfriends said it was rubbish and here's the thing ... One James Rusbridger – a former MI6 man – told the media he was going to investigate Milligan's death because it just didn't stack up. Nine days later, Rusbridger himself is found hanging from a beam at his cottage on Bodmin Moor. Icing on the cake? Shortly before his death, he expressed fears over phone tapping.'

I recall the video of Charles and Diana on the day their engagement was announced. The interview that everyone remembers for the Prince's gaffe about 'whatever love means'. What had been his more important words?

They said the phones are tapped, or something . . .

Cy claims, 'Those are just one-off cases.'

'Yeah, but they form a pattern,' Precious insists. 'And sometimes it's more obvious than other times. Take Nicholas Husband. A GCHQ worker. Found dead with a plastic bag on his head, and then a few months later, fellow GCHQ-er, Kevin Allen, also found dead with a plastic bag over his head. Inquests found nothing suspicious. I mean – really?'

I say, 'Sometimes it's done abroad just to make investigations trickier. British journalist Jonathan Moyle was looking into US gunships and weaponry being sold to Iraq and was found hanging in a hotel wardrobe in Santiago. Only took eight years for it to be officially admitted he was killed by a person or persons unknown. *Eight years.*' I continue, 'And if you think we're just having a pop at the Brits, it's not just us. It's every nation. It's what happens.'

'You must have heard of Alexander Litvinenko,' says Precious. 'KGB defector. Died after drinking radioactive tea. His friend, Boris Berezovsky, was found hung in his Berkshire home. Open verdict returned. The year after that, Scot Young, who had close ties with Berezovsky, was found impaled on iron spikes outside his Marylebone home. I wouldn't say the British police were quick to write it off as suicide, but they didn't even bother to dust his flat for prints!'

There's a dozen other cases I could hit Cy with, but I can see his head is spinning. He's gone through the denial phase and looks to be well into the shock stage.

He says, 'If all this is happening . . .'

'It is,' I assure him.

'Then why's it not in the papers every day? Or all over social media? Or getting wall-to-wall coverage on the news?'

Precious speaks quickly and with force, 'Because it's only one strand of truth. In other words, it's just another story. And other people set the agenda for what stories we should find important and worthy of reaction. They tell us what to care about, what to be outraged about, what to feel aggrieved about . . . and off we go. Ignoring the bigger issues. Ignoring everything we should really be fighting.'

Even I'm surprised by the vigour of her words.

'Everything we've just talked about is officially out there,' I reflect, speaking more to Precious than Cy this time, 'in the public domain. Now, if that's the stuff they don't care that people know about, it makes you wonder about the things they *are* hiding, doesn't it?'

'Jesus,' Cy murmurs. 'It's a bloody nightmare.'

I know how he feels. 'No. Because this is where it gets difficult. When it's done, it's *usually* to protect the likes of you and me. How did President Obama put it? The world is messy.'

'You said usually?'

I recall the Colonel's overturned car, policewomen and policemen rattling around it. I wonder if they were there to help or hinder truth's imperative.

'Yeah,' I reply. 'Usually.'

'And these are the people we're taking on? That's the world we're going into?'

'You don't get it, do you?' Precious's patience is finally wearing thin. 'That's the world we're already living in! All of us! And we're about to challenge the fuckers who run it, hold them to account – or try to! But people who do that tend to end up having accidental car crashes, or accidents in duffel bags, or find themselves mysteriously impaled on iron spikes or unexpectedly the victims of suicides – or suddenly developing terminal cancer.'

I don't know what you'd call the final phase that Cy now enters. Loss of hope, perhaps. 'But all th-these people . . .' he stammers. 'The security services. The police. Politicians. They're supposed to be here to protect us.'

'They are,' I tell him. 'But even amongst the just, there is injustice.'

'But,' Cy shakes his head, 'when they're coming to get you. When you're lost. When they want you dead . . . There must be someone you can turn to.'

'There is,' I tell him. 'Me.'

CHAPTER 52

We book into a modest hotel near the Sorbonne. Precious and Cy traipse off to their double room and I check out my single. As a barometer of how your life is going at any given point, there's seldom anything more depressing than a narrow bed. I dump my bag on top of the wardrobe and head to the bar.

It's dimly lit. A guy at the piano is playing Ella Fitzgerald numbers and the smell of food, wafting through from the hotel's kitchen, reminds me I haven't eaten since morning. My face is also starting to ache from the punch it took earlier today, and as I don't have any aspirin on me, I order a large Napoleon brandy to ease the pain. I knock it back, order another and take a seat.

I phone Anna Brandon. No answer.

Through a window to my right, I can see the Latin Quarter's teeming, vibrant streets. There's a certain irony insofar as when we'd been a couple, Precious had often proposed a trip to Paris, but I'd always been too busy.

The pianist starts playing 'Ev'ry Time We Say Goodbye'.

'Hello.'

I look up. It's Precious. She's alone. And as if she can read my thoughts, she adds, 'Well, here we are.'

'I told you I'd bring you one day.'

'This isn't exactly what I had in mind.'

'Well, the night *is* still young.'

'Novak!'

I grin. 'Mine's a large one.'

Jokingly, she narrows her eyes.

'Brandy, I mean. If you're going to the bar.'

Precious shakes her head. 'You're incorrigible.' But all the same, when she returns to the table she's got herself a large Sav Blanc and a double Napoleon for me. 'Cheers, Novak.'

We clink glasses – 'Cheers, Weeks' – and sip our drinks.

'So, why did you want to help me on the case?'

'You're not the only who likes to see justice done. Besides, it might be interesting. Gotta be more interesting than my current job. Jeez.'

I can see there's something more and press her. 'And . . . ?'

'And when I was doing the research on Diana, do you know what struck me?'

'Tell me.'

'Well . . . What are the headlines from her final year?'

I think back. 'She ends an affair with a heart surgeon. Or rather, he ends it. Starts a new one with a man who's already engaged. I don't know . . . She spends time with him. Some say falls in love with him.' I pause for another sip of brandy. 'She takes her kids on holiday . . . Then has a holiday in France without them, with her new bloke. Dodi.'

Precious nods. 'Exactly! Your perspective is so preprogrammed. It's like all the books and newspaper articles and documentaries about her . . . They all view Diana through the male gaze.'

'Go on . . . Please.'

'She travels to Angola for her campaign against land-mines and politicians react as if she has absolutely no right to get involved. She makes a speech – years ahead of its time – about mental health. Observers are more interested in what she's wearing. She goes to France to strategise what she wants to do in the next stage of her life, and people just report she's running around with a millionaire playboy while she should be at home looking after her sons. I mean, Jesus! Would we interpret what she did differently if she'd been a bloke? We sure as hell would have done.'

'What should I be looking at specifically?'

'Isn't it obvious? What had she done in the final few months of her life that would put her in danger?' Sarcastically, Precious adds, 'And don't think of her as a woman, if it'll help you get your mind around it.'

I ponder the question. 'If a man had done what she'd done, we'd be focusing on . . .'

'Lose the male gaze . . . Think about what she'd achieved in 1997.'

The answer hits me.

Precious grins. 'The penny drops!'

We talk a while longer and she finishes her wine. I say, 'You should stay for just one more.'

'That wouldn't be a good idea.'

'Fair point. Make it two more.'

She stands and I also get to my feet.

'Thanks for coming down to join me. And for your insight. Really. It's appreciated.'

'Good.' She kisses me on the cheek. 'Night, Novak.'

*

I finish my brandy and take a walk through the city. My phone rings. No caller ID. I pick up on the off-chance it's Anna Brandon.

'What the hell are you doing, Novak?'

'Good evening, Miss Winters.'

'You seem to be leaving a trail of destruction in your wake.'

'It's a talent, isn't it?'

'You need to drop this case.' It's not friendly advice. It's a command. A threat. 'You really must.'

I stop. The Eiffel Tower looms ahead of me. 'You put me on this thing. You started it.'

'And I'm finishing it. Matters are spiralling out of control, Novak. We didn't expect you to—'

'To what? Actually do anything meaningful?'

'People are dying. Continue down this path and more people will lose their lives. And you're not precluded from that certainty. Do you understand?'

'Not really.'

'Then let me make it very clear. You get one warning. This is it.'

She hangs up.

Miss Winters didn't ask me where I am or what line of inquiry I'm pursuing because, I suspect, she already knows.

The temperature suddenly feels to have dropped. I turn away from the tower and start back to my narrow bed.

CHAPTER 53

I agreed to meet Leonard Raymond at noon at the Hotel Scarlioni, a luxury establishment in the 16th arrondissement, close to the Champs-Élysées. It's a tall, impressive stone building constructed in the 1920s, still retaining many of its original Art Deco flourishes.

Precious and I walk across its foyer and into a tiny lift. It has old-fashioned bronze-coloured latticework doors that must be closed by hand. I do the honours. Precious presses the top button on the side panel and our ascent begins. We emerge on to the hotel's penultimate floor and, following signage, step through a door that takes us to an outside area. We climb a final flight of steps and we've reached the building's summit.

Ahead of us we see the Scarlioni's four-star restaurant. It's surrounded by terraces, divided into sections by screens fashioned from tall potted plants. We drift to the edge of the rooftop and pause by the low brick wall that runs around its perimeter. The views across the city are impressive. The Arc de Triomphe seems impossibly close and, a mile or so away, I can make out the Sacré-Cœur in Montmartre.

Precious takes in the vista. 'Cy would have loved this.'

He remains back in our hotel. He'd wanted to come along, and argued his presence by his girlfriend's side was

196

the whole point of him accompanying us to France. But Precious reasoned that three strangers might spook Raymond, and that Cy's IT skills could be used to good effect by trying to bypass the security on the Colonel's laptop.

I sniff. 'Paris is a bit grey for me. A little too monotone.'

We cross to the other side of the roof and even I must admit the panorama is a special one. The Eiffel Tower majestic in the near distance, bestriding the sprawling city below.

Precious takes a couple of photos on her phone and we head inside the restaurant. We're shown to our seats by a harassed-looking waitress. I tell her we'll soon be joined by a third member of our party.

When we're alone, Precious asks, 'So this guy. Do you think he'll tell us what Diana was planning to announce? Why it was so big a deal that she was killed over it?'

I reply, 'After what you said last night, I think we both could hazard a pretty good guess as to what it was. But I'm hoping he'll be able to throw more light into the darkness.'

'Do you think we can trust him?'

'Well, we're about to find out,' I whisper. 'Here he is . . .'

CHAPTER 54

Leonard Raymond is a tall, wide man in his late sixties. He wears a cream linen suit with a red silk tie, black armband and a battered fedora. He carries a chipped wooden cane and, as he waddles across the restaurant, he greets the waiting staff like they're long-lost siblings.

He reaches our table and spreads his arms as if embracing an audience's applause. 'My dear boy, my dear girl . . . My deepest condolences for the tragic loss we have all endured. The Colonel was a great man. May he rest in peace.' He closes his eyes and there's a moment of awkward silence.

Precious and me exchange glances. I raise my eyebrows and she tries not to laugh.

Raymond opens his eyes and says, 'Shall we order cocktails? They do an Espresso Martini that's to die for. But where are my manners? I am Leonard Raymond.' He pronounces his given name *lee-oh-nard* and we all shake hands and introduce ourselves. He takes a seat. 'How did our beloved Gerry pass?'

I give him the condensed version and he nods, gravely.

Precious says, 'You don't look surprised.'

'There have been many players in this tragedy. His exit is simply the latest in a long line.'

'The Colonel told me that you and he were the last two people alive who knew what Diana intended to announce to the press.' I pause. 'He also said that whatever it was, it's what got her killed.'

Precious adds, 'We'd like to know, Leonard. We're looking for justice for the Princess. We think she deserves that.'

'Fine words, fine words. But I am a judicious man. It is why I still breathe whilst others who knew Diana's secret now rest in graveyards.'

I ask, 'How did you know the Princess?'

'We met through a mutual passion for the arts. We became good friends. I ran a business out of Paris, and so when she needed to leave the city quickly, she contacted me.'

Precious leans forward. 'So Diana was leaving Paris on the night she was killed?'

'Of course. Why do you think her car was taking her away from the location that the authorities claimed she was heading to?'

'So where was she going?' I demand, but Raymond slowly shakes his head.

'My lips must remain sealed, mon ami. Discretion alone keeps me alive.'

Precious pleads with him. 'You *have* to help us. These people have already killed the Colonel simply for knowing the truth. They're not taking chances any more. You may have been safe. But not now. They *will* come after you next. Your best bet is to tell us what you know so we can expose them and make sure you're safe.' She pauses. 'Who murdered Princess Diana?'

199

'I cannot tell you *who* killed her. As far as I know, dear old Sebby Hughes is the last of us with that information. But I can tell you *why* she was killed. And a little of how.'

I'm desperate to ask who this Sebby Hughes character is, but Precious moves forward, pressing to find out what Raymond knows.

'Those pieces of the jigsaw are incredibly valuable to us,' she assures him.

He nods. 'Very well. To understand why she intended to make her announcement, you must consider how the world was in 1997.'

I reply, 'Clinton in the White House, prior to the whole Monica Lewinsky scandal. Blair's New Labour elected by a landslide.'

'No, no, no! I'm talking about the broader picture! What was happening in the *world*! Diana had already begun addressing the problem, of course, and was succeeding beyond anyone's expectations. That's why they had to stop her.'

Precious says, 'We need details, Leonard.'

He hesitates and murmurs to himself, 'If Gerry is gone, I am no longer safe . . .' He nods. 'Very well. You ask Leonard Raymond for details? You shall have them.'

CHAPTER 55

Raymond gives an enormous sigh, removes his hat and places it on the table. 'But first, I think, a cocktail.' He catches the eye of a waiter who strolls towards us. 'My friends and I require libations!'

The waiter nods. 'Yes, sir.'

'Capital! Now, let me see . . .'

Raymond studies a menu and I say, 'Large gin and tonic for me.'

Precious asks for a sparkling mineral water.

The waiter stands behind Raymond's chair and nods to us both. 'Of course, sir. Of course, madam.'

Raymond finally lowers his menu. 'I must follow my instinct. I shall have a very large Espresso Martini.'

'Of course, sir.'

For a second I think the waiter is going to say something else; he leans forward momentarily before drawing back and walking towards the bar.

I ask, 'Not tempted by the cocktails, Precious?'

'Bit early for me.'

Raymond looks surprised. I wonder whether he thought that 'Precious' was a soubriquet I was bestowing on him. But now I see he's looking down, peering at his own body, as if he's never seen it before. He says, 'I appear to have been . . .'

Precious says, 'What, Mr Raymond?'

He tugs open his linen jacket. On the white cotton of his shirt there's a red circle, about an inch in diameter. 'Stabbed.'

I'm up and moving around the table towards him. In the seconds it takes me to do that, the small red circle has become a crimson slick the size of my palm.

Raymond pants, 'Oh God, oh God, oh God . . .'

I see there's a tiny hole in the back of his chair where he's been stabbed. Precious is on her feet as well. 'You're going to be fine.'

The waiter looks back. Sees us. I shout, 'Stop!'

Other diners glance our way and spot Raymond's injury. He slumps on to the table. The cutlery clatters and side plates are sent crashing to the floor. People around us begin to scream.

I say to Precious, 'Look after him!' and tear towards the waiter who's begun to race to an exit. He dashes through one of the doors that lead to the outside area and I don't pause but follow him on to the terrace.

He's waiting for me and as I hurry on to the patio, he plunges something into my back, or at least, he tries to. A long, thin blade. The combination of my thick suit jacket and the speed I was moving at means the wound isn't a deep one. But still, the blow sends me staggering to one side. I trip and end up sprawled across the paving. He takes a step back and for a bizarre second I think he's bending down to tie his shoelace. But he hitches up his right trouser leg and takes a Beretta Tomcat from its ankle holster.

As he stands, I scramble to my feet and move around the corner of the building. I hear a shot and see part of the brickwork ahead of me shatter.

The gunman tears around the corner in pursuit, but this time I'm waiting for him. I elbow his throat hard and he gets off another shot. I grab the Beretta, but he grips it tight and we jostle over it, both of us locked together in our fight for the firearm.

He's stronger than me, and as we pirouette towards the edge of the building it's clear he's gaining the upper hand. He's trying to point the barrel in my direction, and slowly succeeding. I can see this is a tussle I'm not going to win.

I try to headbutt him. He's too well-trained, though, shifting position slightly, and although I make contact with the side of his face, it's an ineffective move. The Beretta is pointing at me and he tries to pull the trigger back. In a ploy I hope will catch him off guard, I completely relinquish my hold on the gun and him, pushing his body away. He back-pedals wildly. His momentum takes him to the very edge of the terrace and he raises the gun in my direction.

But I'm already hurtling towards him. I bulldoze into his torso, shoving him over the side of the building. He drops the Beretta and grabs the edge of the low wall that runs around the terrace. I seize his left wrist with my right hand, while my left palm presses against his forehead. He's dangling over the side of the Scarlioni and I can either help him up or send him plummeting.

He looks at me. There's no plea for mercy in his eyes. Only anger.

I tell him, 'I'll help you. But you need to tell me – who sent you?'

'Go to hell!'

'Just answer my question and I'll drag you up.'

His smile is cruel and triumphant. 'You're already a dead man! The Muse is coming for you!'

'Who's the Muse?'

'You're a dead man! Do you hear me? A dead man!'

When Precious joins me on the terrace, the gunman is a messy comma on the streets of Paris. A ring of horrified onlookers is already circling his corpse, mouths agape, I imagine, camera phones clicking.

'What happened?'

'He fell.' I touch the back of my shoulder. It's cut but doesn't feel too bad. 'Raymond?'

'Dead.'

'Look, I don't fancy getting caught up in any police investigation right now. We need to get out of here.'

'Agreed.' Without exchanging another word, we march from the rooftop, enter the lift and begin our descent. Precious says, 'You're hurt.'

'It's nothing. Did Raymond say anything before he died?'

Precious nods. 'Just one word. No idea what he meant though. It could have been shock, I suppose. Might not have been trying to tell me anything.'

The lift judders to a halt and I slam open its heavy doors. We walk quickly across the foyer.

'What was the one word?'

As we step into the Parisian sunshine, Precious replies, 'Artemis.'

CHAPTER 56

We catch a cab to the Gare du Nord, phoning Cy en route, arranging to meet him at the station. He arrives, carrying our luggage, and as he hands it out we bring him up to speed about what – and who – went down at the Hotel Scarlioni.

'Christ!' he says to Precious. 'Are you all right?'

She seems mystified by the question. 'I'm fine. Why wouldn't I be? Any luck with the laptop?'

He shakes his head.

'Our train leaves in a minute,' I cut in. 'We can catch up later.' I sling the duffel bag over my shoulder and wince as it digs into my newly acquired wound. 'Let's go!' I transfer the bag to my other shoulder and we hurry across the station's vast concourse.

Less than an hour after meeting Leonard Raymond, we're on a train thundering across France towards London.

Our carriage is full, meaning we can't discuss anything to do with the case until we've reached St Pancras and the three of us are in the back of a black cab.

'Well that,' Cy announces, 'was a tragic waste of time. I mean—'

'What are you on about?' Precious asks. 'It went pretty well.'

'A man was killed!'

I interject, 'Two men, actually.'

Precious nods. 'OK. *Aside* from that.'

'But we didn't actually learn anything!'

Our cab pulls away from the taxi rank and we begin speeding through London.

'We now know,' I reply, 'that Diana was leaving Paris on the night she was murdered. And going off the little that Raymond did tell us, I think we can make an educated guess about what she intended to do next. What her announcement to the press would have been about. Although to be fair, I might not have seen it if Precious hadn't offered us a different prism through which to look at the situation.'

Cy says, 'I don't get it. Do you reckon you know who wanted her dead?'

'Think about what Raymond said, Cy.'

Precious nods. 'And all the suspicious deaths we told you about on the way over to Paris. What was the one industry that connected a whole bunch of them? I mean, we don't have absolute proof, but it's looking—'

Cy interjects, 'Hopeless! Can't you just drop it? People are dying and you're out of leads!'

'We have three,' I reply. 'One, the video footage showing the traffic on the stretch of road where the Colonel was killed. Two, his laptop. That could still prove useful if we can actually access it.'

'Finally, and most importantly,' Precious continues, 'Sebby Hughes. Raymond said that he knew about Diana's murder. So we need to track him down. That's a priority.'

Cy looks away.

Precious asks, 'What is it?'

'Isn't it obvious?'

I say, 'Tell us. Please. What do you—'

He interrupts with a ferocious, 'You're going to get Precious killed! You came damn close last time you got her involved in one of your stupid quests! Don't you get that?'

She says gently, 'I can handle it.'

Cy glares at me. 'You went after Whittaker. He winds up dead within a day. You went after Raymond. Two more people die. You're hell-bent on going after Sebby Hughes. Great. Who's going to get killed this time? Because I'll tell you one thing: keep on digging and more people are going to die. Innocent people, and yeah, probably people even you care about.' He shakes his head. 'But you're still not going to back down, are you? You can't.'

And this time, it's my turn to fall silent and look away.

CHAPTER 57

You could argue that the internet has taken a lot of the romance out of my job. I guess, decades ago, searching for someone like Sebby Hughes would have been a matter of talking to his former colleagues and trawling through his old haunts. But now the hunt is a virtual one.

Sebby, it turns out, is ex-military and, prior to 2010, he crops up in several social media postings. But for the past ten years or so, he's been quiet on regular platforms, and so I plunge into the Dark Web. Yes, I've got *that* piece of software and so visiting darknets is relatively safe, although trading in the various markets they house can be hit-and-miss.

Last year, a breach associated with over ninety per cent of LinkedIn users led to information on 700 million people becoming compromised. And by compromised, I mean, of course, up for grabs. The data was dumped in two waves, initially exposing 500 million individuals, with the remaining users' info following shortly after. It's not something I vociferously condone, but I've taken advantage of it on several occasions and I reach out again to my Dark Web contact who has direct access to the hacked data. I give her the out-of-date info I have on Sebby Hughes and wait for a response. Within an hour, she offers me more recent details for a very reasonable price and, after paying using crypto, she sends me what she's got, which turns out to be pretty extensive.

It's fast, sure, but not as much fun as trawling his old haunts.

Whilst I've been tracing Sebby Hughes, Precious and Cy have been in my front room. They connected a laptop to my TV and have been combing through the footage from Freddie's helmet cam. I walk downstairs and tell them about my success. 'How are you guys getting on?'

Precious replies, 'Well, going off your description of the Colonel and his Defender, we found him fairly quickly. He's got a few plausible tails, but we were looking for a big ol' mama of a vehicle.'

I don't want to be that guy but tell her, 'The car that took out Whittaker won't necessarily have been sizeable. If the driver used the PIT manoeuvre, it could have been done in an anonymous little family four-door.'

Precious smiles and holds up her hand. 'Yeah, but I don't think that's the technique they used!'

'Hold up!' Cy interrupts. 'What's the PIT manoeuvre?'

'Pursuit intervention technique manoeuvre. Also known as tactical car intervention,' she replies.

'It's when the pursuer starts to overtake the target. But actually kind of nudges the side rear end of their car. Result? The target fishtails!' I conclude. 'Usually skids right across the road and ends up facing the direction it came from. But if you get it just right, you can actually flip the victim's car.'

'It's awesome!' Precious enthuses. 'And the pursuer doesn't need to be driving anything enormous! Like Novak said, you can implement the technique in pretty much any ride.'

'It was used extensively in the US, but some states started banning it because too many drivers were getting killed from their car flipping or rolling or what have you.'

Cy asks, 'So why don't you think they used this PIT manoeuvre thing, then? Sounds effective.'

'Oh, it is!' Precious agrees. 'But the Colonel was ex-mil. They knew that. So they also knew there'd be a good chance he'd have been aware of counteractive measures.'

'Such as?'

She taps her fingers as she reels off possibilities. 'Swift deceleration, swift acceleration. Swerving to the other side of the road – a really skilled driver could even manage a small skid and come out of the PIT nudge.'

'You might have a point,' I concede.

'You know I have!'

'So you were looking for a beast of a car just a little way behind the Colonel's Defender.'

Cy says, 'And we found one.' He rewinds the paused footage on my TV, freezes it again and points to the screen. 'A Toyota Land Cruiser 78.'

'And what's the betting it's been Schelled up?' I murmur. 'Schell Industries are armouring, ballistic and survivability specialists,' I explain. 'I mean, they've got their fingers in a lot of pies. Light weaponry, assault rifles, you name it. But they also take cars that people like you and I can buy and transform them into vehicles that can be used in warzones and other hostile environments.'

Precious points to the Land Cruiser. 'One of their most popular units is the upgraded version of that car. Popular because it just looks like a normal set of wheels. I mean, big, sure, but it doesn't look wildly out of place in a normal urban environment. But it's actually got a discreet armament spec and ECM suite to diff locks and—'

Cy interrupts. 'And I got an image vector of the guy driving it, then cleaned it up and sharpened it.' He hands me a sheet of A4 paper. 'Here's the printout. Take a look.'

The page contains a single shot. It's an image of the man driving the Land Cruiser. I stare at his face for a full five seconds before looking up.

'What do you reckon?' Precious says. 'Do you think that could be the guy who killed Colonel Whittaker?'

'It is him. Beyond a shadow of a doubt.'

Cy asks, 'How can you be so sure?'

'Easy,' I reply, glancing down at the driver's face again. 'I know him.'

CHAPTER 58

His pale, smooth features are unmistakable. I recall the look he shot me from the SUV as I sped away from The Lines and I involuntarily shudder.

Precious asks, 'Who is he?'

'An old friend of mine.'

Cy takes my words at face value, 'A friend?'

But Precious reads my expression and gestures for him not to push it.

My phone rings. It's Anna Brandon, asking if I can meet her in London. She doesn't go into details but stresses it's important.

On the train into Waterloo I try calling Sebby Hughes but he doesn't pick up, so I leave him a message. I march briskly from the station, cross the bridge and cut through Charing Cross, meaning I reach the National Gallery, where Mrs Brandon asked to meet, in good time.

I jog up the stairs that lead to the Central Hall, hang a left and make my way through a number of the gallery's larger chambers. Mrs Brandon is waiting for me in one of the rooms full of vivid, sixteenth-century masterpieces. She's sitting on one of those low wooden benches, in front of Tintoretto's *The Origin of the Milky Way*.

In a building full of priceless artwork, she's staring at her shoes.

'Hello, Mrs Brandon.'

She looks up, appears surprised to see me. 'We have to talk, Mr Novak.'

'That's why I came. What's wrong?'

She takes a deep breath and tells me, 'I'm happy with my husband. This has to stop.' She shakes her head and lowers her voice. 'I'm grateful for everything you've done. But I have to move on. You must see that?'

'Is he making you say this?'

'No.'

I nod. Look around at the paintings. There's a gorgeous Titian across from me, depicting the goddess Diana. She looks slight. Passive. But I know that elsewhere in this room, *The Death of Actaeon* shows her commanding a pack of hounds to rip a man to shreds.

Mrs Brandon stands up and seems unsteady. Perhaps she's twisted her ankle. I don't know, but she slips and I catch her, grabbing her upper arm. She takes a step back from me. 'Please just leave me alone.'

She's speaking the words and they're delivered in my direction, but it's as though she's not talking to me.

Reluctantly, I shrug. 'I'll draw up an invoice in the morning and get it across to you. I hope I was of some help . . . Good luck.'

I turn to go and she calls my name.

'Yes, Mrs Brandon?'

And now her words are 100 per cent for me. She looks into my eyes and I see her fear. 'You can't beat them. Just run!'

I move closer to her. 'What do you mean?'

'I'm sorry.'

She turns and begins to stride away. Before I can follow, a burly security guard puts her hand across my chest. 'Why don't you just let her go, sir?'

The woman is only doing her job, but it's as annoying as hell. 'She's in trouble. I'm trying to help.'

'Maybe she doesn't want your help.'

It's a fair enough point. But why did she drag me all the way into London to see her, just to reveal she doesn't want to see me?

I circle the guard and exit the room, but, of course, Anna Brandon has disappeared.

Crossing Trafalgar Square, I try Sebby Hughes' number again. He picks up this time and I tell him my business concerns Diana, Princess of Wales, and ask if we can meet.

'Are you one of them journalists?'

'No.'

'Then what are you after?'

'The truth.'

He ends the call and I head to the Admiral Duncan to meet up with a contact. I give him the Colonel's laptop and he assures me he'll find a way to access it. We share a drink and I leave. I should get back to Waterloo, but when I hail a taxi, I ask the driver to take me to Pimlico. As the cab makes its way along Old Compton Street, my phone rings. It's Sebby Hughes. He's obviously in two minds about helping me but we chat and eventually he agrees to meet me tomorrow.

*

The taxi drops me off on St George's Square and I make my way to one of those short, discreet mews that are impossible to find unless you know exactly where you're heading. It's lined with low, sleek cars and the houses are tiny, but in terms of price per square inch, they're amongst the most expensive in Europe. When I first met Mrs Brandon, it was in one of these residences. She lives with her husband in Windsor, but her place in this mews is – she informed me – her personal town house. 'A bolthole for when I need to get away and indulge in a spot of retail therapy,' as she'd put it.

I knock on her door. No answer. I drop to my haunches, poke open the brass letter plate and peer inside. Last time I was here the hallway was a mass of artwork, coats and clutter.

It's empty now.

I stand. Move along to the ground-floor sash window. Its curtains aren't quite pulled shut, meaning there's a narrow ribbon of space between their hems that I can see through. I move closer to the pane and squint through the double glazing into the front room.

It's completely empty.

A man in a long, ridiculous Barbour jacket steps from the house next door. He's carrying a phone and although he asks, 'Can I help you?' he actually means, *what the hell are you doing?*

'I was looking for Mrs Brandon.'

'Who?'

'Anna Brandon. She lives here. I'm a friend.'

'Never heard of an Anna Brandon. Sorry.'

'She only stays here on and off. That's probably why you haven't met.'

He shakes his head. 'Someone's having you on,' he tells me. 'I've lived here since the 90s and I can tell you that place' – he jabs a finger at the house where I first met Mrs Brandon – 'has been unoccupied for over five years.'

CHAPTER 59

Sebby Hughes lives near Waterloo, in a tiny terrace house just off one of the Upper Ground side streets. Precious, who insisted on accompanying me, rings the doorbell and stands back.

Sebby swings open the door and we're ushered inside. His house is sparse and immaculately clean. The smell of bleach almost makes my eyes water.

'Come through . . .'

He's in his late forties. Painfully thin. His hair is damp, pressed against his skull as though he's wearing a swimming cap. He's neatly dressed and polite to us both, but he's twitchy and there's something haunted about him, as if he thinks he's on the verge of discovering something terrible. As he shows us through to his front room, I ask why he changed his mind and agreed to meet us.

'Ah, well,' he replies. 'I found out we have a mutual comrade-in-arms. Mr Harvey.'

'Frank?'

Sebby nods. 'I met him years ago when he was writing a book on Diana. I asked him about you.'

'What did he say?'

'He said you were a soldier, Mr Novak, sir.'

'I wouldn't say that.'

I introduce Precious and we take a seat.

Sebby asks, 'Now, what can I get you to drink?'

We both ask for a coffee.

'A little firewater in yours, sir?'

'That would be very acceptable.'

'And in yours, miss?'

'Not for me, thanks.'

He zips off to make our coffee and Precious calls through, 'How did you know the Princess?'

'I was part of her security detail. Best job I ever had. Went freelance after that.'

'Freelance?'

I mouth the word 'mercenary' to Precious.

Sebby calls through, 'Then I had a little run-in with . . . well, I can't really call him a man. More of a monster. Tortured me.'

Precious grimaces, but Sebby is speaking quite casually. He could be recounting getting stuck in a jam on the M6.

I say, 'Sorry to hear that.'

'It was a few years ago, now. It made me look at my life. I retired. I think I lost my bottle, to be honest with you.'

He returns with our coffee. It smells good. He hands Precious a white mug with separate pictures of Charles and Diana on it, sandwiching the words 'The Marriage of Prince Charles and Lady Diana Spencer, Wednesday 29th July 1981'.

'Right . . .' Sebby takes a seat. 'Let's get to the main event. The reason you good people are here. You want to know what really happened in Paris on 30 and 31 August, 1997 . . .' He takes a sip of his coffee. 'Like I said, I was working for British intelligence at the time, but I was nothing to do with the Diana job. The first I heard about it was on the Sunday morning, like the rest of the world, I suppose. I got up and took a phone call from a friend. "Have you seen the news?" she says. "No," I say. "Who's died?"' Sebby pauses. '"Better turn the telly on'" she says. So I do and . . .' His voice drops to a whisper. 'I couldn't believe it. That she'd gone, I mean. Just couldn't believe it. But I knew . . .'

Precious asks, 'What did you know?'

'Well, all that crap about it being an accident! It was insulting. It was obviously a job.'

And again, very softly, Precious asks, 'Why was it obviously a job?'

Sebby looks at me as if to say, *Is she for real?*

I explain, 'We just want to hear your take. That's important to us both.'

He gives a nod of understanding. 'Well, none of it made sense. The cover story was laughable, for a start. They reckoned the driver, Henri Paul, was trying to shake the paps that had followed them into the tunnel. What does that even mean? You drive into a tunnel, it's fairly obvious where you're going to come out. And where were they heading? The Fayeds' residence that official sources claim they were going to? All you've got to do is look on a map and it's fairly obvious that's *not* where they were off to. And all that gubbins about Paul being drunk and an alcoholic, when clearly he wasn't. And the footage from the Ritz that doesn't check out . . .'

Sebby covers a lot of the points we already know, but listening to them stacked up, one after the other, it yet again strikes me as odd that there's no public clamour to scythe away the lies that have grown up around the Princess's final hours.

He takes another sip of coffee. 'It had to be in a tunnel, though. They're in Paris. One of the busiest cities in the world, and the accident just happens to take place in the Pont de l'Alma, one of the very few outdoor spots that's away from prying eyes.'

Precious interrupts. 'Not entirely. There were journos and every stretch of road has cameras.'

'Journos? Yeah. I'll give you that. Although a lot of the photos they took of the crash were confiscated and never returned. Funny that. And they also made a useful scapegoat. Even today a lot of people blame Diana's death on the fact she was hounded by the press. Cobblers.'

She presses him. 'But the roadside cameras and—'

His laughter cuts her off. 'Roadside cameras? They were all disabled!'

I've read about this and say, 'It was actually admitted that over ten CCTV cameras were out of action that night, meaning no real record of their approach to the tunnel was recorded – and, crucially, what happened *inside* the tunnel wasn't filmed, either.'

Precious asks, 'Why were they out of action?'

'No explanation was ever given,' Sebby replies. 'But the weird thing is, certain pictures did come to light that look to have been taken from CCTV cameras. But their provenance, as they say, was never established. Tell you what else points to it all being dodgy as hell – they opened up the tunnel tooth sweet.'

I'm assuming Sebby means tout de suite and reply, 'Yeah. Late morning, wasn't it? Ten-thirty-ish?'

'No way. Try 7 a.m.! There was a journalist – Chris Dickey – who went there at seven in the morning. Couldn't believe what he saw and he actually filmed it, so there's proof. They'd already reopened the tunnel! The crime scene was being driven through! Literally! The most famous woman in the word has been killed under mysterious circumstances and they open the site less than six hours after she was taken out of the Mercedes and less than an hour after her death has been announced. There's absolutely nothing about the crash that makes sense if you believe the official narrative. Nothing.'

Precious plays devil's advocate and says, 'But supposing Henri was just driving too fast and that's how it happened? Wasn't he driving at crazy speeds?'

Sebby wags a finger at us. 'They messed up there, too, just like with the doctors. In the hurry to paint Henri Paul as a drunken lunatic, they said the Merc had been rocketing along at 120mph! I mean, come on. They then announced the speedometer's needle proved it, because it was stuck on 120, so that's how fast the car must have been going when the crash occurred.' He smiles. 'That announcement turned out to be a major error . . .'

CHAPTER 60

Precious frowns. 'Why's that a major error?'

'Well, miss, it proves they were deliberately lying. You see, Mercedes blew the falsehood out of the water by announcing that, on impact, the needle would automatically go to zero. So the authorities do a quick about-turn and say, well, the car was still travelling at about 60mph, which is about twice the speed limit for the tunnel. But the truth is, they can't have known precisely how fast that vehicle was travelling.'

I say, 'You mentioned before that they messed up with the doctors on the scene?'

'The doctors and one or two other things, yeah. So, immediately after the crash, there's this doctor who sees what's happened. He's got no idea who's involved but he's a good guy. Goes to help. Tries to treat the Princess, bless him. Then the official doctors take over. The odd thing is, their assessment of Diana's condition and the first doctor's assessment are totally different. Polar opposites!' Sebby shuffles forward on his seat. 'And the people who reached the crash site before the authorities could get there? Well, the majority of them would have been innocent members of the public and can't have been briefed. Which is why accounts of what was happening vary so massively.'

Precious says, 'Give us an example.'

'Take a big one: her final words, or even the state the poor little thing was in. So many versions and different takes were given. By definition, some must have been untrue. By the way, the ambulance got there pretty sharpish. The crash occurred at twenty-three minutes past midnight. The cops arrived at half past and the ambulance arrived approximately five minutes later. So, that's what? Twelve minutes after the crash. Pity they couldn't have got her to the hospital that bloody quickly and—'

I interrupt. 'Frank went through that with me. There's nothing off about the length of time it took to get her to the Pitié-Salpêtrière. The French routine for treating patients is different to the way we do things here. That's all.'

'Beggin' your pardon, Mr Novak, sir. But I've heard all that and it's all my eye. I can buy the fact that she was treated on the scene. Fair enough. But the fact it took over forty minutes to transport her four miles? They had a police escort so, according to the ambulance driver, they were able to maintain a speed of around 25 to 31mph. Let's say it was the lowest of his estimates – 25mph. They should have covered the four miles in less than ten minutes! At some stage you've got to apply common sense and say something is fishy and it ain't just the bouillabaisse.'

I nod. 'You might have a point.'

Sebby continues. 'The ambulance stopped briefly en route and then stopped again for about five minutes just before the hospital. The quack claimed it was because Diana's condition worsened and he was afraid any movement at all could be fatal.'

I do some quick arithmetic. 'So that leaves a credibility gap of about twenty minutes?'

Sebby nods. 'And there's the fact they drove past one hospital! Well, that never sat right with me. If she was so close to death and needed proper attention urgently, why not stop at the first hospital? The authorities said it was because very early on, the medics on site had been told they had space at the Pitié-Salpêtrière. But in those circumstances? You find space at the first available hospital.'

Precious tells him, 'All of this is public domain. All these inconsistences and lies . . . They're already out there in the inquest's findings and Operation Paget. We want something new.'

I lean forward. 'Sebby, we need to know why and how that crash happened. Can you tell us?'

'Of course!'

'And most importantly,' Precious adds, 'we need to know who killed Diana.'

'Look at the facts that we know, miss, that are already out there. The fact that she looked fine when the first doctor reached her. That it all happened in the tunnel and all records of what immediately followed were either confiscated or lost. The massive discrepancies in the witness reports. And the business with the ambulance taking so long to reach the hospital. Don't forget the inconsistencies with the autopsies and the way the crime scene was ruined as quickly as possible . . .'

It's as though he's willing us to make the leap and see the truth as he understands it. But I want unambiguous answers. 'Just tell us why she was killed.'

'You still don't get it? Really?' Sebby takes a deep breath. 'That's just it. The Princess of Wales didn't die in that crash or on the operating table or anywhere else that night . . . Diana wasn't killed in Paris. She was switched.'

CHAPTER 61

Molly's Story (cont.)

Molly Stone stood in the doorway of Frank Harvey's private room in the Royal Surrey County Hospital and said, 'I don't want to say I told you so . . .'

Her former husband looked up. 'But you will?'

'Only if you misbehave.'

He grinned. 'So you will!'

She laughed, walked across the room and sat on the edge of his bed. 'I come bearing gifts.' She handed him a basket of fruit.

Frank gave the apples, grapes and bananas a cursory glance. 'What can I say? I'm underwhelmed.'

'Thought you might be.'

'I'd hoped you knew me well enough to bring me a decent bottle of Scotch, if anything . . .'

The words were a long-standing private joke and Molly replied, 'Well, if you don't want my other gift . . .' She took a sheet of paper from her bag.

Frank sounded more serious as he asked, 'What have you got for me, Moll?'

'Couldn't get anything on the woman. Sorry. Total blank. But slightly more success with the man.'

She handed Frank the sheet of paper and he scanned its contents. 'What? The guy is a ghost but you managed to get all this? How?'

'Me and one of The Next Time Club tracked him down using, shall we say, unconventional methods . . .' Molly related the unlikely sequence of events that had resulted in her uncovering the facts she'd just shared with Frank.

He said, 'That is genius, Moll! You haven't lost it.'

She shrugged. 'Maybe I just misplaced it for a while. Got to admit, it reminded me how much I missed it all. Investigative journalism . . .'

'What's stopping you doing more of it?'

'I wouldn't want to go back to journalism as such. Dealing with twelve-year-old editors who judge a story by how many likes it gets on Twitter? No, thanks.'

'Just the investigative part, then. I can guarantee there's enough unsolved crimes to keep you busy. Make it an offshoot of the club.'

'If I got one or two of them interested, would you join us?'

'Maybe.'

'What would we call it?'

'That's easy,' Frank replied. 'Molly's Mob.'

She laughed again. 'Maybe not. Look, I've got to dash. Meeting the missus at the Frontline. I only popped in to shower you with gifts.'

'Thank you, Molly. For everything.'

She nodded as she got to her feet. 'You're not the only one who fancies a few new stories.'

Frank smiled.

Molly paused at the open door. Turned back to face him. 'I've got the name!'

'Well?'

She announced, 'The Next Time Crime Club!' and Frank responded with an enthusiastic thumbs up.

He heard her footsteps in the corridor outside and felt her absence. The room suddenly felt quiet. He looked down at the basket of fruit. Shook his head.

'Oh, well . . .'

Warily, Frank plucked an apple from the arrangement and smiled. Nestling under the fruit, he could see a bottle of Glenlivet Captain's Reserve Scotch.

CHAPTER 62

'She was switched?' Precious doesn't even attempt to disguise her incredulity.

Sebby replies, 'Think about it! First responders say she looked surprisingly unscathed when she was pulled from the Merc. She was awake and talking, more or less fine. She's whisked away in an ambulance – and the woman taken into the hospital is suddenly on the verge of death and in all kinds of physical trauma!'

'That's because her condition deteriorated. It happens. Look . . .' I try to remain diplomatic. 'Everything you've said up until that piece of fantasy – sure. You make good points and I'll go with most of them. But suggesting she was switched? That's . . . that's simply not credible.'

'Why not?'

'Because we know she died!'

'How do we know?'

'Because, from the moment she left the Ritz to the moment she was laid to rest at Althorp, a lot of people came into contact with Diana, God help her. Are they all part of the conspiracy?'

'Yes! They're either part of it or they've been suckered into believing it!'

'That's insane. Why would she even want to disappear? She had two kids that she was a perfect mother to. She was happier than she'd been for years! Are you saying she just turned her back on her friends and loved ones? Why?'

'I don't know the details. Not all of them, anyway. But I'm guessing a very limited number of people were informed when she felt the time was right.'

'Sebby . . .' Precious's voice is caring but urgent. 'You need to stop this.'

'She's not contacted me. Yet.'

'That's because she died in Paris, twenty-five years ago.'

'She's still alive,' he says stubbornly.

I say, 'What *proof* do you have that she's still alive? Actually, let's take it one step at a time. What hard evidence do you have that she made it out of Paris back in '97?'

'I just know!'

He's becoming agitated, so I nod. 'Go on . . .'

Sebby pauses. 'Look – I'll write you a timeline showing how and where she was switched. Do you have any paper? And a pen? I can quite easily show you.'

I reach into my jacket pocket and pull out a sheet of paper. It's a printout of the photo showing the man driving the car that forced Gerry Whittaker off the road. The same person I'd seen approaching The Lines as I was leaving, having stolen the Colonel's laptop. It's been folded twice so the image isn't visible when I hand it to Sebby. But out of curiosity, I imagine, he opens the sheet of paper and looks at the photograph. The impact is immediate. He looks up, horrified.

'Get out of my house!'

'What is it?'

'Both of you! Get out!'

He's on his feet, tearing the sheet of A4 into shreds.

Precious says, 'Calm down – please!'

'Get out!'

Sebby puts his head in his hands. Palms against his cheeks. Fingertips circling his temples.

I say, 'You know the man in that photograph.'

'Not a man! More a – a monster.'

Precious murmurs, 'That's the person who tortured you?'

He nods.

'Sebby,' I tell him, 'it's vital I know who he is.'

'If I tell you, will you leave my house? Immediately?'

Reluctantly, I nod.

'He's a killer. A hired assassin. And a sadist.' Sebby shakes his head. 'His name is Lee Greenwood. Also known as the Muse.'

CHAPTER 63

We're as good as our word, thank Sebby Hughes for his time, and leave his house. It's early evening and there's a thin drizzle in the air. We start walking back to Waterloo but as we're passing The Mulberry Bush, a pleasant little pub on Upper Ground, it seems a shame not to use it to escape the rain and I suggest a drink.

We head to the upstairs bar. Precious gets an orange juice and lemonade and I opt for a large gin and tonic. We take our drinks to a table and sit down.

'When we were at the Scarlioni in Paris, the guy that killed Raymond told me the Muse was coming after me. At least we now know who it is.'

'Yeah, but knowing what kind of a psycho this Greenwood is . . . I don't imagine it's a comforting thought.'

'I'll find a way to reach out to him. He's a gun for hire. Whatever he's been paid to deal with me – I'll double it. And I'll try to buy some information from him. Information about the people behind the murder of Gerry Whittaker.'

'But the Muse might carry out his contract on you. Aren't you worried?'

'I don't have time to be worried.' I sip my G&T. 'What did you make of Sebby?'

Precious shakes her head. 'Poor guy. I mean, interesting stuff until he goes off on one about Diana still being alive.'

'It's weird. Diana had such a profound effect on people she barely knew. I mean, Frank only met her a few times over a quarter of a century ago yet he told me he still misses her. And Sebby wants her to be alive so badly that he's concocted this whole fiction about her surviving Paris. She must have been a hell of a woman.'

'What's your next move?'

'Reach out to Greenwood. Give Sebby time to calm down and then find out what else he knows.'

'What can I do to help?'

'Walk away,' I tell her. 'While you still can.'

An hour later, we're back in Guildford. I swing by the Royal Surrey County Hospital to visit Frank. We swap news. He's suffering from a ruptured spleen but is otherwise OK. He tells me about a woman called Molly Stone and the information she uncovered for him, which I mentally file away for future use. I bring him up to speed with what happened in Paris and meeting Sebby, but I leave out the fact that a psychotic sadist is trying to kill me. Little things like that can bring the mood right down.

I take a taxi home and phone a contact who works for Special Branch, asking her for anything she can pull together on Greenwood. She says she'll get back to me.

I call Anna Brandon, mainly because I'd like an explanation for her warning to me – 'You can't beat them. Just run!' There's no reply, but my phone is still in my hand when it starts ringing.

'Hello?'

'Novak . . .' It's Miss Winters. 'You saw Sebastian Hughes today.'

'It was just a social call.'

'I told you to drop the case.'

'Yeah, well, I can't do that.'

'Why not?'

'I promised the Colonel I'd see it through to the end.'

'He's dead.'

'Exactly.'

'You aren't helping anybody.'

'This is about justice, Miss Winters. It's about not looking the other way. It's about giving a voice to the fallen.'

'Whatever happens next is on you.'

I hear a click as she hangs up.

I sleep in but get woken up at 10 a.m. when my phone rings. It's my Special Branch contact, Tania Wilde. 'This Greenwood,' she tells me, 'you want to avoid him, Novak.'

'Yeah, I want to. But I doubt I can.'

'He's wanted on suspicion of over a dozen murders. Some of them very nasty.'

'Murder's always very nasty.'

'Don't be a smart-arse. This guy likes to toy with his victims. Really hurt them. He's rumoured to have a torture chamber. You don't want to know what he does there.'

'I can guess. How do I get hold of him?'

'He didn't leave a forwarding address. Sorry.'

'Come on, Tania. Any known associates we do know the whereabouts of?'

She gives me some pointers but I can tell it's against her better judgement. 'Seriously,' she tells me, 'leave it, Novak. Do you know why they call him the Muse?'

'I'm assuming it's not because he's a deep thinker?'

'He has a brother. Equally crazy. And equally well-built. Anyway, someone calls his brother the Mountain, on account of him being so huge. And someone else says, well if he's the Mountain, you – Lee Greenwood – must be the Muse.'

'I don't get it.'

'Mountain and Muse were famous Irish foxhounds, legendarily vicious. They not only hunted down the fox, they then tore it apart. Look, we don't know how he does it, but that's Greenwood's MO. He literally tears his victims to pieces. You do not want to go toe-to-toe with a maniac like that.'

'Thanks, Tania.' I hang up and murmur, 'But I've got no choice.'

I spend a couple of days meeting with Greenwood's friends and alleged colleagues, mainly in pubs south of the river. I make it clear that I want to meet the Muse and pay him a lot of money for information and a favour. I'm met with hostility in the main, and no one agrees to help.

But the evening after another long day of trying to make contact, my phone rings.

Number withheld.

I pick up. 'Hello?'

A male voice replies, 'Is that Novak?'

'Yeah. Who's this?'

The voice is gruff yet strangely monotone. 'I hear you've been asking after me.'

'Who is this?'

'At the pub in Custom House. Don't say my name.'

That was the last place I tried yesterday.

'Yeah,' I say, 'I didn't know if—'

He interrupts. 'Is it a job?'

'Not a normal job. I want information. I've also been told you might want to see me. I'm eager to make it worth your while *not* to carry out any assignment involving me. Do you think that will be possible?'

'If the money's right.'

'Whatever it takes.'

'Listen carefully. You'll get some instructions very soon. Follow them. Don't bring anyone. If I even think you're dicking me about or you're shady . . .'

'I'm not.'

'I'll kill you.'

CHAPTER 64

Greenwood hangs up and less than a minute later I receive a WhatsApp message from him, instructing me to catch a specific coach. I grab my jacket and set off in the Marina. It's a damp, cold night.

I park in town and hurry to the station. I've barely time to buy a ticket and race over to the coach, and as I approach the front of the vehicle, its doors slam shut with a hydraulic hiss. I call out to the driver. He opens them again and I climb aboard, showing him my ticket. The front couple of seats are free and, as instructed, I take them. The coach moves forward.

I stand up and take my time loosening my tie, looking down the rows of seats and scanning the faces of my fellow passengers. I count nine of them. They're all either too young or too old to be Greenwood, but a couple of them, with pale, angular faces, return my surreptitious scrutiny and I guess they could be his watchers. The coach nudges out of the station and joins the flow of traffic, picking up speed. I gaze out of the window. The rain's getting heavier.

We've been travelling for half an hour and we're on the motorway doing about sixty. I hear the driver swear and

I'm suddenly alert and on edge. I'm only a few feet behind him, so I lean forward and ask, 'What's wrong?'

'Probably nothing!'

But he signals, slows and veers on to the hard shoulder, gradually bringing the coach to a halt. The driver stands, grabs a torch from a side compartment and looks down his vehicle, 'Don't worry folks! Just checking one of the tyres. I think it's OK, but never does any harm to be careful.'

I think I'm the only passenger not harrumphing or quietly cursing.

He opens the doors and a blast of cold, damp air swirls into the coach. He says to me, 'Would you mind coming out? Holding the torch for me?'

'I would, but it's raining and I don't have an overcoat.'

He answers quietly, 'I really think you should,' and hands me the torch.

'Then how can I refuse?' I stand. 'Lead the way.'

He alights and I follow him down the steps and on to the hard shoulder. It's bitterly cold and by now the rain is driving hard. I raise the lapels of my suit jacket. There's a steep, grassy incline to my right and the motorway is surrounded on both sides by fields. I wipe rain from my face and ask the driver, 'What's going on? The tyres are fine.'

'You're to head up there.' He gestures to the incline. 'And I want my torch back.'

I hand it over. He hurries back to the coach doors and heaves himself up and inside. I stand back. The vehicle pulls away, gathering speed on the hard shoulder before swerving back on to the inside lane. I've lost sight of it within moments, make my way up the incline and climb the wooden fence that divides it from the expanse of meadow that lies ahead.

I'm already horribly cold. The icy rain lashes at me and the freezing wind isn't helping. I try to look over the field, but it's pitch-dark. The cars below me roar by. I'm alone. I wrap my arms around my torso for the illusion of warmth. Shout out, 'Hello?'

No response.

The feeling of solitude and vulnerability is abysmal.

I start to trudge forward and hear it: somewhere close ahead, a phone is ringing.

CHAPTER 65

I follow the sound of the phone and find it wrapped in a transparent plastic pouch, discarded on the grass. A small, black Nokia. I answer it.

'Hello?'

'After I hang up, check out the map app on this phone.' It's the voice I heard earlier, gruff and weirdly monotone. 'A destination's already been entered. Walk there. I'll be watching you part of the way. Try to talk to anyone – anyone at all – and it'll be the last thing you do. Understand?'

'Yes.'

'Right. Dump your own phone right now.'

'I'd rather not.'

'Do it!'

I take my phone from my pocket and throw it aside.

'It's done.'

The voice tells me, 'I don't trust you.'

He hangs up. I access the map app and press *start*. My destination will take about an hour to reach on foot and I make a start, traipsing into the cold darkness.

I've been walking for just over fifty minutes. The cold remains unbearable and my back and shoulder muscles ache from attempts to fold into myself. I'm sodden. The rain has been relentless and falls so hard that I keep my head at a downwards angle because the water striking my face stings like paper cuts.

I've mostly been tramping across fields – miles of dark nothingness, punctuated by a hedgerow or small road that I have to cross to reach another meadow. Greenwood warned me against speaking to anyone, but I haven't seen a single soul since I schlepped from the hard shoulder.

'You have reached your destination.'

I stop. Look about me. I'm at the edge of a field. No buildings, no vehicles, no roads, no lights. I desperately want this to be a test. Greenwood's way of checking if I'd follow instructions like a good boy. And having walked through a freezing, stormy night, I've sufficiently established I'm to be trusted and our meeting will take place in some crowded bar room with warmth and sound and the taste of bitter. Even that pub in Custom House is looking pretty good round about now.

The phone beeps. A text message. It's a postcode. Another message reads: *Go there. Now.*

I enter the new destination and, again, set off into the night.

Cold. Soaking wet. Alone. At first I tried to think of things to take my mind off the physical pain I'm enduring. Now I try not to think about anything except the phone in my hand and the directions I need to follow. Just walk and wait for it to be over. The rain, if anything, has become stronger. I'm so disengaged with the topography of my route that occasionally I stagger into a hedgerow, or down an incline into a country lane. I hate this. It jolts my senses, reminding me of the cold and my aching muscles.

I should let the Nokia simply slip from my grasp, as if I've dropped it through exhaustion. Then follow the next road I come across, until I reach a village or town. Make a call. I could be home within a couple of hours. The prospect of my bed and fresh linen feels like an unfeasible luxury.

'*You have reached your destination.*'

Another message. Another postcode.

I enter the new end point and stumble onwards.

I don't know how many hours I've been walking. How many postcodes I've been sent. I'm virtually unconscious from cold, but I can't remember any other state. Just this nowness of freezing flesh and skin and every muscle in my body as solid and unworkable as ice. The phone and its directions are not simply all that I have. They are all that I am.

Do not drop the phone. Keep walking as it instructs. Wait for it to be over.

Keep walking.

Keep . . .

I fall. Further, this time. Down a hill? Just an incline? No idea.

I lose my grip on the phone. Hit something hard. A road. Where's the phone? I try not to panic. Without its instructions I'm lost.

Stay calm . . .

I'm on my hands and knees, patting the road's surface with my palms, blindly searching for the Nokia. I'm patient. Thorough. Successful. My fingertips touch the familiar casing and I hold the handset closer to my eyes to inspect it. Its screen is smashed. Useless. After everything, I have no idea where I'm supposed to go and it must be over.

A blinding light feels like a beam being drilled into my brain. I half squint, half turn away from the source. But I can hear it coming towards me at speed.

I'm exhausted, kneeling into the middle of a narrow road, and a van is hurtling towards me.

CHAPTER 66

Sophie's Story

Everybody at the Crownly Ladies' Luncheon Club adored Sophie Grace. If any of the older members ever had problems reaching an event, or getting to a meeting, there was Sophie, hand in the air volunteering to pick them up and drop them off – as long as they didn't mind the mess of her 'scruffy old girl'. By which she meant her Type 2 VW camper. A glorious blue and cream classic with an interior wooden trim, it possessed leather seats that no one knew the colour of, because Sophie always had them covered with tartan blankets.

If there was lugging to be done, Sophie could lug with the best of them. Samovars to the church hall for a midweek coffee morning? Bottles to the recycling centre after that awfully good dinner dance? Or boxes of books that needed dropping off at the jumble sale? Sophie was your woman!

She was always so happy to help. That was the wonder of her. Not like the older ladies who would take on tasks with a world-weary acceptance, as if the slightest element of giving back to the luncheon club was a hideous and unjust imposition. In fact, Sophie was so unwaveringly cheerful, she'd long been known as Smiley Sophie. She was fair-haired, ruddy-cheeked and always took the eye of the husbands attending any of the ladies' bashes.

Her own husband, Christian, was – it was generally accepted – a 'dish'. Six foot two. Dark hair. Blue eyes. A good-natured grin and immaculate skin. Yes, definitely a dish. Maybe even a dreamboat. His conversation, it must be admitted, was invariably a little dull. But he had such a lovely way about him, everybody concurred, that it didn't really matter.

'What does he do, Sophie dear?'

'Oh, he's something in the city. He has told me. Repeatedly. But I just glaze over. You know how it is! Now, let's see, where was I? Oh, yes . . . Pass the whisk, would you, Marjory?'

The topic of Sophie's job, if she actually had one, was seldom broached. But she had children whom she doted on and occasionally brought along to family fundraisers. Twins. Of course Sophie Grace had twins! Two delightful little scamps. Betsy – bossy, funny and a born mimic, who would have the ladies in peals of laughter as the kettle boiled. And Thomas: shy, sweet, thoughtful and helpful. Always racing into the church hall's car park to help carry in plastic bags full of pints of milk. And yes, Sophie did admit to spoiling them. Especially over the festive holidays, but Christmas is for the children, isn't it? Of course, Sophie! Christmas is for the children . . .

What made her *so* perfect was the fact she was imperfect. That's to say, she wasn't too good to be true. The ladies of the luncheon club (although it was so much more than a luncheon club) were always suspicious when newcomers appeared who were just too pristine and flawless. It was so off-putting. So selfish, in a way.

When Sophie had arrived in the parish, all those years ago, she had been admitted into the club and the fact she was eager to help with the donkey work endeared her to other members immediately. Her ability to turn strawberries that had seen better days, and Daphne's plums ('A little tart for me, dear . . . Quite took the enamel off my teeth . . .') into staples of really first-rate jam was another feather in her cap. But she gave no one anything to mutter about. There was nothing to forgive about her, which always put one at an awkward disadvantage.

But it soon started happening.

The men. And occasionally women.

A dinner dance could be in full swing and a total stranger would turn up, hovering in reception, or having the temerity to come through to the hall, and they would want to talk with Sophie. Now, such an intrusion would be perfectly acceptable if the stranger was a good sort. But the strangers were never quite the right class. Rough-looking. Uncouth. Probably strangers to churches since the day they'd had their heads splashed with water.

It wasn't just dinner dances, of course. These chappies – and occasionally ladies – would turn up at bazaars and summer fetes, coffee mornings and even a carol concert, would you believe? A carol concert!

Sophie would excuse herself, and speak to these unsavoury types. She'd pull out her swanky, modern telephone, nod and type notes on the thing. Then she'd send the blighters on their way, stonewalling any and all of the ladies' attempts to find out who the stranger was this time.

This mysterious imperfection of Sophie Grace was her saving grace and the reason she could be universally admired for her erstwhile perfections.

Some speculated that the visitations were made by members of 'the homeless community'.

'Do you mean tramps, Vivienne?'

'One isn't allowed to call them tramps any more, Jean.'

'But that's what they are?'

'Oh, yes. That's what they are.'

Daphne – she of the flawed-fruit fame – piped up. 'But they can't be! Their clothes are terribly expensive. I mean, plain. But expensive. That last chap didn't get his jacket from Asda, if you take my meaning. No. They're not tramps.'

'Members of the homeless community!'

'Sorry, Vivienne.'

Whoever they were, they kept on coming. The last time one made an appearance, he materialised at the garden party, just as the vicar was finishing his speech about Christian values. The fellow sidled up to the tombola, lit a cigarette, would you believe, and quite put the vicar off his timing for his joke about the courgette and the newly-wed. His fluff was terribly unfortunate, and made it sound quite, quite vulgar. Honestly, he didn't know where to look.

Sophie made a beeline for the smirking smoker and it was the usual routine. A hush-hush conversation; notes taken and nodding. Then the man sloped off and Sophie re-joined the throng. Except Marjory bumped into the interloper as he passed the Pimm's stall. She reported to the other ladies that this chap – whom some remembered spotting at the bring-and-buy – was not quite as surly as some of the others.

'He said, "Excuse me, pet",' she revealed to the women on the lucky dip. 'And he spoke with a Newcastle accent.'

The incident was soon forgotten, except for the vicar's unfortunate slip, which became something of a legend for the Crownly Ladies' Luncheon Club. The garden party itself was deemed a great success, and no one even noticed that Sophie Grace had left it early, and alone.

CHAPTER 67

The van must have stopped because I see a figure emerge from the driver's side and walk towards me. The vehicle's headlights are still blazing with impossible intensity, so I can't see his face, just his outline. He's tall, lean and athletic.

He reaches me. Bends down. I expect a question or an offer of help, but he simply plucks the phone from my hand and examines it for a moment.

Now I think he punches me, hard in the face. I don't feel anything, but I'm sent sprawling. My back hits the road and he raises his boot for some reason. Oh, to stamp on my face. I don't register his sole smashing into my head, but the small stones along the road surface cut into my temple and at last I feel something sharp and precise, but it's not pain as such.

I think I'm being dragged somewhere. Then hauled upwards. The van. Yes, the van. I hear him opening its rear doors and he bundles me inside. An inner light shines just above my head and I can make out his face for the first time. He's peering at me, saying something, but I can't process his words.

He punches me again.

I crumple.

The doors are slammed shut and I'm thrown to one side as the van moves forward, accelerating quickly.

AN ACCIDENT IN PARIS

My face is beginning to ache, but in a different way. That's to say, I can feel the force of that last punch. I lie back, eager for the escape of sleep.

I could have been in the van for days. Or minutes. I know the sleep I'm waking from was deep as a well. My clothes remain saturated and I'm still preternaturally cold, but there's no icy wind in the van. There is, however, Lee Greenwood. I suppose he's responsible for rousing me. His face is inches from mine.

'Did you think I wouldn't find out?' he sneers. 'You knew Whittaker. Did you think you'd get me to confess?'

I try to reply but my jaw won't work.

'I'm going to kill you.' He moves even closer to me. 'Not because of the Colonel. And not because of any contract. I'm going to make you suffer because you killed my brother.'

I shake my head.

'You shot him in the stomach at the Colonel's house. He died from his injuries. So I'm going to put you through hell before sending you to hell.'

I try to shrug him off, but my attempts are pitiful. I feel something cold on my left forearm, then the same sensation on my right forearm. Cold and heavy. Metallic?

He pulls his arm back to deliver another punch. Grunting with exertion, Greenwood strikes me with the savagery of an angry man. Once, twice, thrice and . . .

. . . And I come to. But waking up this time feels different. *I can't breathe*. I try to gulp in mouthfuls of air, but my lips won't part. I touch my face. There's tape over my mouth. I try to breathe through my nose.

In, out. In, out.

Calm, calm, calm . . .

The tape covering the lower half of my face feels glued on. I tug at a corner, but it won't budge. My arms are heavy as lead.

I can't see or hear Greenwood, and he isn't punching me, which makes a pleasant change. But if he's placed me here, like this, it must be for a reason, and I'm not keen on hanging around to find out what it is.

I can hear cars in the middle distance. A heavy, fast flow of traffic.

I blink – still unused to the light after such prolonged darkness – and take stock of my surroundings and . . .

. . . *What?*

The panic I forced myself to quell a moment earlier rises stronger and is laced with terror. I know it's not a feeling I can stem, but I'm struck by the thought I could be sick with fear and choke on my own vomit. The panic is unstoppable this time because I can see exactly how Greenwood intends to kill me.

In a way, he already has.

The 'gauntlet' on my right forearm is attached to a thick chain. The chain is in turn attached to a wall immediately behind me, or rather, to a metal plate that's part of the wall. The 'gauntlet' on my left forearm has a similar chain attached to it. This one is slightly longer and affixed to a tow loop on the vehicle in front of me. A massive articulated lorry. A juggernaut.

It's parked now, of course. But when the driver decides to pull away, my body will be torn in half.

CHAPTER 68

I think I'm in a motorway service station, in one of those broad car parks where larger vehicles are sometimes left overnight.

I try my luck and tug the chains but both ends are attached – to the wall and to the lorry – with mechanical expertise. It's not been a sling-and-hope job. It would take a professional to detach either connection.

My heart is racing. I feel hot – so hot I could faint, and my vision is becoming blurry. I try to peel back the tape from my mouth, but my fingers are useless. And then I see him across the way: a man striding towards the front of the lorry.

He's obviously coming from a building across the car park, which the back of his vehicle is blocking from view. And my position is such that I can only see him for a few seconds. I try to shout to gain his attention, but my muffled cries are lost in the ambient roar of nearby traffic. I attempt to wave, but the chains prevent much movement.

The man marches out of my line of sight, but the trajectory of his stride leaves little doubt that he's heading back to the vehicle my chains are attached to. The nausea becomes intense. I can't breathe. Don't want to. I imagine the agony of having my body pulled apart; envisage what's left of me on the ground or being dragged along behind the juggernaut. With any luck, I'll be dead, but I could survive for several seconds as I bleed out and my heart shuts down.

I bang on the back of the lorry but even I can barely hear the noise of my fists. Useless. I hear a beep. A vehicular alarm being disabled. I freeze. The sound of a door being opened and slammed shut.

The driver is inside.

I can't escape this by myself. I look feverishly about me but there is no one. And there is nothing that can help. The back of the lorry is gigantic and although I kick it wildly, again, my actions have virtually no impact. I am invisible and undetectable.

It can't end like this. What happens next feels impossible. But there's no way out.

I claw at the tape across my mouth and, finally, a tiny edge peels away from my flesh. It's been fixed on with an adhesive of medical strength, but I don't care. I rip it from my face, hardly noticing the pain as slivers of skin and lip remain stuck to the tape.

'Stop! Stop! Please!'

For a moment I think he might hear me, but now the worst sound in the world.

The juggernaut's engine turns over.

My cries are again drowned out, this time by the lorry's enormous engine. I keep screaming and yelling and hoping that . . .

The vehicle's lights are switched on.

I feel paralysed. My body's on fire. The sense of impending, excruciating pain and disfigurement effectively shuts me down. Part of me simply wants it to end.

I can't even shout out. My throat is dry and my whole body limp.

This is it. The end.

One chain affixed to the wall. I stare at it, then back at the other chain, attached to the lorry.

Dark fumes splutter from its exhaust pipes.

Make it swift! God, make it swift.

I hear the grind of the juggernaut being slipped into first gear and the lorry begins to pull away from the wall.

CHAPTER 69

Edna's Story

Edna loved Gerry Whittaker. She'd have been the first to admit it. Well, maybe not the first. But after several gins had been enjoyed during a night out with her sisters, she'd nod and, after some sibling banter, say, 'Yes. I do love the Colonel! But not like that. Not in a rude way.'

She had known the news of his death would impact on her, but she'd not been prepared for how hard she was hit by his loss. Edna was an old woman who had faced more than her fair share of grief. She knew it got harder, that the death of friends became more isolating over the years, gradually turning life itself into a war of attrition against solitude.

But there had been something so full about the Colonel, an ability to have an opinion and sway over everything: from what time she set her alarm and what colour nail varnish she wore on a Sunday to how she would spend Christmas and whether that all-inclusive to Portugal was really worth it.

She'd often stayed over at his cottage, but after his death, she more or less moved in. He'd warned her, of course, about the officialdom that would descend in the event of his passing. And, by God, he'd been right on that score.

The men from Special Branch who'd turned the place upside down. The hard-faced ladies from MI something or other who'd interrogated – and that *was* the word – her for over an hour about anything the Colonel might have revealed, even inadvertently.

'Did he ever confide any secrets with you?'

'Well, yes. He did. Just the one.'

'And what was that, Mrs Baker? We need to know. You're legally obliged to tell us.'

'I don't suppose it matters now.' Edna had shrugged. 'He said he thought *HMS Pinafore* was overrated.'

'Is that it?'

'It's considered to be one of their finest, but he didn't care for it at all!'

Their faces became even harder and the interrogation stretched on . . .

And the normal police had done their thing, of course. Very efficiently, too.

Then there was the Family Liaison Officer, or FLO as she was called. She'd telephoned Edna and explained she understood that she'd been close to the Colonel and that this must be a difficult time. She wasn't there to spout mumbo-jumbo advice, but she'd be happy to pop round if Edna felt like 'unloading' over a cup of tea.

Edna wasn't entirely sure what 'unloading' entailed but politely declined. Nevertheless, the FLO was round at The Lines the next day and had such a nice way about her that the time flew by. She seemed to understand so thoroughly everything Edna said and, more importantly, everything she didn't say. As the young woman was leaving, she had asked, 'Would you like me to pop back again? Just for a good old natter?'

'That would be grand. Thanks, luv.'

'My pleasure, Edna!'

'Hang on! I haven't even asked your name! I can't very well keep calling you F-L-O! Unless your name's Flo!'

She laughed. 'Did I not introduce myself? Honestly, I'd forget my head if it wasn't screwed on.' She gave a big, breezy smile. 'Call me Sophie.'

CHAPTER 70

*N*o. *I won't let this happen!* I won't go down like this, battered and bleeding in the back of a motorway service station, just so a sadist can get his kicks and certain members of the upper echelons can pass the port without having to worry about my investigations. My fear becomes anger, not simply drawn from the hell I've been chained to, but about everything.

Everything.

So, no. Not here. Not like this.

I steady myself.

The lorry is starting to pull away. I need to use its power to help me, not destroy me. I pivot my body and turn, arms wide, essentially crossing them and spinning my upper limbs 360 degrees. And again. So the two chains are being connected by a huge, rough knot. I spin my body and arms again. The knot made stronger.

The lorry is moving away and the chains are stretched taut, but they're effectively one chain now, with me affixed to the knot that joins them. The more the vehicle pulls, the stronger the knot is made. The vehicle's horsepower is such that the driver might not even know what's happening at his tailgate. He puts his foot down and the juggernaut eases forward.

The link of the chain closest to its tow bar is prised apart, the lorry moves forward and the remaining links fall to the ground.

Clank!

The chain broken in just a couple of seconds, if that.

The lorry judders into second gear, its driver never knowing how close he came to dismembering a stranger.

Thoughts flood my brain.

The man who tried to have my body torn in two must be close, so I'm still in danger. I begin to yell at the top of my voice. But, clearly, my shouts might be too late, because I spot him. Greenwood. He's laser-focused on me and jogging my way. Our eyes lock. In my peripheral vision, I see he's holding a knife.

I hear laughter. Not his.

For a moment, it's such an alien, unexpected sound that I doubt my own senses. But I turn away and see that a bunch of drivers, who must have heard my shouts for help, are wandering across to me. They're speaking Dutch, and although I can't precisely interpret their meaning, I infer they think I've been chained up as part of a prank. I'm guessing they believe I'm the centre of a stag-party joke that's been carried too far. They can't know, of course, that moments earlier I'd almost been ripped apart.

They're big guys. Jovial, but tough-looking. I see Greenwood's pace slow as they reach me. Our stares meet again and he stops. Turns. I see his van parked a few yards away and watch him approach it. The Dutch guys are laughing and weighing the chains. I stammer something about needing their help.

'Yes, yes . . .' one of them replies. 'We have tools.'

I see Greenwood's van leave the car park. He's in the driver's seat and even from this distance, I can make out he's got his phone pressed to his ear. I wonder who he's calling, and why.

'Thank you,' I say to the men who surround me. 'Thank you.'

One of them asks, 'What happened? Some kind of . . .' He searches for the right word. 'Lark? Yes?'

'Lark. Good word. Not used enough. And yes,' I reply, 'just a lark. But . . .'

'Don't worry. You want us to get you out of . . .' He gestures to the mess of chains.

'Yes, very much. I'd give my right arm to be free of this. Just not literally.'

I don't know if he fully understands my comment, but he laughs again.

'You English! You're all crazy!'

To be fair, he's got a point.

I walk to the service station's main building. It's the normal mix of M&S, WHSmith, a 'Fresh Food Hall' that seems to offer everything except fresh food, and sundry little shops for the driver in need of respite through retail. My wrists ache, but my Dutch saviours did a magnificent job, unshackling me in about ten minutes.

But those minutes could prove costly. I think about Greenwood on his phone. I doubt he was calling his mother to see how she's doing. Not for the first time, I wonder who he reports to.

I reach a bank of payphones. I'm amazed to find I have change in my suit pocket, and even more amazed to find a phone that works. I made a point of memorising Miss Winters' number and I give her a call. The woman with the RP accent puts me straight through.

'Novak?'

'Miss Winters. A man called Lee Greenwood just tried to have me torn in half. Did you pay him to kill me?'

'Don't be ridiculous. If I wanted you dead, you'd be dead.' She sounds like she's telling me the truth, but I can't be certain. 'Tell me what happened.'

I give her a precis and she says, 'Look, stay where you are. I'll send help.'

'I don't need your help. I just wanted you to know that if you're connected to Greenwood, you'd better call him off.'

'Are you threatening me?'

'Whatever happens next is on you.'

I hang up, phone Precious and tell her what's happened.

'Christ!' she exclaims. 'Are you OK?'

'I've had better days. Can you collect me?'

I tell her where I am and she assures me she's on her way. 'And Novak . . . I'm glad you're safe. I wouldn't want to lose you. Again.'

'Well, for what it's worth . . .' I hesitate.

'Yes?'

I'm interrupted by the beeps informing me that I should put more money into the phone. But I'm out of change and the call is cut off. I replace the receiver and try to think.

If Greenwood has backup they could be here at any moment, so I wander into the WHSmith and, out of habit, drift over to the book section. I'm largely hidden by the shelves but can see anyone entering the shop.

The adrenaline is starting to wear off and I'm becoming cold again. Shaky. The ache in my muscles, and especially across my shoulders and back, grows into an acute throb.

The hours of walking through freezing rain, the battering at the hands of Greenwood and the horror of almost being wrenched in half are beginning to take their toll. I need to sit down. Fast.

As I leave the shop, I see a glorious sight: three liveried police cars, blues and twos wailing like they're auditioning for *The Sweeney*, slam to a halt just outside the building's main entrance. If I can make it past the row of shops in between, to meet them, I'm safe.

I should wait here. Let them come to me. But the idea of safety in the back of one of their cars is irresistible and I start making my way towards them. I've almost reached the guy who looks to be in charge, when someone barrels into me. I feel something blunt in my ribcage.

Look down at the damage.

Her cucumber is broken in half. 'So sorry!' she chirps and carries the rest of her M&S shopping to her husband, who mutters something about his wife always bumping into people.

I approach the policeman. Count the stripes. Three.

'Sergeant . . . I'm Marc Novak. I'm guessing you're here for me?'

'Yeah, we're here for you.'

The relief I feel is like a naughty kid waking up on Christmas morning and finding there's a whole heap of presents at the foot of his bed.

'Thank you.'

He looks at me with . . . Well, if he wasn't here to rescue me, I'd say it was a combination of surprise and disdain.

'What are you thanking me for?'

There's an aggressive tone in his question that's hard to miss.

I say quietly, 'You're here to help, yeah?'

'I've no idea what you're on about. Scum like you make me sick.'

OK. Suddenly not feeling like a rescue at all.

I say, 'What do you mean?'

Two officers are at my side. They wrench my arms behind my back, almost pulling them from their sockets.

Click!

I feel the cold metal of handcuffs slapped over my wrists and locked tight. Too tight.

'Marc Novak, I am arresting you for the assault and harassment of Anna Louise Brandon. You do not have to say anything. But it may harm your defence if you do not mention . . .'

He reaches the end of the routine. There's a pause. He adds, 'Well? Anything to say for yourself?'

'I'm being framed!'

He shakes his head in disbelief and I'm frogmarched to the waiting police cars. As we drive towards the service station's exit, across the car park at the entry flow, I see Precious's car. She's heading towards the building I've just been extracted from.

She's here to collect me.

She's also about two minutes too late.

CHAPTER 71

Edna's Story (cont.)

The final time Sophie visited Edna she'd brought some homemade jam for her to sample. The older woman spooned some on to a slice of tiger bread, took a mouthful and declared, 'You'd never know it from shop-bought!'

The FLO picked up on the joke and light-heartedly scolded her, 'You cheeky thing! I'm going to have to watch you!'

Over the next hour or so they chatted about everything from the Colonel's closest friends to the likelihood of a hereafter. Just as Sophie said she was going to have to get off, her mobile rang. 'Would you mind if I took this, Edna?'

'Go ahead, dear!' She hoped it would be the next person she was due to see today, revealing that they couldn't make the appointment, meaning Sophie could spend more time at The Lines. But no.

Sophie had jogged up the stairs to take the call and spoke in a low voice. Yet Edna's hearing remained excellent and she inferred from the FLO's tone of voice that she was talking to a superior. She caught her saying, 'Is it absolutely necessary? All right. Understood. I'll do it. I'll do it now.'

Edna guessed they wouldn't be sharing another pot of tea, after all.

She looked across to the Colonel's old armchair and pictured him sitting there, a serious look on his face.

'*Mrs Baker, that cottage pie was absolutely first-rate! You really have surpassed yourself!*'

Not that he'd ever complained about her cooking, unless she put too much ginger in the chicken soup.

'Edna!' It was Sophie's voice, shouting down from upstairs. 'These houseplants are amazing! What are they?'

'The ones on the landing?'

'Yes!'

'Pink anthurium and a common or garden snake plant!'

'This is going to sound ever so cheeky, but would you pop up and tell me how you manage to keep them in such rude health?'

Edna had assumed her guest would be making herself scarce after the overheard 'I'll do it now' comment, so didn't need asking twice.

She put the kettle on the hob and walked to the foot of the stairs. 'Happy to share the secret, dear! Are you not very good with plants?'

'Afraid not,' Sophie replied. 'Everything I touch dies.'

Edna began to climb the steps towards her.

Sophie listened to Edna's advice as if she was being told the location of hidden treasure. The older woman finished off with, 'Don't overwater them, and I don't care what the experts say, keep them out of the shade!'

'Got it! Thank you so much, Edna!'

'My pleasure, dear.'

'And now I'm afraid I've really got to go.' Then she said something that slightly puzzled Edna, 'Thank you for everything. Everything!' and she embraced her.

'That's all right, dear . . .'

'After you.' Sophie gestured towards the stairs.

Edna shuffled towards them. She paused at the door of the Colonel's study. 'I could show you his yucca plants, if you like?'

'I'm afraid we're both out of time.'

'Maybe next time, eh, luv?' She took another step towards the staircase. 'Yes. Maybe next time.'

Edna felt a violent, forceful push against her back. The pain was fast and unexpected and her vision cartwheeled. Her head struck a step and her spine seemed to curve. She shouted out something but her face hit the floor at the bottom of the staircase and she moaned, but only for a moment.

When her eyes fluttered open she could see only one thing. Sophie's concerned face. She was holding her head. One hand across the back of her skull, the other under her chin. It was probably some technique she'd been taught in the police. Except . . .

Sophie seemed to tense herself and then pause. Almost as if . . . Yes, she'd seen the crucifix Edna wore around her neck. The small gold cross was normally beneath her blouse but the tumble had knocked it upwards and it lay outside her clothing.

Sophie asked, 'Are you Catholic, Edna?'

She couldn't talk and didn't understand why she would be asking the question. Yes, she was badly hurt, but would probably survive the fall. Her eyes, more than anything else, gave a positive response.

Still holding Edna's head, Sophie dabbed her tongue with the tip of her index finger, then gently touched the bridge of the old woman's nose. 'Through this holy anointing, may the Lord in his love and mercy help you with the grace of the Holy Spirit. May the Lord who frees you from sin save you and raise you up.' Then she recited the Lord's Prayer, rapidly and smoothly.

By the end of it, Edna finally understood. She managed to croak, 'No!'

But the nice young lady said, 'Amen,' and twisted Edna's head to a grotesque angle in a swift, single movement.

Sophie closed her eyes at the moment the neck bones cracked.

When she opened them, she saw Edna's dead face. It still looked shocked at the deceit that had been played on her.

The kettle started whistling on the hob.

Sophie turned the gas off, collected her homemade jam and left the cottage without sparing Edna another glance.

CHAPTER 72

We've been driving for a little over an hour, I think. Difficult to tell. I keep dozing off, and sometime during the night my watch was smashed, so it's tricky to know how much sleep I manage. It sounds bizarre to say this as I'm stuck in a stack of trouble, but after the events I've just survived, a warm car with decent upholstery represents five-star luxury. The policemen around me clearly find me repugnant, but they're not actually trying to kill me.

I hope.

So, as we drive through the English morning, I know I should be protesting my innocence, but what would be the point at this stage? I crave rest. That's all. On the occasions I do wake up, I see we've left the motorway for a dual carriageway, then, a little later, that we're moving through minor roads in a verdant, bucolic locale.

'Can I ask where we're heading?'

'You can ask,' the sergeant replies, in a tone that suggests he'd rather give away his pension than give me any facts.

'I'll tell you what. Why don't you keep it a secret so it's more of a surprise for me?'

I close my eyes. The prospect of more sleep is hugely enticing, but before I can nod off, the car slows down.

We're in an attractive country village. There's a pub called The Rose & Crown, a butcher's and, next door to that, a greengrocer with buckets of chrysanthemums, lilies and bellflowers sitting along its frontage.

We pull up outside a baker's shop and the driver turns the engine off.

'Get out!'

'I'll get out.'

My handcuffs are finally removed and we all alight. I'm escorted through the village to what looks to be a small police station. It has bright, cheerful hanging baskets either side of its main entrance and ivy covers most of the front elevation.

I'm 'accompanied' along the short path that leads to the front door and the sergeant ushers us inside, scanning the empty village roads as we traipse past him. He joins us, nods to the woman on desk duty and she slides some paperwork across the counter towards him. The building feels more like a museum than a working station. The room we're waiting in has a teak delft rack, chintz wallpaper and posters so old they're almost quaint. One shows the silhouette of a man running past a row of houses, underneath the words, 'Lock your doors and windows', as if the advice relates to a shrewd new method of crime-fighting.

I smile at the receptionist. 'Love what you've done with the place.'

The sergeant returns the now completed paperwork, a door clicks open and I'm taken further into the building. Another door and a flight of steps leads us to a basement. This area feels more modern. Stark grey walls and steel doors. I'm pushed through one of them.

The chamber on the other side is empty aside from a table and a scattering of chairs around it. The smell of detergent – bleach, I'm guessing – is overpowering. And in the wall adjacent to the table, a dark, matt panel about six feet by four that's clearly a two-way mirror. Towards the top and in the centre of it, the sole spot of colour in the room. A small circle of red light that indicates a camera is switched on and recording what's happening, which I find something of a comfort under the circumstances.

'I hate to be a bore, bringing up human rights and all that stuff and nonsense, but I'm allowed a phone call.'

The sergeant's nostrils flare. He's not happy. 'Did you think about Anna Brandon's rights?'

'I helped her the best I could.'

'You make me sick.'

'Thanks for the update. But that phone call, sergeant?'

'Sit down.'

We're face-to-face and I say again, 'I want my phone call.'

He nods to a couple of constables who manhandle me into a chair. Now he stands opposite me, leaning over the table. 'You're going down for a very long time.'

'Look, sergeant! I'm being set up!'

Ignoring me, he barks at the constables, 'Let's go!'

As they file from the room, I shout, 'It's been fun!'

Yes, I know I'm being a bit of a wiseacre, but if anyone is covertly watching events unfold, or listening in, I'm damned if they're going to think the torture I've been put through has beaten me.

I hear the door being locked from the outside. Stillness. Silence. I'm alone.

In the police car, I'd felt relatively safe. But in a cellar room in an out-of-the way station, where the officer in charge has just denied me one of my legal rights – not so much. I'm grateful for the camera's reassuring red light.

I wait at the table. Stand. Pace to and fro. Peer through the two-way mirror. Check the door remains locked. It does. I sit down again. Try not to inhale too deeply. I guess I've been locked in this room for a couple of hours, but I'm still not used to that strong smell of detergent.

I fold the upper half of my body over the table and rest on my crossed forearms. I need sleep. Close my eyes. I open them again as I hear movement from the corridor outside.

I'm just in time to see the round red light die.

Whatever happens next will be unrecorded. There's a metallic rattle as the door is unlocked. It's pushed open and a woman enters the room. She sits opposite me.

'We really must stop meeting like this, Miss Winters.'

CHAPTER 73

Miss Winters looks as elegant and poised as ever. 'Mr Novak, you're in a great deal of trouble.'

'I know. It's a recurring theme since I met you. Now, why do you think that is?'

'And you look like you've had a difficult few hours.'

'Yes, but why do I have the feeling my day is about to get worse?'

'I told you to drop the case.'

'Why don't you tell me. Or show me?'

'Tell you or show you what?'

'You've got something up your Vivienne Westwood sleeve. Something damaging and horrific. Tell me or show me what it is.'

'Very well.' She removes her laptop from its case and opens it. 'I have something I'd like you to watch. And I should tell you, Mrs Brandon is intent on fully pressing charges and making a splash about this in all the papers.'

I'm starting to feel sick. 'I tried to help that woman.'

Miss Winters purses her lips. 'Did you? Or did you harass her? Become obsessed by her? Assault her? Stalk her husband in order to intimidate him, and even threaten her, sexually?'

'You know damn well I didn't do any of those things.' I lean back in my chair. 'Just me what you've got.'

She presses *Play*.

I'm watching me and Anna Brandon, but I've no idea where we are. The footage has been shot from a few yards away, covertly, judging by the framing, and there's no audio.

She's wearing Jackie-O sunglasses and when she removes them, even from this distance, it's clear her eyes are red and strained. I remember now. The café at the Serpentine. Except the angle from which the footage has been shot cuts out Mishka, who was with us. More than this, her absence suggests I was alone with Anna. I appear angry and she places her hand on my arm, as if to calm me.

'That's not how it happened.'

Miss Winters asks, 'What do you mean? Are you saying that's not you?'

'Well, yes, that's me.'

'Or it's been doctored?'

'Yes! Well, no.' Pointlessly, I'm trying to explain myself. 'The look of annoyance I give. That was directed at Mishka – she'd said something insensitive – and when Mrs Brandon put her hand on my arm, it was a display of gratitude. That makes it look like she's trying to calm me down.'

Miss Winters widens her eyes in mock surprise. 'Really? Because it *looks* as if you're furious with her, and she's putting her hand on your arm in case you're thinking of hitting her . . . Again.'

'What the hell are you talking about?'

She gestures to the screen. The video now shows a succession of photographs. Anna Brandon is on my doorstep and I'm clearly gripping her wrist.

'Is that you?'

'Yes. But it's not what it looks like!'

'You're saying the picture's been Photoshopped?'

'No! But she'd turned up on my doorstep and hit me. I was just . . .' I trail off, knowing how weak my explanation sounds.

'You were just defending yourself? From the mighty and savage Anna Brandon? Yes, I'm sure a jury will believe that.'

The photos that follow show Anna Brandon running down my driveway, as if she's broken free of my grasp and has been forced to flee for her life.

'That didn't happen! Those photos must have been taken at a different time.'

'Of course,' Miss Winters purrs. 'Anything you say.'

The next three pieces of footage are brief and shot at an extreme angle. They're dark and grainy, but what they show is unambiguous. I recognise Anna Brandon's husband in various compromising positions with three young women. Each clip starts with them, blurry, but obviously enjoying non-platonic relations. The camera then pulls back and I can be seen, photographing the liaisons. I know exactly how this looks.

'I was hired to get proof of his infidelity!'

'Really? Because Anna has been quite frank about the fact that she shares an open marriage with her husband. She knew all about these relationships, is on record as having encouraged them. So, I don't know what made you become a Peeping Tom, getting your kicks from photographing her husband as he enjoyed healthy relationships with other women, but . . . it doesn't look good,' she adds firmly.

I recognise the location of the next clip immediately. The National Gallery. CCTV shows me apparently gripping Anna's forearm.

'Grabbing her again, Mr Novak?'

'I thought she'd been about to fall . . .'

The screen now shows the security guard who'd intervened as Anna Brandon had rushed away from me. She's talking to someone off-camera. 'I heard her say to him quite loudly, *I'm happy with my husband. This has to stop!* That's when I went over. He grabbed her arm at one point. Oh, and she said *Please just leave me alone!* I do remember that very clearly. But when she tried to get away, he was obviously going to give chase, so I prevented him from leaving.'

A male voice off-camera replies, 'Thank God you did!'

Most of the remaining video follows these lines. Misleading photographs. Snatches of video footage, which, although not faked as such, deliver a grotesquely skewed version of the truth. There are several photographs from the evening she told me her husband had struck her. We're outside my home. In some pictures I'm holding her face, as if I'm pushing her head back.

'I was trying to assess her injuries!'

In one, it looks as though I'm slamming her against my car.

'She was about to fall! I was trying to prop her up . . .'

The succession of stomach-turning imagery feels never-ending.

Miss Winters says, 'I think you get the picture,' and fast-forwards to an interview with Anna's husband. He talks about how I made contact and began insisting that his wife would be better off with me, before stalking and ultimately threatening him. It's all fiction, of course. He explains how he hired private detectives who assembled the video and photographic proof we've just viewed.

'And now,' Miss Winters announces, 'the pièce de résistance!'

It's Anna. An interview, shot around the time she told me her husband had assaulted her. Her face is badly bruised and she's been weeping. As she speaks, she sounds terrified. It's difficult to watch. She claims I repeatedly begged her to leave her husband for me, even though we barely knew each other. That I was a schizophrenic liar who insisted, even to her, that she'd hired me to watch her husband, when everyone knew their 'adventurous' open relationship was something she enjoyed. I was persistent. Paranoid. Charming on occasions, but dangerous. A fantasist playing at detective.

'Nice touch,' I mutter.

Anna Brandon tearfully stammers details about how I'd struck her. And worse.

'Turn it off.'

'Oh, I think you should watch until the end, Mr Novak.'

I swipe my arm across the table and send the laptop flying across the room. But it doesn't shatter or break. It simply lands on its side and continues playing for a moment. Miss Winters can't conceal her delight.

The final words of the video are spoken by Anna with a kind of petrified sincerity.

'This fantasist . . . Marc Novak . . . He needs help, sure. But at the same time, after everything he's put me and my family through, you must understand . . .'

I close my eyes.

'. . . He's a monster.'

CHAPTER 74

'That video,' I say very quietly, 'is an abomination. An unforgivable insult to the thousands of women who give honest testimony in an attempt to win justice. You're picking over their truth to pluck out bits of camouflage for your own, vile deception.

'That—' I jab my finger at the laptop, 'is a betrayal of the people, predominantly women, who face domestic abuse, or any other kind of abuse, physical or mental, or both. You're weaponising their efforts for a goal that's the antithesis of everything they deserve. That video doesn't simply traduce and incriminate me, it lets down the millions of survivors who've had to battle for respect and humanity and the justice of fairness at its most basic level. It is an atrocity that offends everything we hold dear about our perception of what is right. Which is why I say again: it is an abomination.'

Miss Winters nods sympathetically. 'Yes. Well, there is that. But it's good, isn't it?'

'It's appalling.'

'Yes, yes, yes,' she continues. 'Although . . . it's beautifully crafted. And so moving! I mean, who could watch that and *not* absolutely loathe you? Despise you? Consider you the dregs of society? We'll get a few more people to make complaints about you, of course. Really keep the momentum going when the story breaks.' She nods. 'When you're released from jail, and you've served parole, what do you think you'll do? You'll be forced into a change of job by law, of course. And I really think you'd better leave the country or these stories will keep on surfacing and resurfacing. But emigrating might be fun! If anywhere will have you, that is.'

I shift in my chair. 'You know, Greenwood is psychotic. And I know I should pity him, but I despise him for what he tried to do to me and for the suffering he's wrought on others. But he enjoys watching people suffer for a few moments. And God knows that's bad enough. But you? You're the tawdry type of sadist who relishes the agony being prolonged and extensive. You're *worse* than Greenwood.'

'And you, Mr Novak, are a sore loser.'

'I haven't lost.'

'I don't rate your chances of success too highly. I mean, no offence, but . . .' Miss Winters takes a two-page document from her laptop case. 'Sign this and it's all over. We don't use the video. You can go back to your old life. No one is hurt. A fresh start. Think about that.'

She hands me the document and as I read it, she nods at the two-way mirror. The small red light shines again.

'Do the right thing, Mr Novak.'

The document is extraordinary. It's a statement I'm purported to have made, charting my own mental decline. The crazy conspiracy theories I've concocted about the Princess of Wales and sundry other individuals connected with, however tenuously, the latter days of her life. It also addresses the therapy I've subsequently used to stage a full recovery. My acceptance and absolute certainty that the death of Diana was simply an accident in Paris. My apologies for any distress I have caused.

It offers me a way out. A farewell to the madness of Greenwood and the unseen cohorts that have been mobilised to derail me. A cessation of an investigation that no one wanted or wants, and the harm it's unleashed. Sign this document and I'm free again. It offers me the opportunity to hit the reset button on my own life.

I say to Miss Winters, 'Hand me the pen.'

I take it. Remove its lid. The nib pauses over the second sheet of paper by the word 'Signature'.

Miss Winters tells me, 'You're doing the right thing.'

My mind is made up.

I reply, 'I know.'

CHAPTER 75

I flip the document back to its first page and draw a huge cross, corner to corner, all the way across it. I turn to its second and final page and repeat the defacement. And now, for good measure, I tear the document into shreds and toss them into the air like confetti.

Miss Winters simply turns to the two-way mirror. Shrugs. The red light dies.

'You're a fool, Mr Novak.'

'Maybe. But I think I stand a pretty good chance against you. Even now.'

She laughs. 'Really?'

'Oh, aye.'

'And why is that?'

'Because you're an idiot, Miss Winters.'

'An idiot?'

'No one has called you that for a long time, have they? But you know you're not as bright as you pretend to be. And I'll tell you what your Achilles heel is.'

'Please do.'

'You got where you are too easily. You've not had everything handed to you on a plate, granted, but it's been prepared in a Michelin-starred kitchen and all you've had to do was pick it up. When you were young, you were probably beautiful. That was useful.' I make a play of scrutinising her face. 'You're not bad now. Showing signs of being past it, though; all your fancy face creams and assiduously applied make-up can't quite conceal the inevitable atrophy. I bet you tell yourself it doesn't matter, when in actual fact you know the loss of your looks means the loss of one of your most potent resources.'

'I thought you were supposed to be a gentleman?'

'Never think the courtesy I extend to most is offered to all. And never, *ever* mistake my adherence to old-fashioned values for weakness. As some kind of dusty, dotty intransigence. No. It's the way I purposefully choose to live my life.'

'For richer or poorer?'

'For better or worse.'

'Well, that's fabulous to know. But you were saying? About me. It's fascinating.'

'Oh, yes. Where was I? You did well at school. Mummy and Daddy didn't tell you this enough, but they were proud of you. Well, if they'd spared you any thought, they would have been. Having said that? The type of school you went to? Well, it's in their own best interest to exaggerate the success of their students. Otherwise, what's the point of the exorbitant fees? You wandered into jobs because you had money, looks and contacts – and this one really suited you, didn't it?'

'Yes. Yes, it did. And I'm proud of that fact.'

'I'm sure you are. But let me tell you something, Miss Winters – or whatever your real name is. That coldness you pride yourself on? That ability to take sentiment out of the equation and operate on an impersonal level? That icy ability you're so proud of? That you *think* makes you so unique and good at your job . . . ?' I lean forward and whisper, 'It really doesn't.'

'You're a fool. You don't understand—'

'Oh, I understand,' I tell her. 'I've met dozens of men and women like you. Who believe their callousness has cachet. That their cruelty is a form of rare intelligence. That it makes you one of the elite. Laughable! It really doesn't, you know.'

It's her turn to lean forward. 'So what does it make me?'

I relax back into my chair. 'Not given it much thought, to be honest. Although,' I laugh, 'I guess the irony is that there are so many petty, privileged frauds like you out there that it makes you common, Miss Winters. It makes you a parasite no more extraordinary and no scarcer than head lice. And one other thing.'

'What?'

'Your left eye is starting to twitch. Mummy and Daddy wouldn't like such an obvious sign of weakness. Go to your room, young lady. Daddy will be up later.'

'I think I've heard enough.'

'You've never been pushed, Miss Winters. None of you lot have. That's your weakness. Never had it hard. Not really. Not like others. Not like the majority. And I'm going to push you. Hard.'

'And what?'

'You'll fall.'

'You may not believe this . . .'

'Try me.'

'But I like you, Mr Novak. Which actually makes *this* very hard for me.'

She nods at the two-way mirror.

Two women and a man enter the room. The guy unlocks a door I hadn't previously spotted, located in the room's far corner. One of the women points a Glock G34 at my head, whilst the other has a quiet conversation with Miss Winters.

The man says, 'Get up.' He gestures to the door.

It leads to a corridor. I go first, followed by the woman with the gun. Miss Winters and the other two bring up the rear. I walk. And walk. I'd assumed the corridor would bring us to another room a couple of metres away, but no. We stride down the passageway for a good ten minutes. Its walls, initially plastered with a smooth finish to resemble any hallway in any house, change in appearance. I'm soon marching through something more akin to a tunnel, dug out of earth.

Eventually, we reach a wooden door. I see the Glock remains trained on me, but now the other nameless woman and man are also holding pistols.

Miss Winters opens the door and takes the lead. I join her, and wordlessly, with three guns pointing at our backs, we begin to walk through a wood.

I've read all the Cold War history books and watched enough movies to know how a walk through a forest with three gunmen at my back will play out. But I promise myself that I won't beg, or weep or wail.

I say to Miss Winters, 'This is it, then?'

'The end?' She nods. 'I'm afraid so.'

CHAPTER 76

Maureen's Story

Maureen Shaw began feeling nauseous around 11 a.m. Knowing that nothing puts customers off their sandwiches faster than seeing the person who made them looking sweaty, grey and obviously poorly, she had a quick word with her assistant, who told her to go home. She'd handle everything.

'Thanks, luv. You're a lifesaver.'

Freddie dashed into Rudy the Foodie as she was groggily putting on her jacket.

'How's your Hay fund going?'

The young man beamed. 'What with tips and everything, I'm only twenty pounds off!'

He sounded as though he was announcing he'd scooped first prize on the lottery. Maureen smiled. Rooted out her purse from her handbag and extracted a couple of tenners. 'Here.' She handed the notes to Freddie. 'Mission accomplished.'

'Maureen – thanks! What's this for?'

'Put it down as a gesture to young love. I was young myself once, you know!'

Freddie hugged her. 'You're an absolute ledge!'

She wanted to say that Freddie was the legend. Ever since he'd started working for her, he'd made Rudy the Foodie a sunnier place, and his positivity and sheer energy for life had proved to be a tonic for her personally. But this morning she felt too ill for all that. Besides, she could tell him another time.

He disengaged and she turned, opened the door and enjoyed the feeling of cool air against her face.

'Thanks again, Maureen!'

The last time she ever saw him, Freddie was smiling at her whilst ramming the money she'd given him into his trouser pockets.

'See you tomorrow, Freddie.'

Maureen arrived home at about 11.30 a.m. and began to run a bath. Whenever she felt ill, she would play classical music, drink endless glasses of water and have a soak. She phoned her assistant to check everything was in order at the café.

'We're fine here! You just get yourself better!'

Maureen undressed, placed her ancient portable tape player on top of the toilet and pressed play. Music filled the bathroom. The cassette was a compilation of arias her late husband had made for her, less than a week before he'd died, and the first track was the barcarolle from Offenbach's *The Tales of Hoffmann*. She hummed along to it as she stepped into the bath.

The water felt the perfect temperature. She lay down and closed her eyes. The tape continued to turn.

Freddie was told he had an extra run. An unexpected job to deliver some sandwiches to an address in Foxglove. 'The client will meet you outside. He paid in cash this morning, so don't worry about getting his card details or anything.'

'Foxglove?'

'Yeah. Shouldn't take you too long.'

Freddie took the box of sandwiches and slipped it into his small rucksack.

'It's just I hate that stretch of road now. Where that old guy died.'

'You'll be fine!'

He put on his rucksack. 'I know.'

'If you want cheering up, just think – not long till Hay!'

'Can't wait!'

As he walked to his bike, he took his phone from his pocket and called his girlfriend, primarily to let her know he'd achieved his target and they were both *officially* going away for a few days. The prospect felt dangerous and glamorous and wonderful.

But she didn't pick up.

Freddie decided not to leave a message and set off for Foxglove.

Maureen was beginning to feel better and was even considering going back to work, but decided against it. Her assistant might misinterpret her reappearance as a sign of doubt in terms of her abilities. And besides, an afternoon off might do her the world of good. She hadn't felt this relaxed in a long time.

'O mio babbino caro' from Puccini's *Gianni Schicchi* began to play. She thought of her husband. It had been their song.

The narrow country lanes were never a problem for Freddie. Sure, they meandered, and you had to be careful when approaching a blind bend, but the heavier vehicles steered clear of them, which meant Freddie didn't have to keep half an eye open for lorries or the massive juggernauts.

Occasionally, on main roads like this one, they drove too close to his bike as they overtook. He dreaded that sensation of being knocked off balance by the displacement of air as they thundered by, sometimes only inches from his shoulders. It was the only time he ever felt really worried when going about his deliveries.

Especially now. Especially here. On this stretch where that guy in the Defender had been killed. Accidents happen every day. He knew that. But when they're in a place so familiar, and they end in someone's death . . . Well, Freddie had told Maureen, it just puts the wind up you a bit, doesn't it?

There were flowers by the roadside where the fatal crash had occurred, half a dozen bouquets in plastic wrapping. As he cycled past them, Freddie heard the rumble of a large vehicle. A lorry was approaching from behind. He braced himself, gripping the handlebars a little tighter in case the vehicle came too close.

At that moment, he felt his phone vibrate and he hoped it was his girlfriend, returning his call.

Maureen sank beneath the bath's warm water. She kept her eyes open, looking at the ceiling, then closed them. Her senses were claimed entirely by the music and the comforting warmth of the water. No matter how often she heard this aria, it always made her think of her husband. How he'd proposed to her as Callas had sung it on a 78, in their tiny, grimy, brilliant little bedsit in Manchester, so many years ago.

She opened her eyes.

And saw, directly above her, a man wearing a black balaclava looking down on her.

CHAPTER 77

At Miss Winters' bidding, we link arms and begin to saunter through the trees. There are patches of dazzling snow on the ground and the air is crisp. We could be an old married couple, out on a languid Sunday stroll through the woods.

The armed trio remains several paces behind us, affording Miss Winters and I a degree of privacy. After a few steps, I break the silence. 'Why was I even brought into this? You and your people are resolutely trying to keep what happened a secret. Why did you hire me to investigate if you never wanted it uncovered? I think you can tell me now, surely?'

'Standard procedure. We try to ensure that the operation remains watertight, but we need to check for leaks. People who could potentially reveal too much. We need those checks to be real-world processes. And so we sent you on your way to identify people or organisations we had to . . . address.'

'The Colonel?'

'And Sebastian Hughes.'

I stop walking. 'What? Sebby's dead?'

'He soon will be.'

'Jesus! He doesn't know anything! He's harbouring some crackpot idea about Diana being alive.'

'He is considered threatening enough to be removed from the equation.'

The man behind us clears his throat and we continue making our way through the woods.

'To be *killed*. Use the words, Miss Winters. Don't insulate yourself with euphemisms or jargon.'

We walk a few more paces and she says, 'I'm sorry about Anna Brandon. We set her up as a bargaining chip to use against you, if you discovered too much. None of us believed you'd actually turn us down when we had that at your throat.'

'Who is she really?'

'Anna? Oh, she is who you thought. Which made her perfect. But she has massive gambling debts she doesn't want her husband to know about. You can fill in the blanks.'

'And let me guess. She thought she was serving Queen and Country.'

'In a way, she was.'

'Who do you work for? MI5?'

'God, no! Nothing so prosaic. I'm part of a shadow service. Official but unofficial. The world has changed, Mr Novak. The UK needs an organisation that can operate without the constraints faced by traditional military intelligence.'

'You really think you're the good guys?'

'You must have heard the tales about Churchill. How he had military intel that the Germans were planning a devastating attack on Coventry. Hundreds, maybe thousands of people would be killed.'

'I know the story. He couldn't warn or protect them because that would reveal he had the information, which would tip off the Germans that their security was compromised. Which in turn could have resulted in the deaths of hundreds of thousands of our people.'

'Exactly. Was he right, do you think, Mr Novak? To remain silent as innocent blood was spilt?'

'What's your point?'

'Isn't it obvious? For the good of the many, a few must die.'

'Yeah. That's always easy to rationalise. Unless you happen to be one of the few.'

'I've been faced with that same Churchill dilemma many times, and chosen the solution he himself opted for.'

I'm an idiot. I've only just realised what she's doing. 'Are you looking for my forgiveness, Miss Winters?'

'No. Just your understanding. What you said back in the interrogation room . . . You were right about a lot of it. In the early days, my background . . . my *privilege,* people insist on calling it these days . . . Yes, it did help. But I still had to work bloody hard. And in today's world it's nothing but a setback, let me tell you. In meetings, young eyes watch me with scorn for what I am and where I'm from. Oh, they're professional and prudent, but they want me and my people gone. And like you, Mr Novak, they believe I've had everything handed to me. At the same time, they *expect* handouts, of course, as if it's their birthright. They enjoy endlessly criticising the amusement parks we've created. But, my God, how they bleat if they're not given a free pass for all the rides.'

'I think it's a little more complex than that.'

'Really?'

'The first time I met you, I wondered if you'd trained yourself to sound less posh.'

'Very astute.'

'And I found myself wanting you to like me.'

'Well, mission accomplished. I am very fond of you, Mr Novak. Just as I was fond of the Colonel.'

I can see a clearing up ahead and ask, 'Is this it?'

'I'm rather afraid it is.'

'Is there anything I can say to stop this happening?'

'The three people behind me are not my staff. I'm powerless to prevent what's about to happen.'

What's about to happen.

We've reached the clearing – and this time I have no problem with her inclination to avoid the 'k' word.

The woman with the Glock addresses me. 'You walk ahead. Alone.'

I nod. Like I said, I've watched enough movies to know how this will play out.

CHAPTER 78

We stand on the edge of the clearing.

Miss Winters says over her shoulder, 'Give us a moment,' and, as one, the trio takes a respectful step back. 'When you reach the trees on the other side . . . That's when they'll do it.'

'You know, my mum died on the same day as the Princess of Wales. And now it looks like Diana's death will . . .'

I hear myself trail off, with no idea how to end the sentence.

'The Diana operation is a very unwelcome distraction right now. And you must know it's only a tiny part of a much bigger game.'

'Meaning what?'

'The people who really control the world we live in . . . ? For generations, they've worked together as one, in harmony, pretty much. But after the events of the past few years, those alliances are breaking up.'

'Is that such a bad thing?'

'It could be catastrophic.'

'I'm sure your shadow service will keep it all in check.'

The look in her eyes reveals I understand nothing of the situation's magnitude. 'There's a storm brewing. It will be devastating. We think we want freedom. Choice. But above all, we want order and society. The battles ahead may destroy all that. They may well eradicate everything we hold dear.'

'I think you might be exaggerating—'

'There's a *shadow war* coming.' She takes my hands in hers. 'I'm just sorry we won't be able to fight in it, shoulder to shoulder. I honestly think that we might have been on the same side . . . at last.'

'Miss Winters.'

'Yes?'

'Don't flatter yourself.'

Her smile falters.

I ask, 'Does this have to happen?'

I made a promise to myself that I wouldn't beg, so when she nods, I shrug. Pull my hands from her clasp. 'Fair enough. Well, unfair enough.'

The man behind us grows impatient and for the first time raises his voice. 'You! Start walking!'

I take a look at my surroundings. I've never noticed how many shades of green even a small patch of forest offers up. And that smell of damp soil and foliage is gorgeous. I smile at Miss Winters. She makes a fist of her right hand. Puts it to her mouth and coughs.

I say, 'Well . . . bye, then.'

And I immediately regret my glibness because her eyes have welled up. She offers me her palm and asks, 'Any regrets?'

We shake hands and I say, 'Only that I couldn't see it through. Apart from that?' I shrug.

She gives a deep sigh. 'Marc Novak, you're a knight errant in a world that no longer wants knights errant.'

I turn away and start walking into the clearing. I hear the armed escort move forward and, just for a moment, I spin around, walking backwards as I tell her, 'As epitaphs go, that isn't such a bad one.'

She's weeping. The three people who've frogmarched us here are by her side and they're all standing in a neat little row, watching me.

And the woman who dragged me into this whole mad, miserable, bloody affair says, 'Goodbye.'

I smile and turn, striding resolutely through the clearing, so when they remember this moment, when they put away their guns and discuss it, the conversation won't be tarnished with talk of my fear.

I've almost reached the trees on the far side of the clearing.

I remember Mum used to say, 'Do your best. That's all you can do.'

I did my best. I hope she knows that. I hope they all do.

Just a few steps away now.

And I hope she's been proud of the decisions I made and the actions I took.

Maybe five more paces?

But in the end, I suppose, only we know, and God forgive me, but I pause just before the bank of trees that signals the end of the clearing. Do I look like a coward? Maybe. But it's not that, honestly.

I'm staring at the first tree. A silver birch. I've never stopped to give it much thought, but they're not actually silver. This one is a million shades, but it's predominantly a light, lush amber, the colour of a lion's fur. Its bark is marked with notches. They're natural, not carved into it by a knife, or anything so deliberate. They are there by chance. Four or five horizontal lines. I focus on that patch of the bark.

It reminds me, bizarrely, of tiger bread. Which brings to mind my childhood home. Me as a kid, surrounded by my mum, dad, brother and sisters. Music playing. Laughter loud. The loaf of tiger bread warmed up in the oven, because we all agreed it tasted so much better when it was piping hot. My mum placing it in the centre of the kitchen table and us all cheering. I'd thought that spirit would never end. That the world of warm bread and familial love was a blueprint for life.

I look at the silver birch with its tiger bread markings.

Take a breath. Tilt my head.

Warm bread and loving laughter.

I extend my hand towards the notches . . .

My palm touches the bark.

I hear the gunshot.

CHAPTER 79

Maureen and Freddie's Stories (cont.)

Freddie's girlfriend finished her shift at the hotel and checked her phone. Three missed calls: two from her mum, one from Freddie. She phoned Freddie.

No answer.

She tried again.

He answered this time. Breathless, but obviously pleased to hear her voice.

'I've got good news, Elaine!'

'Are you on your bike?'

'Yes!'

She shook her head. 'Call me back later! You know I get worried when you're chatting away and you're on the road.'

'Yeah. Funny you should say that. Almost got knocked off by a *mahoosive* lorry that swept past me a minute ago! Missed me by less than a foot!'

'Well, you be careful, then! Speak later. Love you!'

She waited. Freddie always echoed, 'Love you,' whenever she said the words, and she angled her head, smiling, thinking he was making her wait for his reply as a joke. After several seconds, she repeated the two words.

Still nothing.

'Freddie? Are you there?'

Maureen tried to scream and raise herself at the same time, but the man gripped her throat and held her below the water. Her absolute terror morphed into a desire to live. She struck her attacker repeatedly, but the blows were ineffective. She'd already swallowed water and needed to breathe . . . Just one breath and she could really have a go at this lunatic, but . . .

. . . But she was too weak and in less than a minute the man in the balaclava felt her body go limp. Maureen Shaw's final thought had been that perhaps, just perhaps, she was going to see her husband again.

Ever the professional, her killer retained his grip for a further ten seconds before he took a small kitchen knife from his pocket. He used it to carve a long diagonal cut into the underside of Maureen's left forearm. He put the knife into her dead grip. Finally, he stood back, glanced at the tape player and decided it would look suspicious if he switched it off.

The woman who scrabbled down the slope, racing towards Freddie's body, later recalled that someone had already reached the poor lad. 'Some big guy was trying to help him. Loosening his clothing, I think. But it was too late. Whatever hit him . . .'

The big guy in question had vanished and was never identified.

The man in the balaclava hurried into Maureen's bedroom. He took several half-empty bottles of gin, vodka and whisky

from his backpack and stashed them in her clothes drawers and behind the paperbacks in her bookshelves. Next,
moving quickly, he poured half a litre of Teacher's over her
duvet and pillows. Satisfied, he carelessly tossed the empty
whisky bottle to one side. It landed on Maureen's bedside
table, knocking over a faded photograph of her with her
husband on their wedding day. It shattered the glass frame
she had kissed before sleeping every night for the previous
sixteen years.

Freddie was dead long before the ambulance arrived and
the coroner said that he wouldn't have felt any pain. But
Elaine did. She never heard him echo her 'Love you,' and
when she visited Hay, alone, it felt like a pilgrimage for a
future torn from both of them.

The camera that she swore he always attached to his
helmet was never found.

He ducked back into the bathroom and gave the body in
the pale, red water a final glance, nodded to himself and
moved quickly into the hallway.

'O mio babbino caro' was still playing as Lee Greenwood
left Maureen's home.

CHAPTER 80

I screw my eyes tightly shut. Hear a second gunshot. And a third, in quick succession. I open my eyes. The sound of the discharges still reverberates through the woods. A sprinkling of snow falls from the upper branches of the silver birch and I turn around.

The woman I knew as Miss Winters is on the forest floor, dead. My first thought is, *Had she known?* and I suspect she had. I begin to walk towards her.

One of her killers gestures with her gun, a motion that tells me to get back. I keep walking. She says, 'Last chance,' and her Glock is aimed at my chest. Reluctantly, I pause and watch them go through the corpse's clothing, searching for something.

After a thorough examination, the man says, 'It's not on her. She might have slipped it to him.'

One of the women mutters, 'They shook hands! We'll search him.' She walks towards me. 'Take your clothes off.'

I'm prepared to argue with her, but not the barrel of her gun. So I strip, handing the other woman my items of clothing as her associate keeps her Glock trained on my torso. After a couple of minutes, the gun is the only thing covering me.

All three of them go through my clothes. The guy says, 'It's not here.'

One of the women reasons, 'She could have secreted it somewhere in the interrogation room.' A thought strikes her and she swears under her breath. 'Or dropped it somewhere in the tunnel. Christ!'

I clear my throat and one of the women throws me my clothes. As I get dressed the man makes a phone call. Immediately afterwards he leans across a fallen tree and brushes a pile of dead leaves from one of its branches to reveal a black attaché case.

I finish tying my tie and fasten my top button.

Without expecting a reply, I ask, 'Why did you kill her?'

One of the women says casually, 'She was supposed to bring you to heel. But she didn't do her job.' And then she adds, 'You were going to join her. But you've got yourself a guardian angel. Swooped in at the last minute and said you weren't to be touched.'

'Who?'

She shrugs. 'No idea.'

The man says to me, 'He said you're to have this, though.' He places the attaché case on the ground immediately in front of me.

I ignore it for the moment. 'What's going to happen to her body? You can't just leave her here like that.'

The woman armed with the Glock replies, 'There'll be people here soon. They'll take care of everything. I suggest, very strongly, you're not here when they arrive.'

To my surprise, the man motions to the case with his gun. I bend down and click open its metallic fastenings. Glance up at him. He nods. I lay the case flat on the ground and open it.

It's fair to say that its contents, including something I've not seen for many years, are not what I anticipated.

CHAPTER 81

The attaché case is full of cash. Bundles of banknotes. Different denominations. I've no idea how much exactly, but as the old joke goes, at a rough guess, I'd say a lot.

On top of the money, there's a bloodstained handkerchief with my initials sewn into it. It stirs a memory from years ago. A deserted warehouse. A woman taken hostage and me helping her, reuniting her with her wealthy and powerful husband . . .

The three people above me are holstering their guns. One of the women says, 'Your guardian angel considers he has repaid the debt he felt he owed you. He has a message for you. You're safe for now, but you no longer have his protection. This was a one-off. Don't be a fool with the money, don't ever contact him – and it goes without saying, you breathe a word about this to anyone and you're dead.'

The other woman adds, 'He also says thank you. And that you really should have taken the job.'

They turn and disappear into the woods.

I'm left in the middle of a forest with a corpse and a case full of cash. This really isn't the way I thought the morning would go. Like I once said, in this job I just never know what the day's going to bring.

I arrange Miss Winters' body, placing her arms over her chest and tidying the clothes her killers disturbed when they searched her. Pointless, I know. It feels strange and unnatural to be arranging her corpse. When I'd first met her, she'd seemed so untouchable. So impervious to—

A thought strikes me. A memory.

Miss Winters coughing. Putting her fist to her mouth and coughing.

I turn her face towards me and part her lips. My finger-tips probe her mouth. I find the item wedged between her cheek and rear molars. Holding it up, to the sunlight, I see it's tiny. The size of a tooth. It's hard to imagine this isn't what her killers were searching for. A micro-USB drive.

A crow caws.

I stand. Scan the woods. The trio are long gone and I pick up the attaché case. Look down on the corpse one last time. Her face has already changed. No longer the woman I knew.

'Goodbye, Miss Winters.'

I slip the USB drive into my pocket and walk away.

CHAPTER 82

Jeremy's Story

Jeremy Simmonds – the man Marc Novak knew as Thom Peters – was in a blazingly good mood. Two days after the shooting in the forest, he'd been informed of Miss Winters' execution and although there'd been a couple of hours for the news to sink in, he remained euphoric. Her death was a blessing on several fronts. It opened up the chance of promotion and he more than fancied himself for her former position. Plus, her fall from grace meant he could blame anything that had recently gone awry on her ineptitude, all his blunders and miscalculations expunged with a simple, 'I was only following her orders, although I did constantly question the wisdom of her modus operandi . . .'

He reached the gated community where he'd lived for the past three years. Waved at the guards.

'Evening boys!'

They opened the complex's huge gate and he drove to his home.

His wife and two kids were downstairs. There were hugs and kisses all around. 'You're in a good mood,' his wife observed.

'It has been a wonderful day! I've just got a bit of work to finish. I'll be in my study.'

As he walked up the stairs, he reflected on the final boon brought about by his former boss's death. He wouldn't have to put up with her any more. As simple as that. She'd looked down on him for years and regarded him with something approaching haughty derision. But who'd stayed the course? Who was going places? And who lay cold in an unmarked grave?

He pushed open the door to his study, sauntered over to his drinks cabinet and fixed himself a large brandy. Why not? He was, after all, celebrating. Jeremy Simmonds intended to read the report that detailed Miss Winters' death and he was looking forward to it as though it was the latest book by his favourite author. He sat in the chair behind his desk and switched the table light on.

He saw the intruder immediately, of course. He'd been hidden by the shadows in the corner of the room, but was now all too visible. He was pointing a Beretta in his direction.

'Good evening, Mr Simmonds,' said Novak. 'It's nice to see you again.'

CHAPTER 83

For a moment, his expression is the epitome of horror. But in fairness to the man I once knew as Thom Peters, he recovers quickly. 'How the hell did you get in here?'

'They have their entrances.'

'And how did you find out where I live?'

'There's a rumour going around that I'm a detective.'

I have Molly Stone and Frank to thank for the information, but I'm not going to tell Simmonds that.

'I've had your study to myself for a fair old chunk of time. I've got to say, you're very comfortably set up. And look! A collection of antique guns!'

I glance across to a display cabinet full of old weaponry. 'Even a gambler's gun. Strap it to your forearm using a spring-loading mechanism and if the card game goes south – click! – the two-bullet Derringer is snapped into the palm of your hand and you can take out whoever's trying to rig the game. Did you think Miss Winters was rigging the game, Jeremy? Is that why – click! – she was taken out?'

'I was nothing to do with that. My God, that decision was well above my pay grade!'

I believe him. Shrug. 'If you say so.'

I hear his wife call from the hallway, 'Everything all right, Jeremy?'

'Fine!' he replies. 'Just on the phone.' And in a low voice to me, 'You go too far, Novak.'

'Oh, you have no idea how far I am prepared to go. Now, I have a friend called Sebby Hughes. I want him to live a long life, untroubled by tragic car accidents or bullets to the head. Similarly, as you're no doubt aware, I've been helped by Precious Weeks and Frank Harvey. I want them all to remain safe. If they so much as stub a toe, I'll hold you responsible, Simmonds.'

He gets to his feet and I take a seat. 'Do you think I'm scared of a nothing like you?' he hisses. 'Some latter-day knight riding into battle on his own? My God, you overplay your hand, Novak. Yes, you know where I live. But you wouldn't dare touch me!'

I idly pick up a framed photograph from a side table. It's a picture of Simmonds, surrounded by his wife and two children. 'I never said anything about touching *you*.'

And there's that reaction I was looking for. Understanding. He realises the threat I'm making and even if he believes I'm bluffing, he can't be one 100 per cent sure.

He says, 'And you have the nerve to castigate me? When you threaten my family?'

'My friends' safety is paramount.'

He keeps his anger in check. 'They'll be safe.'

'And should anything befall me, I've made certain contingencies—'

'Yes, yes, yes! The whole project is finished now, anyway. It was a bloody mess. We can all blame Winters and just plough on with the next crisis.' He pauses. 'Unless . . .'

'That's right,' I tell him. 'My investigation isn't quite finished.'

'You're still not dropping it? Are you insane?'

'I'm close to the truth. And I'm not about to break the promises I made. So when I finally peel back the cover-ups and get to the truth, I'm going to let the world know.'

Simmonds knocks back a mouthful of brandy and asks, 'How do you intend to do that?'

'Oh, not through the normal official channels. I'm going to make a splash. A splash big enough to cause a tsunami that will wipe away the lies that people like you have fostered for decades.'

'You're bothered about wiping away lies? Christ alive, man, you're a relic! That's not how it's done any more. You must see that. Why not join us?'

'No, thanks.'

'Why not?'

'I doubt you'd understand. But I have one more question for you. Greenwood. What do you know about him?'

'He was hired by Winters, I believe, to take care of the Colonel. That was it. He killed the boy and the owner of the sandwich shop because he thought they might have footage that placed him at the scene of Whittaker's death. Their murders weren't sanctioned. And you killed his brother, of course. Very foolish.'

'Where is Lee Greenwood now?'

'God knows.' Simmonds finally smiles. 'But wherever he is, Novak, at some point, he'll be coming for you.'

CHAPTER 84

I meet Anna Brandon for what I assume will be one last time. She's on Bond Street, hailing a cab. As it swerves to pull up to the kerb, I emerge from a doorway and approach her.

'Mrs Brandon. You look well.'

She fixes on me in the same way I envisage French aristocrats must have gawped at the guillotine as they were delivered to its steps. I open the taxi's door for her. She gets in and I follow, saying to the driver, 'Fitzrovia, please.'

As the cab pulls away, Anna Brandon becomes a waterfall of apologies.

I hold up my hand. 'Does your husband know about any of what happened? I mean, what really happened?'

'No.'

'Lucky you.'

'You won't tell him, will you?'

'No. But if you're ever asked about what took place between us, you need to tell the truth this time. Otherwise, when the full story does come out – and I'd make it my business to ensure that it would – you'd be looking at social disgrace and a spell behind bars.'

She nods.

'And if you're ever contacted by someone looking to revive the little wheeze you were a part of, I want you to get hold of me immediately. Otherwise, leave me alone. And leave my friends alone.' I call through to the driver, 'You can drop me here, thanks.'

The taxi slows to a halt.

Anna Brandon says, 'I'm desperately sorry.'

'Go back to your old life. I think you'll find it's better than you remember.'

'It's too late for that.'

'Why?'

She doesn't reply and I get out of the cab. Through her wound-down window, she says, 'My husband and I are divorcing.'

'Maybe it's for the best.' I should walk away now, but hear myself asking, 'Was any of it real?'

'In the National Gallery. I warned you, do you remember? I got into dreadful trouble for that. But I had to. And I once told you the worst thing in the world had happened.'

'Yes, I recall.'

'Well, it had. Just . . . not for me. For you.'

Her head is tilted slightly, so she's looking up at me. It's the first time I've noticed it. Her resemblance to Diana, that is. Another reason, I suppose, why she was selected.

'I was trying to warn you there again, I suppose,' she adds. 'Even then. You see . . . You may not believe me, but I—'

'Good luck, Mrs Brandon. I hope things work out for you.'

She seems stung by my interruption and, as I nod to the driver, she promises, 'We'll meet again.'

The cab begins to pull away.

'I doubt it.'

As her taxi flows into the stream of London traffic, Anna Brandon shifts her position so she can see me through the vehicle's rear window. I want to hold her gaze but, reluctantly, I turn and walk away because, although my case is almost complete, I've still got work to do.

I hail a taxi, climb in and tell the driver, 'The Archduke.'

If I'm to uncover everything about the death of Diana and bring my investigation to a close, I need just one more piece of information. And now, as the skies darken, I'm on my way to secure it.

CHAPTER 85

'Sebby, I have to tell you. I don't think Diana is alive. In fact, it's certain she died on that awful night. But certain people believe you know something important about how she was killed. Which suggests that you do . . .'

'How did you find me?'

We're not far from his house, in a street food market near the Southbank Centre. The good one, just behind the QEH and across from The Archduke. I'd intercepted Sebby as he was about to join a queue and the smell of Indian food, coming from the stall in front of us, is divine.

'I saw some branded packaging in your kitchen bin that suggested you were a habitué of this place. Look, we need to talk.'

He remains silent.

'In your heart of hearts you know, don't you? That she's gone.'

He doesn't reply for such a long time that I suspect he hasn't heard me. But eventually he nods and says, 'She should be allowed to rest.'

'What I do can't harm her. She'd have wanted the truth. Let's remember her for her real achievements. Not as some fairy-tale princess. But as a compassionate, intelligent young woman who deserved better.'

'What I know is . . .' He hunches his shoulders. 'Don't like to talk about it. Only me now. So many others gone. Only me now, so when I die, knowledge of it dies. And that's like it never existed, isn't it?'

'No. Not at all. That would mean they'd won. Just tell me, Sebby!'

'I'm sorry, Mr Novak, sir. But no.'

He begins to walk away. I don't move. But I say one word.

Sebby Hughes stops dead in his tracks. 'What was that?'

'You heard.'

He turns around. Faces me. 'Where can we talk?'

CHAPTER 86

We sit on a bench overlooking the Thames, a little to the side of those second-hand book stalls in front of the BFI. It's a cold afternoon, but it's bright, and light glimmers across the surface of the river.

'It was just another overlooked point at first,' I admit. 'Diana was killed because she'd revealed to the press that she would soon be making an announcement. An important announcement. But there was very little time between her telling those journalists and the crash . . . That's important. How was it done, Sebby?'

'It fell under the Rapid Intervention Procedure Directive. That's why it could be organised so quickly. How the cover-up could be so complete and far-reaching. But it also explains all the mistakes they made with the so-called official version of events.'

'Rapid Intervention Procedure Directive?' I ask. 'What is that?'

'Commonly known as the RIP Directive, Mr Novak, sir. And for good reason.'

'Oh my God. I've heard of it – it's a myth, isn't it? The espionage equivalent of a campfire story designed to scare you . . .'

'It's a lot more than that,' Sebby replies. 'Our society is more fragile than you think, Mr Novak, sir. Or that's to say, bits of it are. One person, if they hold enough power, or they're in the right position . . . Well, they could do massive damage. That could be through an action. The Prime Minister declares war on China. Or seeks to impose military law and suspends elections. Sounds bonkers, doesn't it?'

'It's happened in other countries,' I concede.

'Or the damage could be done through an information reveal. Someone might, for whatever reason, be on the verge of disclosing intel so explosive it would have consequences considered to be catastrophic. Now, those circumstances might arise very, very rarely. No one's disputing that. I certainly ain't. But it's always a possibility. Hence the RIP Directive.'

'Go on.'

Sebby gazes across the Thames. 'Well, it's said that certain security services have a list of key people. Not just politicians, but figures of national and international importance. And for every one of them, they have a Rapid Intervention Procedure planned and on standby, ready to be executed at any given time.'

I stare at Sebby. 'I can't believe that.'

He gives a half-smile. 'Shame that Jeffrey Epstein didn't make it to trial, isn't it? Would've been interesting.'

'You're telling me that they already have a plan in place to assassinate certain people? Just in case they need stopping at a moment's notice? That's horrific.'

He shrugs, 'Well, that's the way it *used* to be. These days, a good old-fashioned murder is an option, sure enough, but problematic ministers might suddenly find child pornography on their home PC, or face allegations from people they've known innocently for years.'

'We've come a long way, haven't we? Developed so many ways to destroy someone. Often more brutal than a bullet.' I pause. 'Look, the idea of the RIP Directive has been swishing around for years. It's never been proven, though. Not once.'

'Not categorically, but a couple of memoirs published within the past ten years hint at it. And let's be honest, would it really be that surprising? I thought you *knew*. I thought that's why you said the word.'

'I suppose I knew but didn't want to believe it.' I'm aware that sounds fatuous, so I press on quickly. 'Look. We accept that Diana's death was linked, in part, to a RIP Directive—'

Sebby interjects, 'Don't go thinking the procedure would be an unchanging thing, set in stone. It was more an outline. A template, if you like, that could be applied wherever she was in the world at the time it was needed.'

I hear myself saying, 'Makes sense,' as if all this grim and gruesome detail is somehow pedestrian.

'With Diana, when it all happened, it had to be tweaked, of course. 'Cos of exactly where she was, and the necessity to do it so quickly. But . . .' It's his turn to ask questions. 'What was she going to announce? And was that really what got her . . . You know?' He stands up and I see he's becoming agitated. 'Christ!'

'Take it easy, Sebby.'

'But why did it have to be implemented in the first place? No one was bothered that she was having an affair with Dodi. Nothing had changed in her life during those final weeks of August. Why did they have to take her from us?'

I stand, too. Clouds are gathering. The light no longer glistens across the Thames.

I put my hand on Sebby's shoulder. Squeeze it.

'Deep waters, my friend. Deep waters.'

I'm walking Sebby back to his house. As we pass the street food market I tell him about the arrangement I struck with Simmonds. He should be safe. He thanks me, but adds, 'I ain't never safe from him, though. Not up here.' He taps his right temple.

'Are you talking about Greenwood?'

'The Muse. Yeah. He gets into your head and does terrible things.'

I confide in him; relate what happened to me.

'So you escaped?'

'Yes.'

He adds, 'For the time being.'

'I'm aware of that.'

'There'll be a reckoning. Are you a praying man?'

'I wish to God I was.'

He smiles. 'Then fight hard. And if you get the chance – kill him. Don't hesitate.'

'You think it'll come to that?'

'No doubt in heaven, sir. And when you do come face to face with that bastard . . .'

'Yes?'

'Tell him I say hello. If you know what I mean, Mr Novak, sir.'

We reach his front door and shake hands firmly. 'I think I do.'

As I head back to Waterloo, I replay his warning in my head and I'm aware he's absolutely right. Soon, very soon, there will be a reckoning.

CHAPTER 87

It's the day after I met Sebby on the Southbank and I'm making a call to Frank Harvey. 'It's time,' I tell him, 'to pull in that favour from Sue Carpenter.'

'Are you sure?'

'Absolutely.'

Sue Carpenter is the editor of one of the UK's best-selling tabloids. She was a young journalist when Frank met her back in the 90s and became her mentor, and the pair retained a strong friendship, even after her career skyrocketed whilst his saw him become an unwilling member of The Next Time Club.

'OK,' Frank tells me. 'I'll reach out to her. But Novak . . . Are you sure you know?'

'What really happened in Paris, 1997? Yeah. I know. Although part of me wishes I didn't.'

He doesn't reply.

I say, 'Let me know how it goes with Sue.'

'What are you going to do?'

'There's a couple of things I need to do,' I tell him, 'before this can be really over.'

I reach out to Veronique, a young woman studying history at the University of Surrey. She's Colonel Whittaker's daughter and although she barely knew her father, I want her to know what kind of man he was, and how he died.

We meet at her University's Stag Hill campus but our conversation doesn't go as I'd anticipated. Veronique doesn't need or want my assurance. She views the man who, along with her mother, had raised her as her 'real dad' and it seemed to me she had very little feeling for Gerry. She wasn't cold-hearted, as such. In fact, when we parted, she said, 'I'm sorry for your loss, Mr Novak,' and I found myself thanking her.

I arrive home, open a bottle of White Horse and pour myself a generous measure, but before a drop of it passes my lips, my phone rings. It's Frank. I ask, 'How did it go with Sue?'

'Well, she played it cool but she's keen to run with it.'

I laugh. 'I bet she is! It's the story of the century!'

'Don't expect too much, lad.'

'Frank, through her newspaper we'll be telling the world the truth about Diana's death. Do you have any idea how huge that is? It'll change everything.'

'Nothing changes everything. Let's take it one step at a time.'

He's right, of course. I take a sip of my whisky. 'OK, Confucius. So what's the drill?'

'Because of the extreme sensitivity of the story I've arranged for us to meet Sue in person, the day after tomorrow. We give her the story at noon. She'll actually write it herself, which is almost unheard of. And then they go big with it the day after. And by big, I mean mega. This will—'

I smile. 'I know.'

'We're not allowed to talk to any other media outlets for three months. That way she can run it as an exclusive.'

'OK. Not thrilled by that, but I'll let it slide. One thing I can't let pass, though . . .'

He knows, but asks the question. 'And what's that?'

'I give her the story on my own. I'm pretty certain we're safe now. But I can't be 100 per cent certain that they won't try to stop me delivering the truth. Look, I started this alone. I finish it alone.'

There's a moment of silence before Frank replies, 'I started this twenty-five years ago, Marc. At least let me be there when she finally gets some sort of closure.'

CHAPTER 88

If Sue Carpenter entered a competition predicated on looking like a newspaper editor, she'd finish in last place. I expect them to be gnarled, monolithic, inelegant and shouty. She's the opposite: thin and angular. Exquisitely dressed. She possesses an attractive air of being in control, and when I talk, she looks me in the eye like it's a first date. She's ferociously intelligent and has more polish than Mr Sheen. If I make her sound poised and glacial, well, that's because she is. But she clearly has a soft spot for Frank. She meets us in the foyer of her newspaper's offices and as we take the lift to her floor, he talks about her early days – and early mistakes – in journalism with a father's biased pride.

Frank brought Precious along. I'd hoped to keep her out of this stage, but can see why she'd want to be there as the story is unpacked. As Frank had gone to introduce her to Sue, his old friend had raised her palm.

'Oh, I know Precious Weeks! You were a rising star of the fourth estate a couple of years back! With political designs, if I recall? Courted by both major parties. The face of the future.'

Precious just nodded. 'All that's having to wait.'

'Not indefinitely, I hope?'

'Oh, definitely not indefinitely.'

*

Sue ushers us into her office. A corner room that's very high up in a very high building.

I take the seat nearest to the windows. Precious sits in between me and Frank. Sue, of course, takes her seat behind her desk and places a recording device, no bigger than a box of cigarettes, on top of it. 'I'm going to record this, of course. Everybody fine with that?'

Precious replies, 'No problem.'

Sue Carpenter presses her device's red 'record' button. *Click.*

'OK,' she says. 'Who killed Diana, Princess of Wales? How did they do it? And why?'

'To understand why she was murdered,' Precious begins, 'you have to understand the world as it was in 1997.' This was one of the steers Leonard Raymond had given us. 'Not how we view it today,' she continues, 'within its historical context, but as it was seen as it was being lived. As the mid to late 90s were unfolding, 1997 was a year of incredible hope. The Blair government was elected by a massive landslide and, sure, we all know how that turned out but at the time it felt like a real force for good. Of modernisation. Equality.'

Frank continues, 'There were meaningful talks about the Troubles for the first time in decades and both sides were well on the way to the Good Friday Agreement, signed just a few months after Diana's death. Peace in Ireland for the first time since the 60s.'

Precious nods. 'And so many positive reforms. It was all "Cool Britannia" and anything was possible!'

I take up the story. 'Over in the US, earlier in the year, Bill Clinton began his second term in office. He was the first Democrat to be re-elected since Roosevelt, over half a century earlier. He talked about putting politics to one side and creating a better future. A bridge into the twenty-first century. And just before his re-election, he announced, and I quote: *I am launching an international effort to ban anti-personnel landmines . . . The United States will lead a global effort to eliminate these terrible weapons and try to stop the enormous loss of human life.'*

Precious adds, 'In a way, things had never looked more optimistic. Like I said, anything seemed possible. Clinton was the youngest president ever to win re-election, by the way. Blair was the youngest PM of the twentieth century. There was this feeling of youth. Of rebirth. Of doing the right thing. It was the best of times.'

'It was the worst of times,' Frank counters. 'Violence on a global scale was escalating to levels humanity had never known outside the world wars. In the previous five years alone, the US had attacked Baghdad and taken a beating in the Battle of Mogadishu – forcing American troops to pull out of Somalia; Bosnia was a war zone, NATO and the States attacked Serbia, and Clinton ordered a cruise missile strike against Iraq in '96. And let's not forget the war of Transnistria, the conflict in Nagaland, the Armenian – Azerbaijani border conflict, the Chechen War, the Cenepa War between Ecuador and Peru, the Caprivi conflict in Namibia and God knows how many insurgencies. It wasn't just a decade of carnage. It had been a half-decade of extreme carnage.'

I take over this time. 'But by the mid-90s, the world wasn't just a mess of these bigger wars with US, UK, European and Asian involvement. There were a frightening amount of what could be termed local wars causing a horrific loss of life. There were civil wars breaking out on an unimaginable level. Again, in just the five years prior to '97, there'd been civil wars in Afghanistan, Tajikistan, the Republic of Congo, Yemen, Nepal and arguably Iraq in '94. But, also, an absolutely grim number of skirmishes. Deadly skirmishes. Massacres were on the rise.'

Frank details a mortifying amount of massacres carried out by paramilitary and quasi-paramilitary forces, in India, South Africa and South America. 'In 1997 alone,' he tells Sue, 'in one country alone – Algeria – let's see, we're looking at the Thalit massacre – 52 killed. The Haouch Khemisti massacre – 93 killed. The Omaria massacre – 42 killed. The Si Zerrouk massacre – approximately 50 killed. And many, many more. Christ, there were similar massacres that year in Rwanda, Sri Lanka and much worse in—'

Sue interrupts with a weary but forceful, 'All right! I get it! The five years leading up to 1997 and 1997 itself: lots of big wars. Lots of little wars. Lots of skirmishes. Lots of massacres. I'm not being heartless, but so what? I mean sad times and all that, but what's it got to do with Diana?' She leans back in her chair. 'Christ, you lot are depressing.'

I say, 'The point is, the business of bloodshed was enjoying a boom.'

'Right . . .' Sue is attempting to sound apologetic. 'You've set the scene. There's renewed optimism in some countries and spiralling violence in others. Great. I'm with you. Now. No more background.' She looks at me. 'Mr Novak. In under a hundred words, tell me, very simply, who killed Diana and why.'

'Fair enough,' I reply. 'Here's what happened.'

CHAPTER 89

'Diana's murder was ordered by a collective of individuals in the arms-manufacturing industry. They had seen the success she'd achieved with her campaign to get landmines banned. That alone cost them countless millions. They were terrified she'd turn her attention to the manufacture and supply of other weaponry, in a bid to de-escalate the rise of wars and bloody conflict the previous few years had witnessed.'

Sue is nodding. 'So you're telling me it was nothing to do with any of the romances she'd had, or wanting to move abroad, or her work with people suffering with AIDS?'

I reply, 'Why would it be? Why would anyone in a position of power care about any of that? Follow the money, Ms Carpenter. Money and might are what drive powerful people to transgress. Not the relative trivia of public perception for matters that don't affect their bottom line.'

Precious says, 'Don't view Diana's story through a prism of the male gaze. People tend to focus on her relationship with Charles or James Hewitt or Hasnat Khan or any number of men who weren't half the person she was. And, God, the media loved reporting on her perceived run-ins with other women, like her mother-in-law or even Camilla. What a way to deflect from her talents and achievements!

I mean, women being pitched against women? Nothing the press enjoys more! No offence.'

Sue gives a half-smile. 'I can't say I disagree.'

'Start looking at Diana,' Precious urges, 'as a successful woman in her own right. Because that's exactly what she was. You acknowledge that truth and start to see the broader truth. What the Princess helped bring about regarding landmines was remarkable. Yet the public tends to forget about it, only remembering her walk through that minefield. But people had been trying to get landmines banned for *decades*. She came on board and by the end of the year, the Ottawa Treaty is signed by over 150 countries, banning the manufacture, use and stockpiling of landmines. I mean, we overlook how huge an achievement that is.'

Frank adds, 'The Canadian Prime Minister called the treaty "without precedent or parallel in either international disarmament or international humanitarian law". My God, if Diana could achieve that in just a few months, what else could she have done? In that brave new "anything is possible" world, how much more of an impact could she have had on the arms and weaponry industry?'

Sue asks, 'She was dead by the time that treaty was signed, wasn't she?'

Frank nods. 'Aye. She was killed weeks before it was ratified. But many of those involved in the process credit her with making it happen and forcing governments to actually confront the problem. It's not just about fans of the Princess rewriting history. The people who were there and involved say, categorically, that after all the work she'd done, the treaty could not fail. It was her doing. That's incredibly significant.'

There's a moment of silence.

'All right.' Sue drums her fingers on her desk. 'This is starting to make some sort of sense. The arms manufacturers, who *had* been making landmines, see part of their business is being disrupted by the Princess. It's a bit of a leap to suggest they thought she wasn't going to stop there, though.'

I say, 'She'd already indicated that she wanted to visit some of the countries we mentioned earlier, and she expressed a desire to help the victims of war and help end the ongoing suffering.'

Sue shrugs. 'But that doesn't mean she was definitely going to go after them.'

'No,' I agree, 'it doesn't. But they couldn't afford to take that chance. It remained a possibility.

So when Diana told the press that she was going to make an announcement that would amaze them, well, certain leaders within the arms business became very nervous.'

'But they couldn't have known what she was going to announce!'

'And that's the whole point!' Precious exclaims. 'They couldn't *know*. But the possibility – or, after what she'd already achieved, the *probability* – was enough to convince some of them that she had to be stopped.'

'I'm inclined to believe she *was* going to announce something along those lines. It would make sense, and Gerry Whittaker's words lend credence to the theory. But the crucial point is, even if no one knew what she was planning, the mere fact that she *might* have been considering campaigning against the supply of armaments to certain countries would have been enough to trigger panic in some quarters,' I conclude.

Frank leans forward. 'Arms manufacture generates billions of dollars a year. That kind of wealth also creates people who will do *anything* to keep the money rolling in. It's worth noting that in the April of 1997 the US Senate ratified the Chemical Weapons Convention, banning the manufacture, use or stockpiling of chemical weapons. That was a victory for manufacturers of conventional weaponry. It meant the biochemists wouldn't be coming on to their patch and taking a slice of their profits.'

Sue says, 'But the US government weren't trying to help the arms manufacturers. Didn't you say Clinton vowed to get rid of landmines and to ban them?'

'Oh, he made the vow,' Frank replies. 'But the US was one of the very few big nations *not* to sign the Ottawa Treaty. Whilst the American President was telling the world how terrible landmines were, the Pentagon was awarding contracts to literally dozens of US companies to manufacture them. And whilst Clinton was preaching about the evils of stockpiling anti-personnel mines, his own nation was stockpiling over 15 million of them. The US government, like many governments, may have talked a good game when it comes to opposing the arms industry, but it encouraged them in private. The amount of money the industry legitimately generates for nations through taxation and other, shall we say, *gifts*, is extraordinary.'

Precious shakes her head. 'It's no wonder so many politicians were pissed off with Diana and openly scorned her for her stance on landmines and getting them outlawed. They were desperate to stop her! They saw her work as an attack on an industry they viewed as a very lucrative cash cow. It was only after Blair came to power in '97 that the

UK government started to support the Princess's aims of consigning landmines to history.'

Sue is nodding. 'OK. I think I can sell that to my readers. Diana – proven and effective enemy of the arms-manufacturing industry. She's already put them out of pocket so they have her killed so she won't spearhead any more campaigns against them.'

'That's a little simplistic, but pretty much dead on,' I admit.

'OK. Let's move on to the next biggie,' she says. 'How was she killed?'

CHAPTER 90

'It was becoming clear,' Precious tells Sue, 'that Diana's campaign to end landmines had been an extraordinary success. British MPs are hopping mad. I mean, the Ottawa Treaty will save the lives and limbs of kids and thousands of other innocent people, but they're more concerned about the financial implication. Pretty standard. But everyone with their snout in the arms trough is now worried to death she'll start campaigning for arms companies to stop selling AK-47s or the like to paramilitary organisations who had a nasty habit of gunning down unarmed civilians. I mean, that would be a disaster, obviously. Lives would be saved, but dollars would be lost.'

I say, 'They probably thought they had time to orchestrate a smear campaign against Diana to discredit her. Maybe they were behind the various attacks against her in the press that were already becoming standard. Like the ugly lie in wide circulation that she was losing her marbles. Spiteful, vindictive stuff designed to belittle her. Hateful. Would be interesting to see how that started?'

'Stick to the point,' Sue reminds me.

'I'll do my best. Now, I have a friend called Sebastian Hughes. Sebby. Not going to lie – he *was* peddling some cockamamie idea that Diana's still alive. Nonsense, of course. But certain people still seemed interested in old Sebby. So I got to wondering what he knows that's so significant. Well, the RIP Directive. And yes, I know it's got a melodramatic name but the Rapid Intervention Procedure Directive is actually very practical and pragmatic. Chillingly so. And I can tell you, without exaggeration, that dozens of services across the globe have it, under one name or another.'

Sue asks, 'But what is it?'

'It's a directive that means every individual who holds a rank of note and considerable power in our society must be considered a potential threat. Now, that potential may be extremely remote. But in the event of that threat being realised, certain organisations have ongoing, evolving contingencies.'

'To do what?'

'To kill them. Rapid Intervention Procedure is just a fancy way of saying kill them in a hurry.'

'And you're suggesting Diana was subject to an RIP Directive?'

'We are,' Frank replies. 'Diana gets to France, tells the press she's about to make a big announcement. Certain individuals think it will impact their business so they trigger the Rapid Intervention Procedure.'

I lean forward. 'They activate it by saying just one word. The trigger word assigned to Diana's RIP Directive.'

Sue's question is the obvious one. 'What was the word?'

It was the last word Leonard Raymond ever spoke. The word that caused Sebby Hughes to shift his perspective and help me. The word that was uttered twenty-five years ago to trigger the death of a princess.

I say it now. 'Artemis.'

Precious nods. 'It makes perfect sense. The way Henri Paul was set up. The way evidence was wiped away so quickly, eyewitnesses turned away, the conflicting evidence reports. Everything. The insane delay for the inquest, the way certain people connected with the crash in Paris wound up dead ... This wasn't a long sequence of coincidences that just happen to keep being played out to muddy the truth about Diana's death. So many inconsistences, deaths, lies and cover-ups can't all be coincidences.'

I say, 'And standard for the RIP Directive, they have off-the-record press releases lined up which are quickly put out. But everything happens so swiftly, some of the facts are demonstrably inaccurate. So there's a news blackout implemented whilst that's sorted. It gets lifted but things have to be cleared away quickly, now. The tunnel is reopened, witnesses told they're not needed, and the lies we'll grow to accept as truth are hastily planted. Henri Paul was drunk. Ridiculous. That he was trying to shake off the paps in the tunnel. Ridiculous. Even their destination – where they were driving. They were actually leaving Paris, as their route suggests, and as we were informed by a Mr Leonard Raymond. My belief is that Diana was heading back to England to make her announcement, but that's guesswork. But even the fact she was leaving France couldn't be admitted, so some clearly nonsense facts are given to us about where they were heading.'

I pause. It's a lot to take in. After a moment, I continue, 'No, the eradication of the truth in relation to that crash was a process. And it was carried out at the behest of several individuals within the arms industry ... by an intelligence agency. A security service.'

Sue looks appalled. 'You're telling me that an official agency carried out the murder?'

Frank replies, 'Well, a state agency was involved. Could have used freelancers. We might never know who was driving the car that nudged the Mercedes off course to cause the crash. But we know who was responsible and how the whole conspiracy was implemented.'

Sue's appalled expression has changed to one of mild disappointment. 'The RIP Directive is . . . bold and I've never heard of it. But everything else surrounding the death suddenly feels . . . tawdry.'

I nod. 'Murder's a tawdry business, Ms Carpenter.'

'It was all about money?'

Frank says, 'Shouldn't come as a huge shock, should it, Sue? That's the way the world works. Didn't I teach you that?'

Precious tells her, 'Putting it very simply – powerful people wanted to protect their interests. Interests that the Princess threatened.'

'The odd thing is,' Sue murmurs, as if to herself, 'most of it feels rather obvious now you've pointed it out.' She looks up, firm voice coming back into play. 'And you have proof for all this?'

I answer that one. 'For most of it. On Colonel Whittaker's laptop.'

She pauses. 'Two more questions. Who were the individuals within the arms-manufacturing industry who triggered the RIP Directive?'

'Most of them are dead. And no, we can't prove who they are. They covered their tracks well. It's what they do. Well, did.' Frank sniffs. 'One or two of them may still be alive. No *court* could touch them. They'll have made sure of that.'

There's something amiss about the way Frank says *court*, but Sue is already asking her second question.

'And the big one. Which nation's security services took out that Mercedes?'

I tell Sue, 'I want your feature to be very clear here. The security services of the world do a magnificent job, by and large. We're talking here about a faction using freelancers. I don't want any agency currently in existence to feel in any way culpable.'

Sue rolls her eyes. 'Yes, yes. But which was it?'

'We can never know definitively, but I strongly suspect it was a joint operation between two nations, which would also explain why some things were overlooked in the cover-up. Each side leaving it to the other and—'

Sue snaps, 'Just tell me!'

Frank gives Sue the names of the two nations we believe colluded in the killing.

Sue repeats Franks words. Shocked.

Precious says, 'It's not that much of a surprise, is it?'

'Maybe not. All right. I'd like that laptop.'

'We'll hang on to it,' Frank tells her. 'When this breaks, we'll need all the evidence we can get. You can trust me, Sue.'

'Can I?'

She's only half joking and Frank replies, 'You know you can! But you only get the laptop when the story is out there. Look, you can attribute the facts to us to cover yourself. Don't worry about that.'

It's my turn to ask a question. 'When will you run it?'

'A story like this?' Sue Carpenter gives a short laugh. 'This is tomorrow's front-page news!'

CHAPTER 91

We're in the lift, descending. Precious says, 'The fourth estate treated Diana appallingly. I saw an early-morning edition of a tabloid rushed out after she died. The main headline was "Diana Dead", but apart from that, every other headline was about Charles's reaction. She was cold in Paris and the papers were focusing on her former husband. I guess this gives them some kind of atonement. Finally delivering her story.'

Frank replies, 'We've done what we can with what we have.'

Precious nods. 'The Colonel's laptop is an absolute godsend!' and now Frank and I exchange glances. 'What?'

'The Colonel's laptop,' I tell her, 'hasn't been accessed yet. My contact is still working on it. But we know the facts, and once they're in the public domain, the truth will catch fire and burn across the world.'

'Very poetic, lad.'

'There's a lot we forgot to tell Sue,' Precious remarks. 'Like about why so many key officials kept changing positions and handing on their role ... because they didn't want to be part of something they gradually realised was a cover-up.'

'And how a certain official said one thing at one point, then completely changed his story. Presumably because he was told to do so by a member of *that* service,' I add.

Frank sounds more sanguine. 'That was a lot of information we gave back there. Any more and she just wouldn't have taken it in. There'll be time enough to add details and more explanations.'

'This,' Precious announces jubilantly, 'is just the beginning.'

We leave the newspaper offices and meet Cy in The Chandos, a busy little boozer just opposite the National Portrait Gallery. As usual, its downstairs snugs are all taken, but we manage to secure a table in the upstairs bar. Precious and Frank trot off to get the first round in, and I'm left sitting opposite Cy.

I like the guy. Mostly. He can be controlling and I get the impression he isn't crazy about me, but I guess that's understandable. He always seems to be watching. I half wonder if he wants me to trip up, so my relationship with his girlfriend is completely ruined, forcing me off the scene. But I'm aware that could very well be an illusion created by my own vanity.

He leans a little closer to me and says, 'I wanted to say thank you.'

'What for?'

'Bringing Presh into all this. It's rejuvenated her. Reinvigorated her. She's even talking about hiring a carer for her mum, now she's on the mend, and coming back to London. Picking up where she left off.'

'That's great news.'

'So . . .' I can see this is hard for him. 'I know we've not always seen eye to eye, but . . . Thanks, Marc.'

He offers me his palm.

I smile. 'My friends call me Novak.'

'Yeah,' he replies. 'Let's take it one step at a time, eh?'

We shake hands and Precious and Frank arrive back at the table to dish out the drinks. After they've sat down, I get to work on my first G&T. But Frank raises his glass. 'It's taken a quarter of a century, but tomorrow, the truth about Diana will finally see the light of day.'

Precious says, 'Here's to the truth!' and the four of us clink glasses.

'Hard to contemplate, isn't it?' Cy reflects. 'The world will be a totally different place tomorrow.'

My phone rings and I excuse myself, taking the call on the rear staircase.

When I return to the table, I say, 'Big news!'

Cy asks, 'What's happened?'

'That was the guy I gave the Colonel's laptop to. He's managed to open it. Look, I'm going to have to break up the celebrations. I've got work to do.'

Frank says, 'Can we help?'

'I need to set something in motion. A means by which I can release a lot of information all at once, across multiple social media platforms. Once upon a time, I'd have asked Mishka to set it up for me, but . . . The release has to be simultaneous, you see, and at an absolutely precise moment.'

'Sounds like a piece of cake.' Cy takes a sip of his orange juice. 'I can help you.'

Precious is more suspicious. 'Wait a minute! Novak, whatever you've got planned, is it dangerous?'

'Of course not,' I lie to her. 'Not at all.'

I can't be honest with her. Obviously. The truth would frighten her too much.

Because the truth is, the reckoning is coming.

Tonight.

CHAPTER 92

Cy arrives at my house just before midnight and I show him through to the front room. 'Thanks for coming. Can I get you a drink?'

'An Americano would be great.'

'Not a proper drink?'

'I'm good, thanks.'

He sets up his laptop whilst I make his coffee. It's going to be a long night, so I fix myself a Vegas Bomb, then drift back into the front room carrying our drinks and an extra shot glass full of White Horse.

'You don't need to do that,' I tell him, nodding to his equipment.

He looks up, surprised. 'I'll need to start work on—'

'I misled you, Cy. I'm sorry.'

'What's happening?'

We both take a seat. 'Some time ago, I got hold of the laptop that belonged to Gerry Whittaker.'

'The one you gave me in Paris? I couldn't bypass its security settings. They were military-grade.'

'Well,' I continue, 'I gave it to a contact of mine and – as you know – he *was* able to hack into it. He had a little more time, to be fair.'

'Yeah . . . And?'

'I've called a few people to let them know that the information the laptop contains relates to the death of Diana. And that the details revealed are absolute dynamite.'

Cy grins. 'That's great news! It means when the article comes out tomorrow we can . . .' He trails off as he sees me shaking my head. 'What is it?'

'I lied. My contact accessed the laptop and found it's empty. Completely devoid of any files or data of any kind. I've checked it myself. Nada.'

'It's useless?'

'Utterly.'

'Look, Marc, I'm not like Presh and you guys. I don't understand stuff like this. What the hell is . . .' He pauses. 'Why did you ask me to come round tonight?'

'Because I need backup and I don't want to get Precious involved in this. So, with her out of the loop and Frank still not 100 per cent, you're the only one I can trust.'

'To do what?'

'I have no doubt that my phone calls are being bugged by the agency that originally hired me. And if my guess is right, they will send someone round to steal the laptop tonight. In fact, I'm counting on it. That's the whole point of this charade. You've got to bear in mind they can't be seen to be involved in any murder attempt on me – I've taken precautions to ensure that. So, they'll send someone with a personal grudge against me. They're hoping he'll kill me, then I'll be out of the way and they can maintain plausible deniability in terms of ordering my death, if it's ever investigated.'

'I still don't get—'

'I'm hoping you'll be my backup.'

He grimaces. 'I think I *will* need that proper drink.'

I nod to the glass of White Horse. 'There's a large whisky on the side.'

He downs about half of it, coughs and splutters, 'I'm really not your guy. This kind of thing . . .'

I go to the cabinet that displays many of my first editions and remove a row of Flemings. There are several guns on the rear of the shelf.

'Where the hell did you get those?'

'Borrowed them from one of the people that put me on this case to begin with.' I remove a small pistol from the cabinet. 'OK, this is technically an antique. It's a Beretta Model 1934. As deadly today as it ever was and in perfect working order. The Italian army were still using these things until about twenty years ago. Here . . .' I offer him the semi-automatic. He shakes his head. 'Have you ever fired a gun before?'

'No.'

'I'll put the cartridge in for you, then all you have to do is point it at the bad guy and pull the trigger. With this model, there'll be some recoil. It's a simple direct blowback pistol with an open slot, but this piece has a steel-backed rubber grip.'

'Is that a good thing?'

'That's a good thing.' I can see he's hesitant, so I withdraw the Beretta. 'You don't have to do this, Cy. I'll be the one in the firing line and I'll confront the man they send. But you'll be close by – and I can't guarantee it won't kick off.'

'Why do you want this guy so badly? Why would you risk your own life to apprehend him?'

'He murdered people who were important to me. And he's vowed to kill me.'

Cy takes a deep breath. 'Give me the gun.'

I hand him the firearm and as he gets used to the feel of it, he asks, 'So, who do you think will be paying us a visit tonight?'

'His name is Lee Greenwood . . .' The man I'm hoping to draw out, so I don't have to spend the rest of my life looking over my shoulder. 'Also known as the Muse.'

CHAPTER 93

The dark hours slink by. I remain seated in the corner of my front room, hidden by shadows. I've got a Webley & Scott in one hand and a G & T in the other. Cy is in the next room along, my dining room. He's under strict instructions to remain silent and even when I confront Greenwood, he's to stay out of sight. If it transpires that I need help, he's to come in shooting – *only* if I call him. But if he can see I'm in trouble and I don't shout for his assistance, he must quietly flee the house by the side door, run as fast as he's able and phone for the police when he feels safe.

I've been over this with him three times already, partly because Cy is doing me a favour and I don't want him getting hurt, but also – if I'm being honest – because I can't bear the thought of Precious's wrath and sorrow if her boyfriend is injured. We broke up because I misread a situation. People I thought I could trust physically assaulted her, simply to make a point that they weren't to be taken lightly. She recovered, although our relationship never did. My error, and what it led to, still haunts me today. So, I really don't need the guilt of getting her current partner shot.

I sip my drink. Glance at my watch. It's 3 a.m. Most night-time attacks, when executed by the military, are undertaken around this hour as people tend to be at their

341

most tired between now and a little after 4 a.m. I put my glass on the floor and raise a mug of cold coffee to my lips.

The wait continues.

My mind drifts back to the clearing in the forest. The gunshots. And Miss Winters' lifeless body. I have the micro-USB drive I took from her safely stored away and although I'm tempted to access it, it could be booby-trapped. It's not unknown for that kind of device to be fitted with a locator, activated when anyone tries to access the information it holds. And so, although I will try to examine the data the drive contains, that's for another day when I can focus on investigating its secrets with a degree of safety. I stifle a yawn . . .

It's 4.17 a.m. and I rub my eyes. It's starting to look like I was wrong. Perhaps I've overestimated the importance of the information I claimed there was on the laptop. After all, in just a few hours the world will learn the real facts about what happened twenty-five years ago. Maybe Jeremy Simmonds' superiors – whoever the hell they might be – have accepted that it's just the beginning and that now, the entire truth surrounding the death of Diana and those around her will percolate into the public arena. In fact, it's entirely possible—

I hear something.

A tiny noise. But in this long, empty silence, it's unmissable. A small, metallic click, coming from the area around my front door. I get to my feet. My eyes are accustomed to the near darkness and I move my Webley to hip height.

Another noise. This one softer. The sound of my front door being pushed open. I feel cold air press into the room. I glance to my left, suddenly fearing that Cy might blunder in, asking how much longer we'll be forced to keep watch . . .

But there's no movement from that direction.

I turn my head back to the door that leads through to the hallway.

I narrow my eyes, focusing on the handle . . .

A couple of silent seconds elapse.

The handle is pressed down.

For a long moment, nothing. What's he waiting for?

Then the door is very slowly pushed open and finally he steps into the room. It's the man who has promised to murder me. The Muse.

I anticipate he'll be wearing night-vision goggles, so I switch on the lamp immediately to my left, expecting the sudden illumination will have a blinding effect on him. But Greenwood's face is exposed, those smooth, alabaster features, so familiar to me now, unshielded by mask or goggles. He doesn't look remotely surprised to see me.

'Marc Novak,' he sneers. 'I'm going to enjoy killing you.'

'Join the queue. And I'm afraid the Colonel's laptop isn't on the menu tonight, either. Put your hands in the air.'

'Laptop? Oh, I heard about that.' He pauses. 'You don't think I'm interested in it, do you? I'm just here for you, Novak. That's all.'

'I said put your hands in the air.'

He's studying my face to gauge how far I'll go. I've seen too many people throw away a tactical advantage because of a reluctance, or perceived reluctance, to shoot a gun; to actually pull a trigger and send a potentially lethal projectile flying towards an opponent at Mach 3.

I've no qualms – and to emphasise the point, I loose off a single shot, sending it a few inches to the right of Greenwood's head. The demonstration seems to amuse him, but he slowly raises his hands, like a teenager begrudgingly complying with a parent's request.

And even as the loud discharge reverberates I hear something else. Cy is opening the door to my left. 'What's going on?'

'Get back into the dining room, Cy. Everything is fine.' I take a couple of steps towards Greenwood and say, 'Get on your knees.'

He shakes his head. 'Who's pretty boy?'

'Cy! Get back, mate.'

'Oh, that's right!' Greenwood nods. 'Cy Hillier. You're Precious's beau. One of your cast-offs, isn't she, Novak? Or was it the other way around?'

'I said, get on your knees. The second bullet goes in your leg. The third, in your brain. *On your knees!*'

Greenwood purses his lips. 'That's my line.'

The words stir a recollection . . . Of course. Greenwood's brother. At The Lines. The sentence I'd spoken before shooting him at point-blank range.

'Oh, yeah,' Greenwood informs me. 'He told me about that and everything else before he died. And I told him I'd make you feel pain like you can't believe is possible. I *promised* him.'

'Your brother knew the gamble he was taking. Unlike your victims.'

'And I'm here to make good on that promise.'

'Well, unfortunately for you, I'm the one holding the gun.'

'Imagine a torture so acute that you're actually screaming and praying for death. You first. Then I might pay Precious a visit.'

Cy snaps, 'Shut up!'

I say calmly, 'Don't let him wind you up. He's just trying to get under your skin.'

'And after Precious, maybe a member of your family. Or maybe that journalist, Frank Harvey. But you first, Novak. Your reckoning is tonight.' He smiles at me and rests his palms on his hips.

'Put your hands back in the air or I swear to God I will shoot you.'

Greenwood replies, 'I don't think that would be a very good idea.'

His confidence is unnerving and I ask, 'Why not?'

'Because,' he tells me, 'if you even start to pull back the trigger of that pistol . . .'

I feel the cold barrel of a gun on the base of my skull and Cy says, 'I'll kill you. Now drop your Webley or I will take great pleasure in blowing away the back of your head.'

CHAPTER 94

Greenwood pulls a Ruger SR40c from his small-of-the-back holster and points it in my direction. It's a compact semi-automatic, no bigger than your unfurled fist, a modest-looking sidearm designed by the FBI to ensure maximum firepower and instant hospitalisation.

He says, 'Drop the Webley.'

I don't react.

Cy drives the barrel of his gun further into my head. 'Do it.'

I try to speak calmly. 'Cy, whatever he's told you is a lie. Whatever threats he's made to you or Precious are just—'

He interjects, 'Whatever he's told me? Oh, Novak, for a bright guy, you can be incredibly stupid. He didn't tell me anything. I'm his boss. Now, drop your gun.'

I let my Webley fall to the floor.

He says, 'Cover me while I take care of him.'

Greenwood nods.

Cy orders me to sit in one of my wooden chairs and starts handcuffing my wrists behind my back.

'What do you mean you're his boss? How the hell did you get mixed up in all this?'

'I've been mixed up in this for a very long time. And you've always been too blind to see it. The people I work

346

for singled out Precious years ago, when her press career was really taking off and she was being courted by both the major political parties. She was identified then as a person of extreme importance to us. One of tomorrow's leaders.'

I try to keep the horror from my voice. 'You're a sleeper!'

'At last! Yes. I'll be there to gently guide her and report back with all the intel that my people can use. But mainly, I'll be keeping her in check when needed.'

'Good luck with that.'

'Her trajectory stalled the moment her mother got ill, but we know a glittering career in journalism and politics still lies ahead for her. Meaning I am a prized asset.'

'Interesting. You can lose that last syllable and the sentence still works.'

Cy stands over me. 'She loved you, you know? And I came up with the scheme that broke you two up. Penny dropped yet?'

Again, I try to keep my voice level. I don't want him to have the pleasure of hearing my revulsion. 'You had her beaten up and made it seem my clients were behind it. Like it was my fault.'

'It was hilarious . . . Really. All your soul-searching. Precious's sleepless nights. Thank God I was on the scene to comfort her.' He grins at me. 'And more besides.'

Something else strikes me and I murmur, 'The laptop . . . I gave it to you in Paris . . .'

Cy nods. 'I had it unlocked in half an hour. Wiped it clean and locked it again. Didn't you think it was weird that when your contact gained access there was nothing on it at all? Jesus!'

'And you were feeding them information about what we were doing all along . . . It's why they were able to set up the assassination at Scarlioni's.'

'I was one of the sources. There were others.'

'Hey, it's a digital world. Am I right?'

Cy says to Greenwood, 'He's secure.'

'One more thing, Cy. How much of this operation was your brainchild?'

'I suggested your involvement in this whole thing on the off-chance it would lead to something like this . . . And those two men you encountered at The Lines? I authorised them to use fatal force on you. Pity they messed up, but when my superiors heard you mention you'd found information on the Colonel's laptop, I told them I could have missed an embedded data cache. I knew I hadn't, but guessed they'd send our friend to retrieve it, which suited me down to the ground. Me being here to see him take revenge for—'

Greenwood interrupts with, 'Get out of my way!' and Cy moves aside. I see the Muse is holding a syringe. He grasps my hair and tugs my head back to expose my throat.

'Can I just say my last goodbye?' Cy asks.

The other man pauses. Steps back. 'Make it quick.'

Cy drops to his haunches. 'This is the last time you're ever going to see me.'

'I believe they call it a silver lining.'

'But as the Muse is slowly tearing your body apart, and you're feeling every sinew being ripped open and every inch of flesh being sliced into bloody chunks . . . Just think about me. And Precious. Oh, and remember this moment.'

He moves his face closer to mine and smiles.

'You know what?' Greenwood raises his Ruger and places it directly behind Cy's head. 'I think he will.'

Cy Hillier's skull explodes. I can feel his flesh and fragments of cartilage and bone on my face. I can taste the salt of his blood on my lips. I try to breathe, spitting smithereens of his skin from my mouth.

I manage to stammer, 'W-why?'

'He told my brother he only needed one other man when he went to the Colonel's place. If he'd told him to take a crew, my brother would still be alive. But I was merciful to him. Made it quick. Believe me, I won't be extending you that mercy . . .'

Greenwood moves forward and stabs the side of my neck with the syringe. Whatever he pumps into me begins to take effect immediately.

He stands back.

I struggle to keep my eyes open but—

CHAPTER 95

A low, electronic hum . . . A gentle *beep* . . . *beep* . . . *beep* . . .

I open my eyes. Regret it. The room about me is in semi-darkness, but I can immediately tell I'm trapped in Greenwood's torture chamber.

When Tania Wilde, my contact in Special Branch, mentioned this place, I'd envisaged something quite different. I'd imagined it would be a chamber full of archaic devices, chains, racks and implements with threatening, gleaming spikes.

Not like this, which is so much worse.

It feels like I'm a captive in a medical laboratory. Ahead of me, under a huge circular light, there's an operating table. It's surrounded by the usual accoutrements you'd expect to find in theatre. Operating lamps angled to shine their beams towards the table. A sternal saw basin, defibrillator unit and an electric suction pump. But ringing this grim parody of a hospital unit, I can make out a circle of mounted cameras. Some are pointing towards the table. Others are aimed at the spot I find myself in. And along the edge of the wall there are banks of computers and a large Belfast sink.

I hear footsteps. Slow but steady.

The whole place is spotless, except for the wide, porcelain sink, which is awash with red spatter marks.

My left arm is raised and handcuffed to a thick metal loop clamped to the wall. I tug it hard but it's obvious the fixture won't budge.

I look across to the theatre. No Greenwood. I desperately try to wrench my hand through the steel handcuff but it's far too tight for me to even nudge it any way along my wrist.

Whatever he drugged me with remains in my system, clouding my mind. I try to focus. Maybe it's the anaesthetic, maybe it's fear, but my thoughts won't hold. I know I need to escape, but it feels hopeless.

The footsteps are getting closer.

My gaze inevitably returns to the operating table. I recall Greenwood's promise to make me scream and pray for death. I pull my left arm again, desperate to feel any kind of give from the fixture above. There is none.

A door opens. The tall, broad figure of Lee Greenwood enters the room. He's wearing surgical scrubs and a surgeon's mask, and he's pushing something . . . My vision blurs. I shake my head. Greenwood moves towards me. He's wheeling a trolley laden with medical implements. Ring forceps, suture scissors, a row of glistening scalpels and a scattering of feather blades. He stops in front of me.

I try not to look at the instruments he is planning to use.

He says something I can't quite process and his voice sounds like a low drawl.

I attempt to move my arms, but a wave of nausea hits me. My limbs feel pathetically frail. Even if I wanted to lash out at him with my free right arm, I'm too feeble to land any blows worth a damn. His face is inches from mine. He scrutinises my eyes. And now, when Greenwood speaks, my brain processes the words:

'The procedure will take as long as it takes, Novak. I'll try to keep you alive as long as possible. In fact, I have all the equipment and medical know-how to *keep* you alive, even when your body is trying to close down, due to the extreme nature of the procedure. We'll begin very shortly and it goes without saying' – he lowers his surgeon's mask – 'that there will be a degree of discomfort as I dismember you.'

He flashes another smile and trundles on his way.

I try to call his name, but feel the effects of the anaesthetic once more, and although I'm fighting it, I sense I'm losing consciousness and might—

CHAPTER 96

I wake up screaming. The nightmare remains real. Greenwood stands beneath the vast circular light, transferring the medical implements from his trolley to the instrument table. He works with care and precision, with the attention of a man who enjoys his work.

The sound of my screams disturbs him momentarily. He shoots me a mock-sympathetic look and I fall silent.

My mind is clearing. I still feel foggy and my memory is sketchy, but my reasoning process is kicking in.

I can see the operating table and for the first time notice thick leather straps on both sides. I know, without a scintilla of doubt, that if Greenwood gets me to that table, and straps me down so I'm immobile, I will die. And my death will be excruciating and slow.

'Greenwood . . .' I croak. 'Greenwood!'

He pauses. Looks up.

'I can pay you.'

'I'm not interested in your money.'

'Anything you want. I can pay you.'

He doesn't respond.

'There's no need to do this,' I tell him.

'No need. You're right. But I relish the thought of hurting you. You killed my brother. Dipping you into hell, and seeing how long I keep your nerve ends alive before you fall? That appeals to me very much.' He returns to his task, lining up the scalpels so they rest in a meticulous row.

'Greenwood!'

'Keep your mouth shut or I'll slice your tongue off.'

He doesn't even glance up from his implements. I try to focus, to reason my way out of this. Because there *is* a way out. My mind is scratching at it, but can't quite grasp it.

'You killed the old man! And the woman! Shot Hillier from behind!' I feel a little strength returning to my body and bellow, 'You're not a hunter! You're a coward! You call yourself the Muse after a foxhound. But you're just a vulture! Circling the weak and defenceless, only swooping when there's no fight to be had.'

Greenwood isn't distracted from his work. 'Your tactics are clumsy and obvious.'

'If you haven't got the balls for it – fine.' I flex my right hand. The anaesthetic is starting to wear off. 'I had hoped you'd be more of a challenge than your brother.'

I finally see him pause.

'You can pretend this is vengeance for him,' I shout, 'but the effort you're going to suggests it's something more. Penance for letting him die! This is on *you*, Greenwood. *Your* weakness. *Your* brother's weakness. It's on you both.'

There has to be a way out of this . . . The debilitating fog across my thoughts is clearing. Slowly. I need to do anything possible to prevent Greenwood shifting me to the operating table. I shake my head. It's obvious I've only got moments left to come up with something.

Greenwood finishes transferring the implements to the table. He plucks an item from the trolley's lower shelf and walks several paces towards me. He keeps his hands behind his back and cuts a strangely formal figure.

That's it . . . Yes . . . I need him to get within reach of me. That's my only chance of escape. If I can somehow overpower him, I'll be able to find a way out. But I need him to be closer in order to stand any kind of chance . . .

I begin, 'Your brother—'

'Shut up about my brother!' he berates me. 'Do you honestly think you're the first man who's stood where you now stand and has tried to insult me? Who's tried to make me lose my focus? So, what? I'll be thrown into a fury and stride across to you? You'll strike me with your right arm and I'll go down and then you'll make good your daring escape?' He gives a short, mirthless laugh. 'Why do you think I left your right arm lose? It's to give you hope. That you still have a chance.'

He's talking. Good. Egomaniacs love to monologue and I know there's a way out of this. Just need to . . .

'But the thing is,' Greenwood continues, 'there's this lovely moment when my playthings realise it's all over and they don't stand a chance. And here it comes.'

He brings his hands in front of his torso. He's carrying a tranquilliser gun. I feel my body physically slump.

'There it is!' Greenwood's delight is evident. 'Here's what will happen now. I will not step anywhere near you. I will render you unconscious using two darts from this . . .' He gestures to the gun. 'When you wake up you'll be strapped to that operating table. The leather fastenings have secured men much stronger than you, Novak, and although you'll fight for a while, you'll soon resort to pleading.'

There must be an answer. A solution. I can sense my mind and memory becoming fluid again. The way out of this feels tantalisingly close . . .

'I'll amputate your lower limbs first. Then your arms. Then we'll take a short break. After the intermission, I'll slice open your eyes.'

I can't let him use his tranquilliser gun. If a dart hits me I'm as good as dead. I need to keep him talking until I can *think clearly* . . .

'Tell me,' I command. 'No, *promise* me that you won't harm Precious!'

He slips the safety catch of his gun to *Off*. 'In a few minutes you will beseech me to let her take your place.'

'Never.'

'Oh, still got hope? Amazing. That's quite impressive. I'll give you that. My playthings are normally whining and begging at this stage. But you will be in a moment. When you realise the agony is inevitable. When hope peters out . . .'

He smiles.

I narrow my eyes. 'What did you just say?'

'That your agony is inevitable. And when your hope peters out you'll—'

'Shut up!' I yell at him.

When hope peters out . . .

I start to laugh as everything hits me.

Greenwood frowns.

Hope peters out . . .

'You! I knew there was a way out of this. Couldn't grasp it until . . . You see, whatever you pumped into me played havoc with my memory but you gave me the reminder I needed. Thank you. Really. You're a star.'

Peters out.

Peters! Thom Peters! Of course! At last, I recall one of the items I removed from the house of Jeremy Simmonds, AKA Thom Peters, on the night I confronted him.

'I'll make you regret that, Novak.'

One of his antique weapons.

'I doubt it.'

'Time to put you to sleep. When you wake up you'll be—'

'They never win . . . people like you.'

'Oh? And what stops us?'

'People like me.'

He hesitates. 'Is that your final message of defiance?' He raises his gun. 'This is it, Novak.'

'Message! Yes. Almost forgot. I *do* have a final message for you, Greenwood.'

In the same way his easy confidence rattled me back at my house, I can see my assuredness is unnerving the Muse. In his last moments, like every other bully who's finally being stood up to, Lee Greenwood is frightened.

'Message? What message?'

'It's from a friend of mine.' I raise my right arm. Flex my radial muscles and feel the spring-loading mechanism of the gambler's gun click forward. The weaponry I'm wearing on my lower right arm is over 100 years old but still works perfectly. The tiny, two-bullet Derringer moves smoothly from the sleeve of my suit jacket and slides snugly into my hand. I feel its mother-of-pearl handle against my palm and my finger curls around its steel trigger. Its barrel is pointing at the spot between Greenwood's eyes. 'Sebby Hughes says hello.'

I pull the trigger.

CHAPTER 97

I use the second bullet to shatter the chain of my hand-cuffs, then find the key on Greenwood's corpse. I'm tossing the handcuffs aside as I leave the torture chamber and jog up a flight of stairs.

I've no idea where Greenwood brought me but expect I'm in a house in the middle of nowhere. Probably a rural location, miles from any neighbours, village or shops. I push open the door at the top of the steps and walk forward cautiously. I'm in an expensively furnished house, maybe an apartment. The décor is modern and sparse. I listen for a moment or two, then, satisfied I'm alone, hurry through to the kitchen. There's no booze in the fridge, but I find half a bottle of cooking brandy in one of the cupboards. I take a couple of mouthfuls to calm my nerves, then move through to the hallway. I snap back the locks on the wooden front door and swing it open.

A black cab roars along the road directly in front of me. I see a small, pretty park across the way, and a church that I recognise to my right. I take a step forward and find myself in a narrow portico, lined by cream, Tuscan columns. I glance back at Greenwood's house. It's a stucco-fronted, two-bay terrace building in . . .

I look across to the church again – St Peter's – to confirm my suspicion.

AN ACCIDENT IN PARIS

I'm in Eaton Square, Belgravia, London.

Sue Carpenter explained that she'd break the Diana story in the newsstand iteration of her paper, as opposed to the online edition. That way, nobody could hack the article. It feels like a sensible precaution. Flood the country with hard copies of the truth, then run with the exclusive online, gradually adding more detail over the days ahead, including the peripheral facts we supplied her in writing.

Frank claimed that the first copies of any daily newspaper's editions are dropped off between five and six at a small stand in the heart of Soho, close to Berwick Street market. He told us that back in the day, when a really big story was breaking, journos would wait at the stand as dawn broke, just to get their hands on the first papers that carried the scoop.

I'm not sure whether I believe that's true, but I'm in no doubt that he does, so we'd agreed to meet there, early, the three of us, so we could be among the first to read the story that would dominate headlines for weeks and years to come.

My taxi is stuck in traffic on D'Arblay Street so I hand the cabbie a couple of notes and walk the rest of the way.

Precious is already waiting at the stand. She asks, 'Where's Cy?'

I know I'll need to address the fallout of the last few hours, but not yet. 'He had a tough night,' I reply, careful not to lie to her.

'He can get tired if he stays up late, poor thing.'

I nod. 'Last time I saw him, he was dead on his feet.'

'I'm guessing you could use this . . .' She sticks a cup of coffee in my hand. 'You look like an extra from *The Walking Dead*.'

I spot Frank, striding through Berwick Street market. He reaches us and asks, 'Are the papers here yet?'

Precious hands him a coffee, too. 'No. Expected any moment, though.'

I ask, 'Anything broken online?'

'Not a thing.'

Even as she replies, a beige-coloured van screeches to a halt by the stand. A guy leaps from the passenger side, darts to the rear of the vehicle and opens its doors.

'This is it,' Frank whispers.

I've no idea how he knew, but when the guy walks around the van, I see he's carrying bundles of the newspaper edited by Sue Carpenter. He flings them towards the woman running the stall. Precious and Frank rush to her side to buy the first available copies.

I notice the bloke that delivered the papers has a copy himself, rolled up in his back pocket.

'Excuse me!'

He's hurrying back to the van, but pauses. 'Yes, mate?'

'Have you read this morning's paper?'

'Not cover to cover but given it a quick shufty. Why?'

'Does it lead with a royal story?'

He raises his eyebrows and sucks in some air. 'Does it ever! A royal story that I reckon everybody will be talking about! You won't believe it!'

'Thanks.' I smile. 'You know what, my friend? On this one occasion . . . I think I might!'

CHAPTER 98

Precious tosses me a copy of the newspaper. I catch it awkwardly and put my coffee on the pavement. See Frank doing the same. Take a breath. Straighten my back. We all take in the front page at the same time.

I can't quite believe . . .

Check the masthead. Yes, it's the right newspaper. Sue's.

And it's a royal story. Just not the one we've risked our lives to tell.

I glance at Frank. He looks old. Beaten. Tired and translucent. At Precious. Angry and devastated. Close to tears. I peer at the front page.

The headline reads, HAIR TO THE THRONE? and below it, there's a photograph of Meghan Markle, or the Duchess of Sussex, or whatever she's calling herself these days. For a moment, I don't see what the big deal is. She's looking as healthy and as photogenic as ever. She's clearly not ill. So . . . ? One side of her long, dark hair is in dreadlocks. It looks good. I continue to scan the picture for the important element. *Hair to the throne.* I understand. That *is* the important thing. Her hair. Her bloody hair . . . The way a young woman has decided to do her do has merited a front-page splash in a national newspaper.

Apparently the photo of Meghan is an exclusive. An EXCLUSIVE!

All that's different about her is the way she's done her hair. The accompanying text seems to think it's an earth-shatteringly huge deal, but I'm mystified. Sue must have decided to save our big story for another day. Maybe she's fact-checking or—

'There it is.' Precious's voice is a low monotone. 'Page eight.'

I quickly flick there. In the lower right-hand corner, there's a short, four-paragraph story. Even the headline is repugnant. CRACKPOT CONSPIRACY THEORIST CLAIMS 'I KNOW HOW DI DID DIE!'.

With a growing sense of disbelief, I speed-read the brief article.

It's a mess. It claims Mark Novack [sic] believes the British Army killed Diana because she was on the verge of putting the brave men and women who supplied them with defensive weaponry out of business. That isn't what we said – nowhere close. I never intimated the armed forces were involved in any way.

I hear Precious murmur, 'This is a joke!'

The article covers some of the elements we discussed. The amazing work Diana achieved in getting landmines banned. The announcement she teased journalists about. Those facts make it. They're there. And the third paragraph even mentions Henri Paul, but it belittles our argument that he was not drunk and couldn't have been an alcoholic, as official sources claimed. It doesn't mention the booze that so mysteriously turned up at his home after barely any had been discovered in initial searches. It ignores the fact that close friends swore he was sober, and that his post-mortem shows he had a perfectly healthy liver. No, they pretend my assertion that he was sober rests solely on the fact he could tie his shoelaces on the evening before his death.

The article is a masterpiece. A masterpiece of reductive, barely true trivia. It takes our presentation of the truth, sits it in a chair, plonks a dunce's cap on its head and daubs its face with a clown's garish make-up. The resultant mess is a cruel but effective distortion.

There's enough of our words to ensure we can't complain that Sue or her people have entirely concocted the story. But certain facts are wildly off and the entire tenor suggests I'm a conspiracy nut whose grasp on reality was relinquished decades ago. Yet thanks to our agreement, we can't go anywhere else to publicise the reality for another ninety days.

By the time almost three months will have elapsed and our findings, as distorted by Sue Carpenter, will be old news, derided and consigned to the slush pile of ludicrous theories, just below 'aliens killed JFK' and 'Elvis engineered Covid'. We can revive it, sure. But it will have no currency. No weight. No worth.

I say, 'Who got to her, Frank?'

He shrugs. Picks up his coffee and mine. Takes a sip of his. He's already looking better. Amused by the turn of events. 'Oh, well. Some you win . . .'

I remember his warning. '"Don't expect too much, lad." You called it, Frank.'

'Not my first rodeo.' He gives Precious a reassuring smile. 'And it won't be *your* last.'

'Damn right,' she tells him.

Frank hands me my coffee. 'You'll be OK.'

I suspect he'd known all along that if the forces we've been up against saw me reach Sue Carpenter, they would have a contingency plan. Perhaps they believe this approach will prove more effective that a bullet to my brain. Rather than kill me, they've killed my credibility.

It's over. We all know it.

Precious asks, 'What do we do now?'

Frank puts his shoulders back. 'We move on.'

She nods.

Just across the road, the market traders are setting up their stalls on Berwick Street, and there's a cheerful sturdiness about them. The sound of their shouts and laughter interrupts my thoughts.

'Come on.' I throw my coffee and the newspaper into a bin by the side of the stand. 'I think I know where we can get a proper drink.'

EPILOGUE 1

The Mourner's Story

The inquest of Gerry Whittaker faced several delays, but ultimately concluded there were no suspicious circumstances surrounding the crash that killed him. The coroner also noted, in a pointed aside, that the Colonel was a known alcoholic, although some journalists observed that his post-mortem indicated his liver was perfectly healthy.

His funeral took place three weeks after Marc Novak's final confrontation with Lee Greenwood. The intervening days had seen Jeremy Simmonds ensure that the circumstances arising from his death, and that of Cy Hillier, were handled quickly and discreetly. Greenwood's connection to Novak's investigation was never made public. Hillier's 'tragic end' was officially the result of a robbery gone wrong. One major online news outlet even reported that the young man had fought off two thieves, but had been fatally wounded when a gun accidentally went off at point-blank range.

Novak had been offended by the story, but not surprised.

It had also been a time of funerals for Novak. He'd attended services for Maureen Shaw and Freddie Clarke; Edna's would be next.

But the Colonel's funeral was the first time he'd returned to the hilltop church where he and Whittaker had talked, weeks earlier, about delivering justice for Diana. Now it was packed with mourners. Novak took a seat at the edge of the pew furthest back from the altar. He scanned the congregation and was disappointed not to pick out Whittaker's daughter, Veronique.

After the service, 'A Wand'ring Minstrel, I' from *The Mikado* was played and mourners started to weave their way through to the graveyard. The woman Novak had quite by chance sat next to began to weep. 'He absolutely adored Gilbert and Sullivan . . .'

Novak nodded. 'Yes . . . We bonded over a love of the Savoy Operas. Even sang along to this together. Feels like forever ago. Here . . .' He offered her a handkerchief. 'Take this.'

'Thank you.'

They drifted from the church and sauntered to the spot where Whittaker would be buried. 'He picked out this plot himself. Actually showed me it.'

'It's got a very pretty view.'

Novak asked, 'How did you know the Colonel?'

'Oh, just through work.' She sniffed. 'And you know his lovely housekeeper?' Her face crumpled. 'Did you hear? She passed, too.' She paused. Blew her nose. 'Odd them going so close to each other, isn't it?'

'Yeah . . .' Novak half shrugged. 'One of life's little mysteries.'

It was a warm, bright day and they circled the church together, taking in the views and sharing stories about Whittaker. The woman then revealed she'd recently lost her own husband. Novak offered condolences. He mused that a good many people he'd been close to had passed in the last few months.

'Life happens quickly,' he reflected.

As if on a whim, she asked, 'What are you?'

'A work in progress.'

'Aren't we all? I mean, what do you do for a living?'

'I'm a private detective.'

'How exciting!'

'I could do with a little less excitement.'

'How so?'

Novak hesitated. Looked over the Surrey Hills. Attending the funeral had made him consider his own mortality and the state of his life. Almost as if he was figuring out the problem for himself, he said, 'Not so long ago, I told a friend it was time I moved on. Found a different path. I didn't and . . . Well, it got bloody.'

'So do you think you've worked your last investigation?'

'Yes.' The affirmation wasn't simply a reply to her question. It felt more like a vow to himself. 'It's time to find that different path. Time to stop being a knight errant in a world that no longer wants knights errant.'

'Change is always hard, you know. Harder than you think.'

Novak's phone began to ring. 'It's a work call.' He shrugged. 'I'd better tell whoever it is that I'm no longer available. Would you excuse me?'

'Of course.'

He answered his phone. 'Novak & Stewart. Private Detectives. Can I put you on hold for a moment?' He pressed mute. 'I'm going to have to take this, and I really need to go. But it was lovely to meet you.'

The woman handed him a piece of paper. 'I've just scribbled my name and phone number down, in case . . . Well, I'd love to continue our chat. Call me, maybe?'

'Sounds good.' Novak smiled. Looked down at the paper. 'See you soon, Sophie.'

He slipped her details into his suit pocket and began to walk away.

As Sophie watched him follow the path from the church, she saw him speaking to whoever had called. She was about to turn away when a couple of elderly ladies sidled up to her. It didn't surprise her. Sophie had a way with older people.

'Such a shame, isn't it?' one of them said to her. 'And his housekeeper dead, too. Did you know her?'

'Well . . . I knew her at the end.'

The other older woman nodded towards Novak. 'He seems very nice, dear. Is he your young man?'

'Mr Novak? No.' Sophie Grace smiled. 'Not yet.'

EPILOGUE 2

Novak's Story (cont.)

Novak unmuted his phone. 'Hello? Sorry about that. And I'm also sorry to tell you I've just retired so I'm no longer—'

'Mr Novak?'

He half recognised the voice. 'Yes?'

'It's Veronique. The Colonel's daughter.'

'Is this about your father?'

'This has nothing to do with him . . . I'm calling about a murder.'

'Whose?'

'Mine.'

'Are you in immediate danger, Veronique?'

'Not immediate. But imminent. There are some men . . . I think they intend to kill me.'

'Yeah. It's a recurring theme in my line of work.'

'Your line of work?' There was a degree of relief in her voice. 'You said you were retired.'

'Then you said you were in trouble. Where are you?'

Novak reached the end of the path. Looked back towards the church and the fair-haired woman he'd just met. She was watching him from the edge of the graveyard. He turned away and walked the final few paces back to his car.

'The cathedral. Guildford Cathedral. Will you help me, Mr Novak?'

'Of course.' He climbed into his Marina, slammed the door shut and gunned the engine. 'I'm on my way.'

Marc Novak will return.

CLOSING STATEMENTS

I personally believe that the fatal crash in Paris, August 1997, warrants further investigation by an official organisation sanctioned to uncover and confirm the full truth. But this book, as previously mentioned, is a work of fiction inspired by real-life events.

If you're interested in those events and their aftermath, there's a world of material for you to explore. I always think 'Further Reading' sections that go on for half a dozen pages are a bit showy offy. (Is that just me?) So, I'll keep it brief. I'd recommend starting off by reading the official report that summarised the findings of Operation Paget and the various transcripts and reports arising from the inquests into the deaths of Diana, Princess of Wales, and Mr Dodi Al Fayed. All are available to view online and are simply a search engine and a couple of clicks away. Links and related resources can be found on my site, gavincollinson.com

I'd like to thank my family and friends for their support and forbearance as I wrote *An Accident in Paris*. I'm especially grateful to those who read the book as it evolved. Barry, Gabriella, Lucy, Helen, Andy, Merle and my brilliant agent, Kerr – thank you all for commenting, advising, spurring me on and calming me down. Jonathan Zane – you're dangerous and kind, and as you requested, I'm not going to thank you for all the insight you so generously provided. But the next couple of rounds are on me.

Big thanks also to the Welbeck Publishing team, including Jon, Mozidur and Kati. I'm immensely grateful for your faith and guidance. And diamond-encrusted thanks to this book's editor, Rosa. Witty, patient, diplomatic, ruthless and armed with an uncanny ability to determine what needs expunging and what needs expanding, you are truly a Miracle on Mortimer Street.

Finally, my old friend Rik . . . I once said you had a mind like the Black Museum. But that was before you became even more knowledgeable. Thanks for your humour, positivity and constant willingness to help by sharing your extraordinary experience and know-how. You absolutely rock.

This book is dedicated to Mr Nick Tomlinson. A gentleman, but more importantly, a good man. Thank you, sir.

Gavin Collinson

ABOUT THE AUTHOR

GAVIN COLLINSON

Before becoming a full-time writer Collinson's career lurched from campsite management to journalism and marketing within the movie industry. He later enjoyed stints on *Coronation Street* and *Emmerdale* as an Online Producer before working on *Doctor Who* for over eight years. Since leaving the TARDIS, he's written for the stage, radio, computer games and Virtual Reality experiences. He scripted the 2021 interactive thriller *The Lonely Assassins* (starring Jodie Whittaker) which was hailed by *Engadget* as 'the best *Doctor Who* game ever made'.

A fan of classic film and TV he's delivered talks and events on topics ranging from James Bond, Sherlock Holmes and *Ghostwatch*, to Leni Riefenstahl, Charles Dickens and Alfred Hitchcock.

He was raised in Blackpool, Lancashire and now lives in Guildford, Surrey.

WELBECK
PUBLISHING GROUP

Love books? Join the club.

Sign up and choose your preferred genres to receive
tailored news, deals, extracts, author interviews and
more about your next favourite read.

From heart-racing thrillers to award-winning historical
fiction, through to must-read music tomes, beautiful
picture books and delightful gift ideas, Welbeck is
proud to publish titles that suit every taste.

bit.ly/welbeckpublishing

WELBECK

ANDRE
DEUTSCH

MORTIMER

MORTIMER

WELBECK